Finding Jess

Nicole Maser

Contents

Chapter one

Sam barely moved a muscle as she stared down at the speakerphone in the middle of the wide wooden conference room table.

"Well Sam," the man's voice buzzed through, "I have to hand it to you. Everything looks great so far. The software you've developed seems very promising, and I think there's a good chance your company could make a great addition to our portfolio."

Somehow, her body both tensed and relaxed as she shot a glance at Caleb across the table. His eyes widened slightly, a sharp contrast to the calm expression he usually wore. The loose waves of his ink-black hair fell into his eyes as he ran a hand through it—a nervous habit she'd seen countless times over the years.

"We'll need to really dive in and test things out, though, of course," Howard added, his deep voice booming through the speaker.

"Yes. Absolutely," she replied immediately, leaning forward in the office chair, as if being a few inches closer would somehow speed things along.

"So," he continued, "that could take a while."

Caleb shifted again, adjusting the cuff of his shirt beneath his jacket. His tall, thin frame practically folded itself into the chair as he leaned forward, one hand fidgeting with the pen he always kept nearby.

Sam glanced away, refusing to read the look on his face. It was pointless, anyway. She knew he had the same thoughts running through his head that she did.

Caleb had been with her from the start. They'd met fresh out of college after being hired by the same company. Sam worked as a software engineer, while Caleb was in finance and administration. And despite their different areas of expertise, the connection had been immediate—Caleb's sharp analytical mind balancing her own relentless drive for innovation.

They each only made it through two months of grueling sixty-hour weeks, bonding over their tyrannical managers during rushed coffee breaks. And one day, they'd both had it. They decided that if they were going to be working that hard for anyone, it would be for themselves and not some huge corporation that cared even less about them than they did about it.

Sam had already been working on the first version of the financial reporting software in her spare time, which would later turn into a company more successful than either of them could've ever imagined.

And after they officially quit, those sixty-hour weeks instantly turned into hundred hour weeks. Although neither of them minded much. Working on something for themselves was a different level of satisfaction. One they both desperately craved.

But then, reality hit.

They needed money. *Badly.*

No matter how much she wanted to code all day, they also had to get clients to pay for and use the software.

Luckily, that's where Caleb excelled. And the more clients he signed, the more work it brought.

At the beginning, the constant work had felt more like excitement. But after four years, that excitement had dwindled into something far less enjoyable.

No matter how hard they tried, it seemed like they could just never quite keep up. If they weren't dealing with development issues, then they were moving to new cities to integrate clients onto the platform. And if they weren't doing that, they were courting new potential clients.

And although they'd built it into a substantial company, every day still felt like a never-ending struggle.

So when the large corporation reached out to them with an interest in acquiring the company and software, it felt like they'd finally found an answer.

She'd known a handful of classmates from MIT who had gone that exact route. Creating a startup, then selling a few years later. And every single time, it launched them onto bigger and better things.

They could get funding for new ventures with a single email to the right person. They could do anything they wanted. Overnight, they'd proven themselves. They'd proven their worth. A worth that no one could question.

"What would the next steps be?" Sam asked, trying not to sound too eager.

"Well, I'll reach out to a few of our investment firms," he replied. "We'll need to find one that would be a good fit for doing a trial run with integrating the software."

Sam nodded to herself, mentally calculating how long that might take. The due diligence that typically went along with a buyout definitely wasn't a quick process. Adding on weeks or potentially months of trial and integration just for testing would delay things even further. Not to mention they'd most likely need to pause work with existing clients in order to free up their workload to make it happen.

"You said you're open to travel, correct? And no limitations on the length of the travel?"

"Yes," Sam answered. "That's right. We just arrived in Seattle last week for a new client, and we'll be here for another couple of months at least. But after that, we're flexible."

They'd moved cities constantly, packing up every few months to move to the next location of their new clients and help their teams get started with using the software. And although it never bothered them much, this time felt different.

Never once in the four years since starting the company had they ever landed somewhere so close to her old home.

Being in Seattle meant they were still a couple hours away, but even then, it felt odd being back. Or at least, *close* to being back.

"Oh," Howard muttered, as if having some new realization. "That actually might be perfect. We own part of a financial firm in Seattle, and they've had a lot of issues this year with their analytics and reporting. That might be a good way to test things out and make sure everything would integrate well and be productive for our teams."

"That's great," Sam beamed, not bothering to hide the eager excitement this time. "Yes. We can do that."

It was perfect. Better than she could've hoped. If they managed to finish up with their current client over the next month, then they could begin the process right away and cut out potential months of delay.

"Can you go meet with them today?"

Sam blinked once, staring down at the small black speaker. "Today?"

"Yes. I can call them now to confirm, so they'll have a team member available to meet with you."

She shot a look at Caleb and could practically see the problems spinning in his head.

If they started that day, before they finished up work with the new client, they'd have double the workload for a few weeks at least. And doubling an already stretched schedule sounded nearly impossible.

But the alternative of possibly missing out on their one opportunity to sell the company and solve their problems also seemed impossible.

They couldn't let that happen. *She* couldn't let that happen.

"Yes," she answered. "Of course. Send me the address and I'll head over right away."

***

Sam approached the tall modern building, shielding her eyes against the sun that reflected off the glass exterior. She pulled open the heavy door, squinting as a swoosh of cold air blew out against her face.

She glanced around the wide, empty lobby, adorned with black leather chairs and couches that led up to a milky white desk that formed a crescent moon around half the room.

"Can I help you?" A young brunette woman greeted her from behind the desk with a soft smile.

Sam gave the woman her name and a brief explanation of why she was there before being directed to wait in the lobby.

She settled into a large leather sofa as she pulled out her phone to shoot Scarlett a quick text, letting her know she wouldn't be able to meet for dinner.

Scarlett had been in Seattle for a few years, having moved there after finishing college. They'd kept in close touch since high school, talking every week. And now Scarlett was one of her closest friends. In fact, she was really the only thing Sam had looked forward to after finding out they needed to move to Seattle for the most recent client.

She finished typing out the text, then hit send before scrolling through the endless stream of new work emails. In the middle of replying to one particularly urgent message, she spotted someone approaching.

"Hi," the woman said. "You must be from the—"

Sam glanced up as she stood, tucking her phone into her back pocket.

The woman paused, cocking her head. "Sam?"

Sam stared at her for a moment, blinking as a sudden stream of memories she hadn't recalled in years began trickling in.

"Lizzie?"

An amused smile crossed the woman's face, her eyes lighting up with recognition. "Wow, it's been a minute since anyone called me that," she said with a laugh that made her straight red hair skim the tops of her shoulders. "I go by Liz now."

Sam nodded, her mind slowly working to merge the image of her long-forgotten childhood best friend with the composed woman standing before her. Even now, the faint smattering of freckles dusting her cheeks and nose gave her a youthful air despite her polished appearance.

"I can't believe how long it's been," Liz said with a wide grin as she casually tucked her hands into the pockets of her light gray suit pants.

"Yeah," Sam said, forcing a smile onto her lips as she thought of the last time she'd seen her, in the few days after her mother had passed. The days she'd stayed with Lizzie's family before going into foster care.

"So, you work for that software company?"

Sam nodded. "Yeah—well—" She cleared her throat, pushing away those old memories. "Sort of. I mean—I own it."

"Oh," Liz exclaimed, a look of surprise filling her features. "Wow, look at you! I never would've expected that."

Sam gave her a tight smile as she nodded, scratching the back of her neck. Somehow, even as an adult, she still reminded her exactly of the young girl she'd spent endless days and nights with. Hell, she'd probably spent more nights at Lizzie's house than her own.

"Well, I'm relieved," Liz said with a chuckle. "When they called on such short notice, I thought they might rush over some intern or something."

"Oh, so you run the—"

"I manage the reporting department here," Liz cut in quickly with a broad grin.

"Great," Sam said, hoping her feigned enthusiasm sounded more convincing to other ears. It wasn't an entirely unwelcome surprise. But still, being forced to be around a constant reminder of the days after her mother had died wasn't exactly what she would've chosen.

Especially with how things had ended. Liz's face alone, no matter how much it had grown and changed, was still enough to transport her back to the day.

"Well, come on back," Liz said with a wave as she turned around. "Lets get right to it since it's already a little late. But maybe we could catch up afterwards?"

"Mhm," Sam hummed, slinging her backpack over her shoulder.

Liz led her through a long hallway, past a string of offices and cubicles as people left for the day.

"I don't know how much you want to go over today," Liz said over her shoulder as they turned into one of the mid-sized offices. "Hopefully not too much, though. I was trying to make it out of here in time for my cycling class."

Sam sat in the chair on the other side of her desk, pulling her laptop out of the backpack. "That's fine. We can just start with an overview of how you're doing your reporting now and what kind of issues you're running into. Then we can pick things up again tomorrow."

They spent the next several minutes going over things, with Sam occasionally prodding for more details or asking additional questions. She wanted to keep all conversations entirely work related, and luckily, Liz seemed content to do the same.

Maybe Liz wanted to avoid those memories just as much as she did.

Sam typed notes on her laptop as Liz checked her phone for the third time that minute.

"Sorry," Liz muttered. "Keep going. I'm listening. Just need to text my girlfriend real quick."

Sam nodded as she continued typing.

"She's gonna stop by and drop off some food," Liz mumbled as she typed something into her phone before finally dropping it back on the desk. "I'm lucky," she said with a chuckle. "She's actually here at the office most days. She's with the PR agency that works with us."

Sam hummed, only halfway paying attention as she tried to ignore the string of new urgent emails popping up on the screen as she typed.

"Working with someone you date can be—interesting," she said with a snort. "But also has its perks."

"What tool do you use right now to funnel all your data over?" Sam asked, finally tearing her eyes away from the screen.

"Oh—uh," Liz squinted, tilting her head back in thought. "I can't really remember the name. Starts with a 'P' I think. I can show it to you tomorrow."

Sam glanced back down, highlighting that portion of her notes to come back to the next day.

Faint footsteps echoed in the hall outside the door, and a moment later, Liz stood from her chair with a smile.

"Hey babe," she said, stepping around the desk.

Sam continued typing out a quick note as a bag crinkled behind her.

"Babe, this is Sam."

Sam set her laptop on the desk, standing to turn and quickly introduce herself so she could finish up and get out of there as soon as possible.

"Sam, this is my girlfriend, Jess."

Every word and sound instantly evaporated as Sam stared into the doorway.

Jess stood there, eyes wide and lips slightly parted as she stared back.

"Funny story," Liz continued with a chuckle as she peered down into the bag, "we actually knew each other when we were kids."

Tension instantly thickened the air. Sam's pulse quickened, but she kept her expression neutral—or tried to.

"Hi," Sam said, her voice low and even, a faint edge of disbelief slipping through despite her best effort.

Jess' lips pressed together into a thin line, her eyes narrowing slightly, like she was bracing herself. "Hi," she replied, her tone flat and clipped.

Liz arched one brow, looking between them both. "Do you guys already know each other?"

Sam looked back at Jess, who seemed to finally be emerging from the daze she'd entered.

"Yeah," Jess replied, blinking as she shook her head slightly, long wavy blonde hair drifting across the top of her tight white blouse. "Yeah, we—" Jess trailed off, her eyes flitting back to Sam, as if asking a silent question.

Sam cleared her throat, reaching a hand up to scratch the back of her neck. "High school," she said, forcing a smile as she looked back at Liz. "We're friends from high school."

She glanced back at Jess just in time to see an unreadable look pass over her face.

"Oh," Liz said with a surprised grin. "Wow! What a small world."

Sam gave a slight nod, unable to muster a response.

"So how long has it been, then?" Liz asked, looking at Jess. "High school was what—eight years ago, right?" She looked back at Sam then. "So it's been eight years since you've seen each other?"

Sam's eyes skipped back to Jess, who met her gaze for only a split-second before returning to Liz.

Jess offered a smile that somehow wasn't a smile at all as she said, "Four years since we last saw each other."

Sam watched her carefully for another moment before tucking her hands into her pockets to keep them from fidgeting.

Liz nodded, and Sam wondered if she was picking up on the way Jess' smile seemed to stay miles away from her eyes.

The brief silence that settled between the three of them would've been the perfect chance to excuse herself. She could have easily lied and said she'd gotten everything she needed for the day and left.

But something else deep down inside wanted her to stay.

"I didn't know you were living here now," Sam said, trying to keep the words light, as if she was talking to any friend she hadn't seen in years.

Jess looked back at her, and by the look on her face, she could tell she was attempting to do the same.

"It hasn't been long. Less than a year." Jess gave a small shrug that made the ends of her blonde hair sway. "Scar always talked about how much she loved it here, and I needed a change." Her eyes flicked away for a moment before locking with Sam again. "I got a job offer here and decided to take it."

Sam gave a small nod, suddenly wishing she'd returned the missed calls from Scarlett that week sooner. If she had, Scarlett definitely would've given her some type of heads up.

"I'm sure Scar's happy to have you here," Sam said.

"We're all happy to have her here," Liz said with a smile as she wrapped one arm loosely around Jess' waist.

And with that, whatever was keeping her there suddenly reversed. Now instead, it wanted to get away—*begged* to get away.

"Well, I think we covered enough for today," Sam said as she managed to force her professional persona back into place.

"Oh, good," Liz replied with a sigh of relief. "I really didn't want to miss cycling tonight."

Jess turned toward her with a quizzical look. "Cycling?" she asked, her voice lowering a few notches. "I thought we were going to see that movie after you finished work?"

Sam could hear Liz let out a deep groan as she stuffed her laptop into her backpack.

"Shit, sorry, babe. I forgot. Can we do it another night?"

Sam swung the bag over her shoulder, looking around awkwardly.

"Yeah," Jess answered with a small nod. "No big deal."

When Liz looked back down at her phone, Sam saw her opportunity.

"Want to pick things up again tomorrow?" she asked.

Liz hummed, not looking up as she typed something into her phone. "Email me a time, and I'll make sure I'm free."

Sam nodded as she slipped her hands back into her pockets, turning to Jess, fully prepared to give a polite goodbye. But as their eyes met, the intensity of Jess' stare dissolved the words about to roll out.

She swallowed, desperately grasping for that last thread of composure to stay for just a few moments longer.

But in those deep blue eyes, she could see unspoken words, and she wondered if Jess would've said something else if they'd met again under different circumstances.

"Sam," Liz continued, finally peering up at her. "I meant it about wanting to catch up. Maybe we could all meet up for dinner or something sometime soon?"

She knew she should look away from Jess then. That she needed to listen to what Liz was saying.

But Jess was still holding her gaze, and something in her eyes kept her from looking anywhere else.

"I know you're probably busy with all this stuff going on now," Liz continued, "but maybe we could plan something next week?"

Sam blinked, shaking her head slightly as she finally looked at Liz. "Uh—sorry—what?"

Liz held a slightly amused look. "I know. My brain is fried too, after all that," she said with a laugh. "Do you want to get dinner or something next week? To catch up?"

"Oh. Yeah, uh—sure," Sam replied, still not fully understanding what she was agreeing to. Her brain seemed to be moving at half speed, still barely processing the last few minutes.

"Great!" Liz said with a wide grin. "Maybe we could all do something together. A big reunion!"

"Yeah," Sam muttered as Liz took the paper bag of food back around to her desk.

Sam took a step toward the door where Jess still stood, unmoving, as she watched her.

Sam gave her a small smile as she stepped past, keeping her hands firmly in her pockets. "It was good seeing you again."

Jess' eyes flitted to the floor before looking back at her. She opened her mouth to say something, then paused, closing it again. "You, too."

***

Sam barely made it through the front door of her apartment before pulling out her phone.

She stepped over the half-unpacked cardboard boxes littering almost every inch of the floor as she scrolled to Scarlett's phone number.

She tossed her navy blue blazer onto the marble countertop and clicked the call button before putting it on speaker.

The phone rang three times, then Scarlett's voice came through.

"Seriously," Scarlett muttered. "You cancel on me at the last minute, then decide to call when I'm trying to sleep?"

Sam leaned her elbows against the countertop, letting her head droop above the phone.

"Sorry," she muttered, running a hand down her face. "I had a long day."

The sounds of the phone shifting around on the other end crackled through the speaker.

"It's fine," Scarlett murmured, her voice slowly awakening. "I couldn't really sleep, anyway. The florist for the wedding backed out. I guess they overbooked our date or something. So now, on top of everything else, I have to find a new one."

Sam hummed. "Having any luck?"

"No," Scarlett groaned. "But I'm gonna look again tomorrow when I'm not half asleep."

Sam nodded. "Let me know if I can help."

Scarlett muttered something she couldn't quite make out before falling quiet.

Sam swallowed. "Scar," she said quietly, "when were you going to tell me she'd moved here?"

"What?"

Sam exhaled, rubbing a hand over her tired eyes. "Jess." Even saying her name aloud felt weird after so long. "When were you going to tell me?"

A few beats of silence passed.

"Wait—how do you know that?"

Sam held back the groan that wanted to come out as the memories of the last few hours replayed in her mind. Her eyes flicked to the motorcycle helmet by the front door. With how exhausted she was, it probably wasn't a good idea. But really, a late night ride to clear her head sounded like heaven.

"We ran into each other at the office her—" She paused, the next word feeling uncomfortable in her mouth, "*girlfriend* works at. Oh, and if that wasn't bad enough, that *girlfriend* also happens to be an old friend of mine."

The line went dead for a few seconds. Then Scarlett's booming laughter broke through.

"Scar," Sam warned.

But the laughter continued, and as it did, Sam found herself slowly smiling as well. The first real smile she'd felt all day.

If she really thought about it, the whole situation was at least a little funny.

Sam shook her head, laughing along with her.

"You can't be serious." Scarlett said, still choking back bursts of laughter.

"Oh, I am," Sam replied, picking up the phone and ambling down the short hallway to the bedroom.

"Was it as bad as what I'm imagining?"

Sam snorted, tossing the phone onto her bed. "Worse, probably."

Scarlett's laugh vibrated through the speaker. "Fuck, I wish I could've been there to see that."

"Yeah, I don't know if I've ever been that awkward in my whole life," Sam muttered, stripping her shirt off and dropping it into an empty cardboard box on the floor.

Scarlett's laughter died off into a light chuckle. "I'm sorry."

Sam pursed her lips, grabbing one of her looser t-shirts off the bed. "Its fine."

"So really," Scarlett started, her voice going somber, "how was it?"

"I don't know," Sam muttered. "It was weird, obviously. But it was also—good—I guess. To see her again, I mean."

"I bet," Scarlett said quietly.

"Why didn't you tell me she'd moved here?"

Scarlett hesitated for a moment before releasing a deep exhale. "I didn't think it mattered. I mean, once you told me you were moving here, then obviously I was going to tell you when the time came. But after the last time, when you guys—" Scarlett paused, and Sam could tell she was searching for the right words. "When you guys stopped talking, it just seemed like you didn't want to hear about her. So I figured it was better not to mention anything."

Sam pursed her lips, leaning forward to rest her elbows against her thighs. "Yeah."

***

Four Years Earlier.

27

Sam crossed the busy intersection, wiping a bead of sweat off her temple as the New York summer sun beat down against her forehead.

She narrowly avoided a crowd of people as she stepped onto the next sidewalk. The wet heat she could do without, but the swarms of people were actually sort of enjoyable. There was something surprisingly nice about the packed city feeling. She never ran out of new people to meet or talk to. And those random interactions were something she thrived on.

Her thigh vibrated, and she pulled her phone out as she weaved the horde of people.

When she finally glanced down at the buzzing screen, a wide smile broke out across her face.

"Hey," she breathed, tucking the phone tightly against her ear.

"Are you done working yet?" Jess asked, excitement pouring through her words. Just the sound of the smile in her voice was enough to send warmth blooming within her chest.

"Just finished."

"Finally," Jess exhaled. "Can you meet up now?"

Sam chuckled. "Yeah. Where?"

"There's a restaurant a couple blocks from my apartment. I'll send you the address."

A rustling noise crackled through the phone for a few seconds before Jess' voice came through once again.

"Did you get it?"

"One sec," Sam muttered, pulling the phone away from her ear as the new text popped up on the screen.

She copied the restaurant name into her maps app and waited as the directions slowly filled the screen.

It wasn't close by any means, and paying for a cab was out of the question, given that she'd just sunk most of her remaining money into the new computer she needed.

She lifted the phone back up to her ear. "Okay. I got it."

"Is that okay?" Jess asked. "Or do you want to meet somewhere else?"

"No," Sam replied. "No, that's perfect. Just—uh, give me like thirty minutes to get there."

The walk took much longer than expected, even after she'd practically jogged the last few blocks. But when she gave the hostess her name, and she led her to a small table on the outside patio, every step was immediately worth it.

Jess sat at a small table, peering out into the busy street.

But when she glanced over and saw Sam, she instantly shot up.

Sam smiled, bracing herself as Jess rushed toward her, throwing both her arms around her neck.

And for the first time in a year, she felt a sense of home.

Jess let out a soft hum, curling her head into the side of her neck. "I missed this."

"Me too," Sam breathed.

After another moment, Sam finally pulled back. Jess slid her arms away, trailing one hand down until it wrapped around her own. Then she turned, leading her back to the table.

Jess sat down, and Sam pulled the other chair around the table to sit right beside her.

"The server will be right over," the hostess said with a polite smile, leaving two menus.

"Thanks," Sam replied, pulling her phone and wallet out of her back pocket to set on the table.

When she turned to look at Jess, she was already staring at her with a smile she couldn't quite decipher.

"What?" Sam asked with a laugh, all too aware of the way their knees rested against each other.

Jess shook her head, glancing down at the table. "I just can't believe you're finally here," she whispered. "I can't believe it's been a year since I last saw you."

Sam laughed. "You see me on FaceTime like every day."

Jess smiled, rolling her eyes. "You know what I mean. It's not the same."

Sam watched the way Jess leaned back in the chair, pushing her long hair over her shoulder.

"No," she breathed. "It's not the same."

Jess looked back at her as she placed a hand on the edge of the chair, just inches away.

A voice cleared beside them, and Sam turned.

"Hi guys," the young woman said with a smile. "I'll be your server this evening. Can I get you started with something to drink?"

"Oh, yeah," Sam muttered, looking down at the menu on the table in front of them.

Jess' warm hand slipped onto her forearm. "They have the best margaritas here, if you're in the mood for tequila."

"Yeah, sure," Sam replied. "That sounds perfect."

"I'll have one of those, too," Jess added.

"Two margaritas. Got it. I'll put those in now for you."

***

Sam laughed so hard her cheeks ached as she set the margarita glass down beside the other two empty ones.

"I can't believe Scar would do that," Jess said, laughing as she leaned her shoulder against Sam's.

"Really?" Sam asked, raising an eyebrow. "Because Scarlett would be the first one I would expect to take me to a beach party like that."

Jess chuckled, shaking her head. "Yeah, I guess you're right." She sipped the last of her drink before setting it down on the table. "I'm really glad you guys got so close."

Sam nodded, her lips tugging into a small smile. "Yeah. Me too."

The server approached the side of the table, placing a black leather check holder down in front of them.

"I'm just dropping this off now," she said. "But there's no rush. Take your time."

Jess reached forward, grabbing it as the server walked away. "I got it."

"What? No way, I—"

Jess shook her head. "You always pay for our dates, so—" She paused, looking down as she tucked a card inside. "I mean, every time we hang out, you always try to pick up the check." Jess cleared her throat, glancing back up at her. "So it's only fair."

Sam smirked, letting her eyes linger and watch the way Jess shifted in her chair as she glanced out at the people passing on the sidewalk.

After a moment, Jess turned back, finally meeting her gaze.

And Sam couldn't help it when that smirk grew into a wide grin.

Jess shook her head like she was trying to keep the smile off her own lips. "Don't," she muttered in a half-hearted warning tone.

Sam beamed. "Don't what?"

Jess rolled her eyes, but shifted so her arm brushed against hers. "You know what."

Sam watched her for another moment, leaning into the warmth. "Can I at least walk you home, then?"

Jess' eyes flicked up to hers, and Sam instantly detected a hint of familiar heat within them.

"Definitely."

Chapter two

Sam yawned as she stepped off the elevator, the faint scent of stale coffee and lemon cleaner filling the air as she made her way toward the office.

Luckily, there weren't any early meetings or calls scheduled that morning. She'd stayed up late catching up with Scarlett, and once she'd finally gone to bed, it was basically pointless. Jess' shocked face replayed in her mind on an endless loop, making sleep a near impossible task.

She pushed the office door open and stepped through.

Caleb spun his chair in her direction, pushing away from his crowded but meticulously organized desk. "Hey," he mumbled. "I thought you'd be here like two hours ago. What happened?"

She let out a dry laugh, moving to hang her motorcycle helmet on the hook by the door. "You're always telling me I shouldn't work so hard," she replied. "I took your advice and slept in."

Caleb wouldn't buy that lie. He never did. But even though she'd been up hours before sunrise, that didn't mean she wanted to talk to him about it. And he'd also know that.

"Right," he muttered, his sharp eyes flicking to the helmet as it swung slightly on the hook. "Haven't seen that in a while. You rode in today?"

She adjusted her backpack on her shoulder, avoiding his stare.

"Thought you were only riding late at night now, when there's no one around," he said softly, his tone holding more concern than judgement.

"Had a weird day yesterday. Just needed the ride to clear my head."

He nodded, looking away. Caleb cared about her enough to ask, but also knew a boundary when he saw one. And in instances like these, she was endlessly grateful for that particular trait.

"So," Caleb started, his voice taking on a slight edge of apprehension. "I guess this is as good a time as any to add on to the bad news."

She glanced up at him wearily. "What is it?"

He loosed a breath, offering the small apologetic smile he always did when he had bad news to share. It reminded her of the first time he'd done it, when the company was just a few months old and they didn't have enough cash to cover the bills.

"Andrea just emailed her two weeks' notice."

Sam groaned, leaning her head back. "Seriously?"

"Yeah," he drawled. "Sorry."

The PR manager had resigned the month before, along with another developer. And now with Andrea leaving, that made it three people in just the last month.

"None of them seem too happy about us moving forward with a potential buyout," he continued. "They don't want things to change. They like it how it is now."

Sam pursed her lips as she nodded. They'd kept their entire team remote, with open schedules. And a buyout would change that. She couldn't blame them for leaving before it happened.

"Besides," Caleb continued, his tone adding a slight edge, "she said she didn't feel needed."

"What do you mean?" Sam asked, her eyes narrowing. "Of course she was needed?"

He exhaled, giving her a somewhat pointed look. "Well, you don't really let any of the other developers have control over the bigger projects." His eyes bounced away for a moment. "You can't blame them for not wanting to stick around too long."

Her jaw clenched as she shook her head. "You want me to give them control over bigger projects when they can just leave at any moment? This just proves that point even more."

"So what," he groaned, "you'd rather keep working yourself to death instead of trusting them to help you?"

Sam crossed her arms over her chest. "That's better than risking them bailing and leaving us to pick up the pieces."

He let out a deep sigh. They'd had that conversation many times before. And it always ended the same.

Every time someone on the team left, it stung. But it would've stung much worse if they were even more involved—if she let them in on the more important things.

"Remember when we were small and didn't have any of these issues to deal with?" she muttered.

He snorted a laugh. "What I remember is working out of a glorified closet and how you could barely afford to pay either of us anything."

"I definitely prefer things the way they are now," he added. "Even with the stress."

Sam took a deep breath, stretching her sore neck. "Yeah."

She took a step down the hall as he called after her.

"Your friend is back there, waiting for you."

Sam paused, turning to look at him. "What? Who?"

He shrugged. "She said you knew she was coming."

Sam cocked her head, thinking back to her conversation with Liz the day before. She'd been distracted, but she was almost positive she would've remembered if they'd agreed to meet at her office instead that day.

Sam loosed a breath, trudging down the hall.

If it was Liz, then at least she'd be able to get through the work without running into Jess again.

She stopped outside the conference room, peering through the glass paned wall.

Empty.

Sam half turned, ready to go back to her office, but then stopped as a familiar laugh floated in from further down the hallway.

She continued walking until the area opened up into the large workspace they'd set up for when remote developers in the area wanted to come in.

Two developers sat at adjacent desks, smiling up at a woman sitting atop one of the desks in front of them.

She said something that Sam couldn't quite make out, and they both burst into laughter.

"Oh, if you think that's funny," the woman started, and Sam stopped, immediately recognizing the voice.

"No way," Sam said, a wide smile expanding on her face.

The woman instantly turned around, her face already holding its familiar teasing grin, as if she'd been waiting a while to catch Sam's reaction. Her dark skin glowed beneath the harsh fluorescent lights, her expression radiating the kind of warmth that instantly drew people in.

"Ah!" she squealed before hopping off the desk and striding forward with her usual confident bounce. Her long box braids, tied up in a high, perfectly styled bun, swayed as she moved, a few loose pieces framing her face in playful contrast.

Sam dropped her backpack, knowing exactly what Tiana was about to do.

And a second later, she jumped up onto her, wrapping her legs around her waist and her arms around her shoulders in a tight embrace.

"What are you doing here?" Sam asked with a laugh.

Tiana pulled her face back, her bright brown eyes sparkling as she gave Sam a cocky, teasing look. Then the wide grin grew mischievous before she dipped her head down and kissed her.

Sam smiled, laughing through the kiss that she also half-expected.

A moment later, Tiana pulled back, unhooking her legs as Sam lowered her to the ground.

She shrugged, her arms dropping, but still holding onto the sides of her t-shirt. "I missed you," she said with a wide smile. "I couldn't wait."

"Right," Sam replied with a laugh, shaking her head. "I thought you were staying in Dallas for another month?"

Tiana gave her a teasing push. "Dallas got boring quick. I was ready to come home."

Sam snorted, reaching down to pick up her backpack. "Everywhere is boring to you after a couple months."

"Exactly," Tiana replied with a smirk, crossing her arms over her tight sky blue tank top. "Which means it was a perfect time to come back here for a little while."

Sam smiled as she rolled her eyes. "Of course it was."

Tiana laughed, lightly shoving her shoulder. "Oh, don't act like you're not ecstatic to see me."

Caleb cleared his throat as he turned the corner toward them.

Sam shook her head, giving him a semi-apologetic smile. "Caleb, this is Tiana."

Tiana wrapped an arm around her waist, leaning her head into Sam's shoulder. "Old friends."

Caleb nodded slowly, raising one eyebrow as he gave Sam a questioning look.

"Sort of grew up together," Sam elaborated. "We were in the same foster home for a while."

"Oh," Caleb replied with a small nod.

Tiana laughed and Sam watched his professional demeanor finally begin to soften, the way people always did around her warmth.

She glanced around the office. "So if this company is such a big deal, why do you have like zero people working?"

"Most are working remotely," Caleb answered before Sam could.

Tiana nodded. "Well, could you use one more amazing employee in the office?" she asked, shooting Sam a broad grin.

Sam smirked, shaking her head as she caught the slightly horrified look Caleb threw her way. "How did I know that question was coming?"

"Because," Tiana replied with a coy smile, "you know I'd be the best hire you could ever get. Really, I'd be helping you out."

Sam chuckled. "That's so kind of you."

She glanced back at Caleb, who gave her a look that said *absolutely not.*

"It's his call," she said, nodding toward him. "He does the hiring."

But before Tiana even looked back at him, Sam already knew how it would end up. When she wanted something, most people couldn't resist her charm.

To his credit, Caleb kept his usual tough demeanor in place for at least a few seconds before finally giving in.

He loosed a breath, tilting his head back in defeat. "Fine."

Tiana smiled widely, turning back to Sam as she pushed up onto her tiptoes and pressed a quick kiss against her cheek. "Thanks."

She pulled away and ambled back to the desk she'd been sitting on before grabbing a large duffel bag off the floor that Sam eyed warily.

"Don't worry," Tiana said with a chuckle. "I'm not gonna ask to stay with you. I have a friend here who said I can crash at her place 'til she moves."

Tiana threw the bag over her shoulder. "So," she said, smiling between them both, "when do I start?"

***

Sam ran a rough hand down her face, blinking at the laptop screen.

"Sorry," Liz mumbled from behind her desk, giving her an apologetic frown. "Is that going to be too much work to set up? I don't know anything about the software stuff, just the reporting we handle."

Sam shook her head, blowing out a breath. "No, it's fine. Just a little more than I was expecting."

After spending another hour with Liz going through the details, she quickly realized why Howard had picked this firm as the one to test out the software on.

The systems they had in place were archaic, to say the least. So if it worked there, it'd be all but guaranteed to work at every other firm they owned.

But that also meant that the project would be twice as much work as they anticipated. If they wanted to stick to the two-week timeline they'd planned on, she'd need to carve out a few more hours of work each day.

"I know the feeling," Liz said, leaning back in her chair. "I wasn't expecting this on top of all my other work."

Sam glanced up at her as she continued scrolling mindlessly through her phone, only stopping to take the occasional sip of her pink smoothie.

The day before, when she'd first seen her, it'd felt impossible to stop thinking of her as the twelve-year-old girl she'd last known. But after spending a couple more hours together, she knew why.

Turned out, she actually hadn't changed all that much.

"So," Liz said suddenly, setting the phone down on her desk. "You and my girlfriend—" Sam's eyes flitted up, catching the slight emphasis she placed on that word. "You guys had a thing?"

The look on her face somehow seemed both oddly amused and challenging at the same time.

Sam held her stare for a moment, wondering how Jess would've broached the subject. She also couldn't help but wonder if a *'thing'* had been Jess' exact description, or Liz's altered version.

"Yeah," she answered, leaning back in the chair as she blew out a breath. "Sorry. I was caught off guard yesterday and didn't really know how to say that."

Liz stared at her for a moment, her hardened gaze morphing into an amused smirk.

Then she waved a hand in the air, as if brushing the awkwardness away. "Don't worry about it. Everyone is someone's ex's ex. Especially in the lesbian dating world."

She let out a laugh, and Sam forced a smile as she nodded.

Then Liz glanced up at the door behind her with a smile. "Speaking of."

Sam turned around, stopping as she saw Jess freeze in the doorway.

"Oh," Jess said, a stunned look adorning her face. "I'm—I'm sorry," she stuttered, eyes bouncing between Sam and Liz. "I didn't realize you were in a meeting." She glanced back at Sam for a split-second before her eyes returned to Liz. "Are we—still on for lunch today?"

Liz's eyebrows knitted together as she peered down at the silver watch on her wrist. She groaned, shaking her head. "I completely lost track of what time it was."

Sam stayed partially turned around, watching Jess, who carefully avoided her gaze.

"That's okay," Jess said, with a small shake of her head. "Its fine if you're too busy."

Liz looked at Sam then. "Wanna come with?" she asked, although it seemed more like a polite formality than an actual invite. "So we could finish—"

"No," Sam replied, just a bit too fast. She smiled, shutting her laptop. She dropped it into her backpack before grabbing her helmet off the floor. "That's okay. I have to get going, anyway."

She glanced back at Jess, whose eyes now seemed to be fixated on the motorcycle helmet in her hand.

Sam swallowed, moving it slightly out of view as she looked back at Liz. "I think I have enough to get started, so we probably don't need to meet again until Friday."

"Oh, okay," Liz said, standing from her desk. "What time on Friday are you thinking? We're hosting a networking event for some of the other firms we work with at the conference center down the street, so I might need to cut out a little early that day."

Sam frowned. Howard had told them about it that morning and asked if they could attend so they could meet some of the executives at the other firms they owned.

"I forgot about that," she muttered. "I guess we'll need to meet earlier in the day."

"You're coming?" Liz asked, her eyebrows raising.

Sam nodded. "Yeah. They emailed us about it this morning."

"Oh thank god," Liz breathed. "I always get so bored at those things. At least I'll have you guys to hang out with."

Sam gave her a small smile, nodding. "I'll message you later about figuring out an exact time to meet up that day."

"Sounds good," Liz said, stepping out from around the desk and making her way toward the door. "Well, I guess we'll walk out with you."

Sam followed silently behind Liz and Jess as they all made their way back out of the building, exiting out onto the sidewalk. The office building loomed behind them, its tall glass windows gleaming faintly under the muted afternoon sun.

Her bike stood parked just off the sidewalk, its black and chrome frame catching the reflected light.

Sam took a step toward it, setting her helmet on the seat as she adjusted the backpack straps over her shoulders.

Liz stepped forward behind her, letting out an impressed hum.

"I've always wanted to learn how to ride," Liz said, her heels clicking softly on the pavement as she bent slightly to examine the bike. She trailed a hand just above the handlebar, not quite touching it, as if afraid to disturb its pristine shine. Then she let out a soft chuckle, straightening up. "But Jess says she refuses to date anyone who rides a motorcycle." She snorted a laugh, looking up at Sam as she rolled her eyes. "You know, danger and all that."

Sam looked at Jess, the words spurring some unrecognizable feeling.

And this time, Jess didn't avoid her gaze. She looked up at her, mouth opening and pausing with unspoken words.

"I don't blame her," Sam said softly before Jess could speak.

Their eyes remained fixed on each other as Sam offered her a small, understanding look.

Then, without another word, she swung her leg over the bike, the leather seat creaking faintly beneath her. In one smooth motion, she pulled the helmet down over her head.

The bike's engine roared to life, its deep growl cutting through the hum of the city. Sam's gloved hand gripped the throttle, her gaze flicking up to Jess one last time before she pulled away.

***

Three Years and Eleven Months Earlier.

Sam awoke to an arm shifting around her torso.

Soft gray light glowed through the wide cracked window on the opposite wall. She turned slowly, feeling Jess' chin resting on her shoulder. And by the way her chest rose and fell against her back, she knew she was still asleep.

She tapped her phone screen where it laid on the bed beside her pillow, checking the time.

Then, ever so gently, she slid Jess' arm out from around her, scooting her body forward to rise off the bed.

Sam grabbed her t-shirt off the floor and slipped it on before tiptoeing out into the main area of Jess' tiny apartment.

These days had become her favorite. The ones where Jess' roommate left for the weekend to stay with her boyfriend, who lived a few hours away, giving them the space to themselves.

She made her way into the small kitchen area and began prepping a pot of coffee while she checked the string of texts Caleb had already sent her that morning. An endless stream of problems only she could fix.

Within a few minutes, a noise floated out from the bathroom, and Sam followed it.

A light in the bathroom seeped out through the open door, where Jess stood at the counter brushing her teeth.

Sam walked up behind her, sliding both arms around her stomach as she kissed the back of her neck.

Jess relaxed into the front of her body with a soft hum.

"You should've slept in longer," Sam whispered against her warm skin.

Jess leaned forward, rinsing out her mouth. "You should've slept in longer," she said, turning and sitting on the edge of the countertop beside the sink.

Sam rubbed the palm of her hand into her tired eyes. "Caleb texted about some urgent error that keeps popping up for the new client."

Jess frowned, tilting her head. "According to Caleb, there's an urgent error every other day."

Sam chuckled. "Yeah. Maybe I'm not as great at this whole software engineering thing as I thought."

She stepped in front of her, and Jess wrapped a leg around her waist, pulling her closer. Then she leaned forward, kissing her cheek.

"What I mean," she mumbled into her skin, "is that Caleb considers just about every minor inconvenience to be urgent."

Sam pulled back a fraction, a knowing smirk tugging on the corner of her lips. "He just knows how important it is to me," she said, pulling her t-shirt up her body and over her head.

Sam caught the way Jess' eyes flicked down to the thick scar running from the base of her neck to the edge of her sports bra.

"I just," Sam started, her voice lowering into a soft whisper. "I just want it to be worth something, you know? I want it to be worth—everything."

Jess stared at her for a long moment, as if searching for something in her eyes.

Then she pulled Sam close again, trailing a light finger up the scar and stopping when her hand rested around the back of her neck.

"You *are worth everything.*"

Chapter three

Caleb blew out a breath, leaning his back against the wall of Sam's office.

"That's a lot," he muttered.

"Mhm," Sam hummed, eyes raking over the copious notes she'd taken during her time with Liz.

They'd just finished going over all the extra changes they'd need to make in order for things to run smoothly. Caleb seemed more stressed than before. But Sam actually felt better. Now that it was organized, and she'd gone through it aloud, it all began piecing itself together. Everything began forming in her mind, flashing through in different images and lines of code, the way it always did when she started a new project.

And that was the part she loved. The part that made her feel calm. Made her feel in control.

A light knock on the door frame pulled her attention, and she looked up to see one of the developers.

"Hey Sam," she said, "someone's here for you."

But before she could ask who, Jess stepped around her.

She blinked, staring at her for a moment.

"I was wondering when you were going to show up," Caleb said, chuckling as he pushed off the wall toward her.

Jess jumped slightly, as if she hadn't noticed anyone else in the room. Then a wide grin broke across her face.

He crossed the few feet between them and leaned forward, pulling her into a tight hug.

"It's good to see you," she said, smiling over his shoulder. "How've you been?"

He pulled back and threw a nod over his shoulder where Sam still sat, watching.

"Same stuff. Helping our girl take over the world one step at a time."

Jess' eyes flicked to her, and Sam could see the slight apprehension that passed through them.

He looked back and forth between them, then his smile fell. "Sorry," he muttered, shooting Jess an apologetic look. "Old habits."

Jess nodded once, giving him a tense smile that stayed far away from her eyes. And even without that, Sam could see that something was bothering her. Something that had been present even before Caleb's slip up.

Sam closed her laptop, standing and stepping toward her as an edge of concern bubbled in her chest.

Caleb cleared his throat, glancing between them. "I—uh—better get back to work. But let's catch up soon?"

Jess smiled back at him, squeezing his arm. "Definitely."

He smiled at Jess one last time before walking out.

"What's up?" Sam asked, not caring to hide the edge of worry that came out with the words. "Is everything okay?"

She let her eyes rake over Jess' features, searching for signs. Searching for what she needed.

Jess stared back at her for a moment. And then something seemed to shift within her.

She loosed a breath, and with it, that tension that had been present each time she'd seen her over the last few days seemed to release.

Jess smiled softly, shaking her head. "Yeah—sorry. Everything is fine." Jess cleared her throat, her eyes bouncing apprehensively around the office. "I just wanted to talk. I know I should've called or something." She released a laugh that sounded almost nervous in a way. Then she crinkled her face slightly.

"Now that I'm here, I realize it was probably weird to just show up."

Ever so slowly, Sam's concern morphed into amusement.

She shrugged, a small smirk tugging on her lips. "Not the first time you've shown up unannounced to talk."

Jess faltered for a second, before a wide smile crossed her face and she shook her head with a laugh. "Don't remind me."

And just like that, the Jess she knew reappeared. As if the last four years of distance completely evaporated and she was still the person she could tell anything to. The person she could always count on.

Sam's smirk grew into a teasing smile then as she laughed with her. Then she nodded over her shoulder to the desk. "Wanna sit?"

"Yeah," Jess answered, following to sit in the chair beside her.

After a moment, Jess settled and cleared her throat again. "I just wanted to apologize for being so weird the other day when we ran into each other."

Sam chuckled, pulling her phone out of her pocket and setting it on the table beside her laptop. "I think if there's any time where you get a pass on being awkward, it was that day." She leaned back in the chair. "Besides, I wasn't much better."

Jess nodded slowly. "Also, though, about what Liz said yesterday." She swallowed, glancing away. "The motorcycle thing."

Sam ignored the slight pang in her chest at the memory, forcing a rueful smile.

"You don't have to apologize for that."

Jess looked away, an obvious conflict playing out behind her eyes. And Sam hated herself for being the cause.

"Really," Sam continued, "it's okay to know what you want or—" She swallowed, eyes bouncing away. "*Don't*—want in a person."

She had no idea what it was, but something about those words must have been the wrong thing to say. Because the darkness in Jess' eyes seemed to grow then.

A sense of unease filled her chest. Her brain began running through anything she could say or do to make it better.

Jess looked back at her with a small smile that did nothing to calm the rising worry.

"So," Jess said, releasing a breath as she glanced around the large office, "I guess all those early mornings and late nights were worth it, huh?"

Sam chuckled, forcing down the urge to beg Jess to tell her what she'd said wrong so she could fix it. "Yeah. I guess so."

"I'm happy for you," Jess continued. "It's impressive. Everything you've done and accomplished."

A small, shy smile crept up against the edges of Sam's lips as all the conversations with Caleb came flooding back. Every issue that seemed to arise daily. The employees quitting. The new workload. The software problems.

It was an odd feeling, being congratulated while everything constantly felt on the brink of falling apart.

"Thanks," she replied. But even she could hear the way it fell flat.

Jess cocked her head slightly. "You don't think so?"

"No—I mean—yeah," Sam continued, rubbing a hand over the back of her neck. "It is. It's just—different, I guess."

Jess continued watching her, waiting.

"We're um—" Sam paused, clearing her throat. "It looks like we're gonna be acquired by a larger company."

Jess blinked, her lips parting in surprise. "Really?"

"Yeah," Sam drawled. "I mean, it's not official yet. We're still in the early stages," she said, shaking her head. "But that's why I've been at Liz's firm the last few days. It's kind of a trial run to see how things go before they make an official offer."

"Wow," Jess said, a wide smile breaking out across her face. "Sam, that's amazing!"

Sam shot her a smile, although she could feel the hint of apprehension twist with her lips. She nodded, crossing her arms.

"Thanks," Sam continued. "It's just—a lot. It's a big change and some people here aren't happy about it. We've lost some people, so it's been harder lately."

Jess nodded slowly, her eyes flicking down as they trailed over her body. "I could tell," she said softly. "You're crossing your arms the way you do after you've been at your desk for too long the night before."

Sam blinked, a flicker of surprise passing through her. Then she quickly uncrossed her arms.

Even after four years of no contact, Jess was probably the only person who could really see those things in her. Things that she could easily hide from everyone else.

She couldn't remember the last time she'd felt that same sense of vulnerability. As if every problem in her life was out on display, no matter how hard she tried to hide it.

Sam cleared her throat, shaking that uncomfortable feeling away as she pulled her lips into a wide grin.

"So what's been going on with you?" she asked, her brain instantly latching onto Jess instead, as it forced out every other thought.

Jess looked hesitant for a moment, as if she didn't want to let that conversation end. But luckily, she did.

Jess let out a breath, tilting her head back in thought. "Moving here was the biggest thing. I just moved into a new apartment, though, that I love," she said with a pleased smile. "And obviously, getting the new job when I moved here was a big change."

"What are you doing for work now?" Although Liz had already mentioned something about it, she still wanted to hear it all straight from Jess.

"PR," she answered. "I'm at a big agency, so we have a lot of clients here in the city." She paused, clearing her throat. "Liz's company is one of them."

Sam tilted her head, her smile turning curious. "I thought you hated that PR internship you had in New York."

Jess chuckled, her nose wrinkling. "I hated my *boss*. I ended up liking the job, though, once he left."

Sam nodded. "Well, if you want any extra work, let me know. Our PR lead quit a few weeks ago, and I'm pretty sure Caleb is gonna lose it if we don't find someone new soon."

Jess let out a dry snort. "Caleb is *always* about to lose it over something."

Sam laughed, a full genuine smile finally returning to her face. And that seemed to put Jess at ease, too.

"But yeah," Jess said, leaning back in the chair. "Just tell me what you need."

Sam's eyes flicked up to hers. "Really?"

"Of course," Jess said, as if there wasn't any other possible answer. "I'll always help you."

Maybe it was the wording she'd chosen, or the way Jess looked at her in that moment, but something familiar snapped back into place between them. Some feeling of ease and care and—friendship. Something she didn't realize how much she'd missed until then.

"Thank you," Sam whispered.

Before she could say anything else, the office door behind them swung open.

"Hey boss," Tiana's voice floated in.

Jess turned around as Sam looked up to see Tiana striding in.

She leaned back in the chair, casting a quick glance at the time. "It's your first day, and you're late."

Tiana huffed, brushing her long, dark braids back over her shoulder. "I thought tech companies were supposed to be chill and not care about stuff like that," she said, placing a coffee on the desk in front of her.

Sam picked up the cup, taking a small sip as she mumbled, "Don't let Caleb hear that."

Tiana rolled her eyes, pushing Sam's hand off the arm of her chair before sitting on the edge, letting her back rest against Sam's shoulder. "Caleb needs to relax."

Sam took another sip of the coffee, catching the way Jess' eyes flicked curiously between them.

"I'm glad you're selling the company," Tiana continued as she grabbed the cup from Sam's hand and took a long drink. "You were more fun before you were stressed all the time about some letters on a computer screen."

Sam chuckled, shaking her head. "Remind me to not let you into any client meetings. Not sure they'd be happy to hear they're paying as much as they are just for some letters on a screen."

Tiana set the cup down on the table before finally turning to Jess.

Sam cleared her throat, nodding between them. "Jess, this is Tiana. She's an old friend."

Jess gave her a polite smile, holding a hand out.

"Tiana," Sam continued, "Jess is—" She paused, searching for the right words. "Also an old friend."

By the look that passed over Jess' face, she could tell those probably weren't it.

Tiana reached out, shaking her hand with a dazzling smile before shooting Sam a teasing glare. "Another gorgeous girl in your life. Should I be jealous?"

Jess' eyes flared in surprise, but Sam couldn't help the laughter that escaped her lips. Leave it to Tiana to break the tension by causing more of it.

"We both know you'll be jealous regardless," Sam mumbled with a smirk.

Tiana shrugged as she picked up the coffee once more. "So, what am I interrupting? You guys looked way too serious."

Sam exhaled softly, leaning back in the chair. "Just catching up."

Jess cleared her throat. "I should actually probably get going." She stood from the chair, giving each of them a tight smile. "I have to get back to work."

Sam nodded, hating that she felt slightly disappointed.

"But," Jess continued as she took a step toward the doorway, "I guess I'll see you Friday?"

Sam cocked her head. "Friday?"

"Yeah," Jess replied, running a hand through her hair. "You said you're gonna be at the conference, right?"

"Oh," Sam muttered. "Right. Yeah. I'll be there."

Jess gave her a small smile as she nodded. Then she looked at Tiana. "It was great to meet you."

Tiana gave her a warm, but curious, smile as she replied, "You too."

Jess nodded once more before turning to leave.

Tiana remained quiet for a few moments before turning to look at her. "Is that the one you told me about? From a while ago?"

Sam looked down at the desk as she gave a small nod. "Yeah."

***

Three Years and Ten Months Earlier

"And cheers to us for absolutely crushing it and closing our third official client," Caleb said, grinning from ear to ear as he clanked his glass messily against Sam's.

She laughed, pulling her glass back to take a sip.

Jess squeezed her thigh under the table of the booth. "Congrats, babe," she said with a proud smile, before placing a gentle kiss on her cheek.

Sam's stomach fluttered the same way it did anytime Jess called her that.

"Thanks," she replied softly, taking in the beautiful girl beside her.

"And cheers to me," Caleb continued, raising his glass in the air, "for being your permanent third wheel every time we go out."

Sam laughed, rolling her eyes.

"Hey," Jess said, "don't blame us. I tried to set you up twice, but you're the one who said no."

Caleb took a long drink before setting it down with a shrug. "Someone at the company needs to stay focused and not get distracted by pretty girls."

Sam snorted. "Right. We'll just pretend that's the reason you said no, and not because you got nervous at the last second before meeting them."

Caleb shot her a mild glare. "Anyway," he drawled, leaning back against the red cushioning of the booth. "I think we need to find a way to meet with more clients in person. I have a prospect in Austin who wants to use the software, but only if we can spend a few months there with their team, training them on how to integrate it with their workflow."

Sam nodded slowly, looking down at her drink.

They'd already had that conversation twice that week, and each time she'd cut it short. They'd just finally started to settle in New York. Moving again didn't sound appealing.

She looked back at him, catching the way his gaze bounced between her and Jess.

"I mean," he continued, softening a bit, "we can still grow without doing that. But it would definitely take longer."

Sam pursed her lips, scratching the back of her neck. "Yeah," she mumbled.

Jess shifted away from her, sliding out of the booth. "Gonna go to the bathroom real quick."

Sam turned, watching as Jess crossed the busy bar.

"Is that why you don't want to do it?" Caleb asked.

Sam looked back at him. "What do you mean?"

Caleb gave her the look he always did before he was about to give her a hard truth. "Jess. Is she the reason you don't want to go?"

"No," Sam answered automatically, although it sounded hollow somehow. Like her own voice knew the truth better than she did.

"I—" she started, clearing her throat. "I'd never be selfish and put myself before what we're working on." She twisted the glass in front of her, watching the way the ice swirled in the remaining bit of liquid. "I just— I want to be worth some—" She shook her head, slightly frustrated. "The company, I mean. I want the company to be worth something."

She kept her gaze fixed on the drink in front of her as she felt Caleb's stare burning into her.

After a few moments of silence, she looked up at him.

He gave her a small, understanding smile. "Do whatever you think is best, then. You know I'm with you, whatever you decide."

Chapter four

"Wow," Sam mumbled, looking down at Scarlett's engagement ring. "It's even bigger in person."

"I know," Scarlett replied with a grin, her hazel eyes sparkling. "I'm still not used to wearing it. It feels weird. But like—good weird? I would've been happy with anything, but Terrence wanted to go all out."

Sam leaned back in the leather chair, the murmurs of people in the small coffee shop floating around them. "I still can't believe you're getting married."

"I know," Scarlett said, exhaling as she swiped her glossy, dark brown braid over one shoulder, the ends brushing against her fitted denim jacket. "I can't believe I'm never gonna be single ever again."

Sam chuckled. "Yeah, I sort of thought you'd never get married." She reached forward, picking up her mug and taking a small sip. "I mean, who else is gonna take me to crazy beach parties every summer?"

Scarlett shot a mischievous look over the edge of her cup. "Oh, I'll still be taking you. I just won't take anyone home afterwards."

Sam smiled, shaking her head. "Well, I'm happy for you. Terrence is a very lucky guy."

"I know," Scarlett said, taking another deep drink of her coffee. "So you're for sure coming to the wedding, right? I know you're busy with work and everything but—"

"I wouldn't miss it."

Scarlett paused before a genuine smile tugged at her lips. "I'm glad you're here," she said, setting the cup down and reaching across the table to give Sam's hand a light squeeze. "I missed you. A lot."

"Me too," Sam replied with a smile.

She was glad. Really glad, actually. It wasn't until she'd seen Scarlett that morning that she fully realized just how much she really missed her. Even if they called and texted, there was no substitute for seeing one of her best friends in person.

Sam took a sip of her drink, glancing once around the coffee shop before looking back at Scarlett.

And this time, she wore a new, almost teasing smirk.

"What?" Sam asked.

"So, who's this Tiana girl?"

Sam cocked her head. "How did you—"

"Oh please," Scarlett interrupted with a wave of her hand. "Jess tells me everything."

Sam hummed, not entirely surprised. "She told you she showed up at my office a few days ago?"

Scarlett nodded. "Yeah, but that's the boring stuff. I wanna hear about the apparently beautiful girl you had hanging off you."

A dry laugh huffed from Sam's lips. "I wouldn't say she was hanging off me."

Scarlett shot her a pointed look, one brow arching.

The coffee cup turned in her hands as she cleared her throat. "She's a friend. We were really close when we were younger. Still are, I guess. We just don't see each other much anymore."

Scarlett stared at her, slowly cocking one eyebrow. "And?"

Sam chuckled, swirling her drink. "We had a thing for a little while when we were in a foster home together." She paused, taking another sip of her coffee. "We hook up sometimes when we see each other. But it's nothing serious. Never has been."

Scarlett hummed, as if searching for a lie in her words. "Yeah, I've heard that line before," she mumbled.

Sam smirked, keeping her eyes on the drink. "She's a good friend. You'd like her. She kinda reminds me of you, actually."

Scarlett smiled, taking a drink from her mug. "Well, then I can see why you'd like her so much."

A loud group of people entered as Sam let out a soft chuckle.

Scarlett tapped the screen of her phone on the table between them. "Oh—shit," she muttered. "I have to go. I have an appointment to go look at flower arrangements at one of the new places I found."

"Fun," Sam mumbled, taking another sip of her drink.

"Can you come with me?" Scarlett asked, standing from her seat.

"What?" Sam asked, frowning as she peered up at her from behind the cup. "Why?"

"Because," Scarlett started, shooting her a look that left no room to argue, "I wanna keep talking and hear about all this new stuff you have going on."

Sam grunted. "You mean you wanna keep grilling me about Tiana even though there's nothing more to tell?"

Scarlett crossed her arms with a stern look. "Please?" she asked, in a way that was definitely not a request. "It'd be more fun with you there."

Sam sighed quietly, checking the time on her phone. She'd already gotten the most urgent tasks done early that morning, so taking an extended break wouldn't be the end of the world. Although Caleb might not agree.

"Fine," she said, grabbing her mug off the table and downing the rest of the coffee.

"Oh, and—Jess will be there, too."

***

"I know, I know," Scarlett said as she rushed through the door, her shoes tapping lightly against the polished wooden floor as she hurried toward the front counter. "Sorry. We were having coffee, and I didn't realize how late it was."

Sam lingered near the entrance, letting the door swing closed behind her. The cool draft from outside faded away, replaced by the almost stifling humidity of the shop.

"It's fine," Jess answered, her voice drawing Sam's attention.

She turned and found Jess standing near a table piled high with vibrant bouquets. Her eyes flicked to Sam, widening slightly in surprise before softening, and a small, easy smile formed on her lips.

"Hey," Jess said, cocking her head slightly. "I didn't know you were coming too."

Seeing her the day before had felt different than she'd expected. Like a tiny thread had been tugged in her chest, and then it was just left dangling there, waiting to be unraveled.

Sam offered a quick smile as Scarlett strode ahead toward the front desk. "I didn't know either until like ten minutes ago."

Jess smirked, her head turning to where Scarlett now stood. "Well, I'm glad you're here. I could use a second person to help keep her on track."

Sam blew out a breath, nodding to where Scarlett was already speaking with an employee at the back of the shop. "You sure two of us is enough?" she muttered.

Jess chuckled, her eyes crinkling into a playful smile. "Probably not."

"Guys, come on," Scarlett called out, waving them over.

They spent a few minutes listening to the women explaining different arrangements and the logistics of having live versus fake flowers for different things throughout the wedding.

Then, when she was finished, she left the three of them to look over an assortment of beautiful bouquets.

Sam scanned over them, pointing out the few that caught her eye. Although she really had no idea what she was supposed to be looking for.

"So, according to Sam," Scarlett cut in suddenly as she eyed one vase, "Tiana was *not* hanging all over her."

Sam caught Jess as she stiffened before shooting Scarlett a mild glare.

Then she picked up a bouquet as she muttered, "Sam is also oblivious to women hitting on her."

"What?" Sam jerked her head back. "That's not true."

"It's definitely true," Scarlett said as she ambled over to the next row of flowers.

Sam pursed her lips. "Okay, maybe it's been true a few times before." Scarlett gave her a pointed look, arching one brow. "But Tiana's different. I've known her for like half my life. She's like that with everyone."

Scarlett walked further down the aisle, muttering something beneath her breath that Sam couldn't quite make out.

Jess stayed close by, eyes trailing over the flowers before them. "You guys knew each other before high school?"

"Yeah," Sam answered with a nod as she rested her hands in her pockets.

Jess hummed, tilting her head back as if thinking something through. "Did she know Liz, too?"

Somehow, in the few minutes since arriving, she'd managed to forget about Liz entirely. With how easily they'd slipped back into a sense of normalcy, she'd forgotten exactly how much had really changed.

"Uh—no," Sam replied, shaking her head as she moved further down the aisle. "Liz and I were friends a couple years before I met Tiana."

Jess nodded slowly, and Sam could see the wheels turning in her mind. She knew that look. It reminded her of when they'd first met and she would ask her questions about her past, careful never to push too hard. Which made it all that much easier to open up.

"We were in one of the same homes together," she continued, giving Jess the answer to the question she knew she wanted, but wouldn't ask.

"Oh," Jess said quietly, glancing up at her with a slightly surprised look in her eyes.

Sam cocked her head. "Why do you look surprised?"

Jess shrugged lightly. "You never mentioned her before."

Sam turned, looking back at the row of arrangements. "We don't get to see each other often. She bounces around a lot. Never really liked to stay in one place for long."

Jess nodded slowly, her lips tightening in the way they always did when she wanted to say something, but held back.

"What about these?" Scarlett called out.

Sam looked up to see Scarlett making her way back toward them with an enormous bouquet clutched tightly between her hands.

"Oh, those are gorgeous," Jess replied, stepping around the end of the aisle toward her.

Sam looked them up and down, and although they looked almost the exact same as half of the others she'd pointed out so far, she nodded along anyway. "Yeah," she said, trying to add some enthusiasm to her tone. "They're great."

The corner of Jess' lips quirked upward as she shot her an amused glance.

"Ugh," Scarlett groaned. "But it's not exactly what I was picturing."

"What did you have in mind?" Sam asked, trying to find any possible way to be helpful.

"Something with greenery," Scarlett muttered, eyes narrowing as she twisted it in her hand, examining them meticulously.

Sam stared down, scanning the countless green leaves poking out of the bouquet. "Is that not what that is?" she muttered, throwing a nod at it.

Scarlett huffed, shaking her head. "Yeah, but—not like that."

Sam arched a brow as she nodded slowly. She could understand some of the most complex software and mathematics problems known to man, but apparently figuring out wedding arrangements was where her brain drew the line.

"Right," she muttered.

"What about this one?" Scarlett asked, holding up a new bouquet.

Sam held back from pointing out that it seemed to have even less greenery than the last one.

"Pretty," Jess said with a nod, looking it over.

"Sam," Scarlett said, glancing up at her, "what do you think?"

She cleared her throat, raking over it as she tried to find any detail that seemed different from the others. "Honestly? It looks basically the same as the others, but bigger. Too big. It'd probably block most of your dress."

Scarlett cocked her head, peering down at it again. "Hmph. I think you're right." She set it back on the shelf beside her. "See. I told you I needed you here. You think of all the things I never would."

Jess leaned closer into her side, lowering her voice as she whispered, "hope you cleared your afternoon. We might be here a while."

Sam blew out a breath. "Pretty sure Caleb's gonna call me any minute to come rushing back."

Jess gave her a look, then glanced away, the muscle in her jaw ticking. "Guess some things never change."

***

Three Years and Ten Months Earlier

Sam frowned, looking down at the text from Jess asking about their plans for the night.

She typed out and sent a quick reply, letting her know she'd be working late and wouldn't be able to come over.

That was the third night that week she'd had to cancel. And although she knew Jess understood how busy she was, it hurt to go that long without seeing her.

The early mornings and late nights had begun to pile up. Every day it seemed like the already never ending list of things to do grew further and further. And each time she cancelled their plans, the guilt was almost unbearable.

But that wasn't even the worst part. It was watching Jess try to conceal her disappointment that really twisted the knife.

Sam dropped her phone on the desk, forcing herself to ignore the now familiar surge of guilt in her stomach as she focused back in on the work she needed to finish that night.

The steady tapping of Caleb typing behind her drowned out her thoughts. And she couldn't tell how much time had passed before she eventually heard the door to the tiny apartment creak open.

"Hey," Jess said with a smile as she stepped past the threshold, balancing a paper bag beneath her arm.

Sam blinked once, then twice, as her tired eyes slowly absorbed the sight. Then a smile tugged across her face.

"You're here," she said, in more of a statement than a question.

"I hope that's food," Caleb mumbled from where he sat at the second small desk in the far corner.

Jess crossed the few steps toward Sam, placing a gentle kiss on her cheek before setting the bag on the desk in front of her.

"I figured you guys hadn't eaten dinner yet."

Sam's lips curled into a contented smile. "Thank you."

Jess rounded the back of the chair, running her hand up Sam's arm and onto her shoulder before giving the tense muscles a gentle squeeze.

Sam leaned back, releasing a deep exhale as she rested her head against her chest.

"I'm glad you came," she mumbled.

Caleb stood and strode toward them, plucking the paper bag off the desk.

Jess ran her other hand across Sam's chest in a soothing motion. "Three days was too long to go without seeing you."

Sam couldn't help the way she stiffened slightly at the words, each one reminding her of the conversation she'd had with Caleb earlier that day. Reminding her of the near impossible decision she'd had to make.

Caleb shot her a weary glance, and by the way Jess' hand stilled against her chest, she knew Jess had caught it, too.

He cleared his throat in an unusually awkward way. "I'm gonna go stretch my legs," he mumbled. "I've been sitting at that desk for too long today."

He made his way out the door, avoiding both their looks as he closed it behind him.

Jess remained still behind her, staring after him. "Well, that was weird," she mumbled.

Sam shifted in the chair, running a hand across the back of her neck, her brain sprinting through the million different things she could say.

But in all those options, nothing felt right.

Jess weaved around the chair, brows furrowing slightly as she peered down at her. "What's wrong?"

Sam exhaled slowly, but it failed to quell the anxiety bubbling up in her chest. "We've been talking more about the idea of going to Austin to sign that new client and work with their team."

Jess' throat bobbed as she swallowed.

She waited for Jess to say something. Anything.

But she remained silent. And within her eyes lay something deep. Some sadness that looked eerily familiar. Something she'd only seen once before.

The day she'd told her she was leaving for MIT.

"You're gonna do it, aren't you?" Jess whispered.

Sam closed her eyes, releasing a breath before finally looking up at her.

She nodded once.

"How long?" Jess asked, and the fragile tone in her voice instantly made her want to change her mind. To rush out and tell Caleb they couldn't do it. That they had to figure something else out.

But she couldn't.

They'd already had that conversation. And she knew how it would end.

They needed this. She *needed this. She needed to make something of herself. And this was her chance.*

"A few months," she answered. "Maybe more."

Jess nodded slowly, closing her eyes. "What does that mean for us?"

"Nothing has to change," Sam answered, the words rushing out as if the speed would make them true— would cement them into being. "We can go back to how things were. We can—we can call and Facetime and—"

Jess shook her head, and the look on her face was all she needed to see to know the answer.

"I can't," she whispered. "I can't spend another four years—"

Jess paused, tilting her head back as she squeezed her eyes shut.

And all at once, Sam felt the one thing she'd held onto all that time slipping away.

"I can't do it again, living my life around texts and calls," Jess whispered, opening her eyes to reveal two pools of wetness. "I can't wait anymore."

Chapter five

"Lets give it up for our amazing panel guests," the host bellowed into his microphone from the side of the stage at the front of the large banquet hall. "These are some of the most brilliant minds in finance today, shaping the industry."

Sam clapped politely, her eyes flicking toward the stage as the panelists exchanged handshakes and goodbyes. Conversations hummed as people drifted toward the back of the room, the stage at the room's center now empty under its sharp spotlight.

She sat near the back of the room, watching as attendees stood, stretching and gathering their belongings. A few rows ahead, Jess and Liz rose from their seats, Jess brushing a strand of her long blonde hair behind her ear as they turned to head toward the exit.

Liz caught Sam's gaze and smiled, lifting a hand in a casual wave.

Sam nudged Tiana, and they both stood, stepping into the aisle to meet them at the end of the row.

"Ready to make small talk with a million different people you'll probably never see again?" Liz asked with a light laugh, smoothing the lapel of her tailored blazer.

Tiana groaned. "Seriously, this thing isn't over yet? I feel like we've been here forever, and it's already five. Isn't that supposed to be the end of the day when you work an office job?"

An amused smile passed over Jess' lips as Sam shot Tiana a pointed look. "You're the one who asked to come. You could've hung back at the office instead."

"Yeah, well, I thought it'd be more of a party here," Tiana muttered, mirroring the look right back at her.

Sam shrugged, watching the swarms of people as they made their way toward the back of the large banquet hall where the networking part of the evening would be held.

"They usually serve drinks at these networking things," she said, nodding toward the small bar where people had already begun lining up.

Tiana brightened slightly at that. "Good. Everyone here needs to loosen up."

Liz gave Tiana a surprised smile as she let out a laugh. "I couldn't agree more."

"Well," Tiana said, turning toward the bar, "you know where I'll be."

"I have to go talk to a few important people," Liz said, looking back at Jess. Then she looked at Sam with a grin that seemed to feign embarrassment. "I'm up for a big promotion, so they want me to meet more of the executives." She let out a short laugh. "You're so lucky you never have to deal with that, doing your own thing and all."

Sam hummed, keeping her face neutral as she nodded in agreement.

Liz gave her another smile as she placed a hand on Jess' lower back, turning her to leave.

"I'll wait here," Jess said, staying in place.

"Are you sure?" Liz asked with a questioning look. "I don't know how long I'll be."

"Yeah," Jess said with a small smile. "You go do your thing. I'll find you after."

"Okay," Liz muttered, frowning as she turned to leave.

A few seconds of silence ticked by before Tiana turned back to them from where she stood at the bar, holding a beer up and tilting her head in question.

Sam shook her head, holding up the bottle of water she'd swiped at the beginning of the event.

"She's good for you to have around," Jess said from where she stood beside her.

"She's something," Sam muttered with a chuckle as she turned back to Jess. "She always got into trouble when we were kids. And she was always dragging me along, so her trouble turned into mine, too."

The corner of Jess' mouth quirked upward. "Maybe you need that. Someone to remind you to take it easy sometimes and have fun. Especially now."

Sam blew out a breath, laughing. "Well, if you're the one giving that advice, it must mean I really need it."

Jess bumped her shoulder against Sam's, the small smile growing on her lips. "Hey, I eased up a little after college. But you—" she paused as the smile fell from her eyes. "You did the opposite."

It was true. And if anyone were to see it within her, she knew it'd be Jess.

"Okay," Tiana said suddenly as she approached. "So they're only serving beer, apparently," she said, holding a second beer bottle out to Jess. "Hope you're a fan of fruity IPAs."

Jess turned to Tiana, giving her a small smile as she took the beer. "Thanks."

"She hates IPAs," Sam said with a smirk.

Jess' smile grew into an amused grin as she took a sip. "Not as much as I used to. They've grown on me."

"Well, I think they're absolutely disgusting," Tiana muttered before taking a large gulp of her own. "But I'm not about to listen to one more guy tell me about his boring finance job without having a drink first."

"Sam!" Liz called out from somewhere across the room. She looked up to see her weaving through the crowd of people.

Liz grinned, looking over her shoulder as she said something Sam couldn't hear.

And then she froze as two familiar faces trailed behind Liz, emerging from the crowd.

"Mom, dad," Liz said excitedly as they approached, "you remember—"

"Sam?" the older man said as he stared at her wide-eyed.

"Oh my gosh!" The woman exclaimed, surging forward and pulling her into a tight hug.

Sam stiffened. Then, slowly, she reached one arm around the woman.

"Mr. and Mrs. Jacobs," she mumbled, fighting to gain her composure as she took them both in.

"Oh, get out of here with all that," Mrs. Jacobs said, chuckling. "You're all grown up now. You can call us by our first names."

Sam pulled away, nodding as she planted what she hoped was a convincing enough smile on her face. Even if she wanted to call them by their names, she couldn't. She'd never known them as anything else.

"Gosh, how long has it been?" Mr. Jacobs asked, looking her over. "I can't even remember the last time we saw you."

Her smile faltered as she instantly recalled the memory. She could still see the moment in her mind, as if it had only just happened. The day the social worker came and picked her up from their house, even after she'd begged them not to go. After she begged them to take her in.

"Yeah, I can't remember either," she lied, glancing away as she took a sip from her water bottle.

The woman turned to Jess. "Hey honey," she said, giving her a hug. "It's nice to see you again."

Sam watched Jess greet them both. If she'd already met Liz's parents, they must've been more serious than she originally thought.

Mrs. Jacobs turned back to her. "Well, you look great!" she gushed, squeezing Sam's arm.

"What brings you to our company's event?" Mr. Jacobs asked.

Sam cocked her head, but before she could clarify, Liz cut in.

"He's one of the execs at the firm," Liz said matter-of-factly.

"Oh," Sam muttered, trying and failing to gain back her professional demeanor.

Mr. Jacobs smiled proudly, bumping his shoulder against Liz. "Got this one her first job there right out of college."

Liz's smile faltered. "I had other offers," she said quickly, with a laugh that sounded just a tad too forced. "But—it just—made sense to work there, you know?"

Sam nodded, not entirely caring to hear the details.

"It was hard to get her to focus on anything other than soccer in college, but we did it!" he said with a boisterous laugh. "Sam, where did you play in college?

You were so talented, I'm sure you had recruiters all over you."

She glanced away, avoiding his gaze. And her eyes met with Jess' instead, who seemed to be watching her intently. Sam shifted a fraction closer to her. Maybe it was out of some long-lost habit, or maybe it was something else. But either way, it made her feel better.

She cleared her throat, looking back at him. "I didn't play in college."

He jerked his head back, as if it somehow offended him. "What? Why?"

She shifted another inch closer to Jess, scratching the back of her neck. "Uh—I couldn't play in high school. So—" she trailed off, wracking her brain for any way to change the subject.

He either didn't care to hear the rest, or was entirely oblivious.

He turned to Jess instead. "You should've seen these two when they were kids," he said with a grin as he shook his head. "They were incredible on the field, even from a young age. They were at the same private school, and they went undefeated for three seasons in a row until—"

He paused, as if finally catching himself, before continuing what he was about to say. A sheepish look crept over his features.

"Well," he mumbled, throwing his wife a quick look that said he needed rescuing, "the team was much better when you were on it."

Mrs. Jacobs let out an awkward laugh as she waved a hand dismissively. "He likes to reminisce too much. And once he starts talking about sports, you can hardly get him to stop!"

Everyone in the circle laughed, and although Sam tried her hardest to join, nothing came out.

She raised the water bottle to her lips, tilting it back far enough to get a couple of big gulps down.

She was only vaguely aware of Liz changing the subject to something work related, before they all began talking again. She followed each person as they spoke, trying to smile or laugh at all the right moments. But the tightness in her chest didn't recede.

It was as if she was suddenly twelve years old again. Nothing more than an outsider looking in.

Mrs. Jacobs said something to her before laughing, and Sam smiled, forcing a response to come out of her mouth. She wasn't entirely aware of what she'd said, but it seemed to be the right thing, because the older woman burst into laughter.

Sam planted a wide grin on her lips as if she didn't feel like nothing more than a shell of a human being at that moment. The laughter buzzed in her ears, and she couldn't tell if it was theirs, or her own, that she was hearing.

Suddenly, a soft hand squeezed her bicep.

She blinked, looking to where Jess stood beside her.

"Hey," Jess said, a nonchalant smile on her face. Although the look in her eyes was anything but. The concern in them seemed to ask some sort of silent question. "I'm gonna step out for a sec and get some air. Wanna come?"

Sam swallowed as the world came rushing back to her. "Yeah," she nodded slightly, emerging from the daze she'd entered. "Yeah. That sounds good."

They excused themselves as the rest of them continued talking, the laughter fading with every step they took toward the nearest exit.

Jess kept a hand placed gently on her shoulder, leading them to the door that led to the main lobby area. And the instant they stepped past the threshold, a calming quiet greeted them. The lobby had mostly emptied, leaving only a handful of people saying their goodbyes.

Jess led her out to a vacant part of the lobby before she stopped, dropping her hand.

"You okay?" she asked, turning to look at her with that curious concern she'd seen in her eyes just a few moments before.

"Oh—yeah." Sam shook her head lightly, with a tight smile. "Yeah. All good."

Jess' features hardened then, as if they were deflecting the obvious lie. And it was hardly a surprise. She always seemed to have some deep sense of how she was feeling, like their emotions were tangled together as one.

Sam swallowed, hating how transparent she felt beneath Jess' gaze. Or maybe she didn't hate it at all. And maybe that's what she really hated so much.

"Yeah," Sam said softly, looking away. She fiddled with the bottle in her hand. "Its just a lot, I guess."

Jess' eyes traced her face. "Seeing her parents, you mean?"

Sam nodded.

It'd been one thing to see Liz again after all those years. It felt odd, but not necessarily in a bad way. Just different. Unexpected.

But seeing her parents was something else.

As a child, she'd never understood why they hadn't let her stay with them. Why she couldn't have kept the life she'd had. The school. The friends. They'd been her only hope of that.

And—they didn't want her.

As she got older, she understood more of what a big commitment it would've been on their part. And she didn't blame them. Not really. Or at least, she never thought she did.

But seeing them like that—so happy, so unbothered—stirred those old, repressed feelings.

"You haven't seen any of them since your mom passed?" Jess asked softly. "Not even Liz?"

Sam shook her head, avoiding her gaze.

Having her there in the moment had felt like a life raft. But now, knowing that Jess had seen her fumble and lose her composure in front of those people—her *girlfriend's* parents—made it worse. Like she was nothing more than that same powerless child she'd once been.

Like she'd never changed. Never become anything.

"I'm sorry," Jess said, giving her an earnest look that held no ounce of pity. Just pure empathy.

She loosed a breath, scratching the back of her neck as her brain worked to push out those bad thoughts and reset itself.

"It's fine," she breathed, smiling a little too wide. "No big deal."

She looked away, scanning the empty lobby, but she could feel Jess' eyes raking over her, the way they had so many times before.

She looked back at her and saw a slightly curious expression adorning her features.

"What?"

Jess pursed her lips into a tight line. "You know you don't have to do that with me."

She frowned. "Do what?"

Jess stared at her for a moment, her intense gaze softening a fraction. "You know what."

Sam faltered for just a second, but luckily, her brain had already switched gears. She could feel it forcing her confidence back, searching for something to latch onto and take her far away from all of those memories.

"Why are you so good at reading me?"

Jess instantly rolled her eyes, but the corners of her lips turned up slightly. "Why are you so good at changing the subject?"

Sam didn't bother suppressing her grin. She couldn't help it, anyway. That teasing tone in Jess' voice was one of her favorites.

"You know your charm won't distract me like it does with everyone else," Jess continued, a challenging, but amused, glint in her eyes.

"Oh, I know," Sam muttered with a chuckle. "It never worked on you."

Jess watched her for a moment, opening her mouth before closing it again and glancing away. She crossed her arms over her chest before looking back at her, the seriousness returning to her warm eyes.

"So?" she prompted once more.

Sam blew out a breath, running a hand over the back of her neck. "I'm fine," she said. "Really."

By the look in her eyes, she could tell Jess wanted to push her on it. To get a deeper explanation. But instead Jess just nodded slowly, giving her a soft, understanding smile. "Okay."

"Okay?" Sam asked slowly, cocking an eyebrow.

"I didn't bring you out here for an interrogation. You were getting enough of that in there," she said, glancing toward the auditorium.

Sam hummed, nodding slowly. "Yeah. Thanks for giving me an excuse to leave."

Jess' lips twitched into a faint smile.

"Oh, thank God. Are you finally ready to go?"

Sam turned, seeing Tiana walking toward them with a new drink in hand.

"Not yet," she replied, taking one more swig of the water before screwing the cap back on. "I should head back in and talk to some more people before we leave."

Tiana let out an exaggerated groan. "Alright, well, come on," she muttered, motioning her over. "Let's get it over with. I'm not trying to spend my whole Friday night here."

Sam chuckled, shaking her head. "Right," she said, throwing Jess an amused glance as Tiana grabbed her hand to pull her away. "You coming?"

Jess shook her head. "I'm all talked out. I'll find you guys later, though."

They made their way around the crowd, stopping to meet and talk with different people Sam recognized from the few times she'd been at the office.

And as the time ticked on and the drinks flowed, the conversation devolved along with it.

But she played her part to perfection. She put on a smile, giving her thoughts and telling some relevant story that had everyone in the group laughing by the end. As she finished, though, the smile felt more forced than it had before. As if just standing there between them all, pretending to care and have fun had become the most enormous task in the world.

She cleared her throat, letting the painful smile melt away as she excused herself from the conversation.

"Okay, I've hit my breaking point," Tiana muttered from beside her. "I can't do this small talk anymore."

And this time, she agreed.

"Me too. Let's head out."

They made their way through the thinned out room of people before exiting the building to the sidewalk in front of the event center.

"Done for the night?" Liz's voice called out from behind them.

Sam looked over her shoulder to see Liz and Jess walking toward them.

"Absolutely not," Tiana quipped. "I'm ready to go out and have some real fun."

Sam shot her an amused look. "You just spent all day out talking to people, and now you want to do it even more?"

"Of course," Tiana replied as if it were obvious. "It's a Friday night, and I just worked all day."

"You know," Jess cut in beside them as Liz took her hand. "I actually kind of agree. I thought I'd be more exhausted, but going out sounds like fun."

Tiana squealed, a wide grin breaking out across her face. "Yes!"

Sam caught the slight frown that passed over Liz's features as Jess turned to her.

"I don't know," Liz muttered, stifling a yawn. "Its been a long day. I kind of just want to head home," she said, offering Jess an apologetic look.

"Oh," Jess replied, a hint of disappointment in her voice. "Yeah—no, that's okay."

"Oh, come on," Tiana groaned. "Its barely even six. Just come out for a few hours, at least."

Jess looked back at Liz, who pursed her lips, but seemed to be considering it, nonetheless.

After a moment, she let out a low exhale. "Okay. Fine. Yeah, I'm in."

Tiana grinned, looking back at Sam. "You're coming too. And don't even try to say you have to work in the morning."

Sam chuckled. "Hey, I was already gonna say yes." She rolled her stiff shoulders back. "I think I'm gonna take the morning off."

"Perfect," Tiana said, grabbing her hand. "There's a gay bar downtown that I've been dying to go to."

Jess pulled her phone out of her pocket. "What's the name? I'm gonna text Scar and see if she wants to meet us."

Chapter six

"He said that?" Jess asked, her head jerking back in amused shock.

"Oh yeah," Tiana groaned, her words just loud enough to hear over the music and swarms of people in the surrounding bar. "And that wasn't even half of it."

Sam laughed into her drink as she listened to Tiana recount another one of the conversations she'd had that evening.

"I've only talked to him a few times," Liz said with a laugh, finally looking up from her phone, "but that's exactly the kind of thing I'd expect him to say."

Sam had nearly forgotten Liz was still with them. She'd been so quiet, her focus fixed on her phone for most of the evening, that the sudden interjection was surprising.

Jess turned toward Sam, her fingers trailing along the rim of her drink as the laughter settled. "So," she started, her tone casual, "do you still need help with that PR stuff you mentioned?"

Sam exhaled, the words drawing her focus from the comfortable rhythm of the bar's noise. "Yeah. I can use any help right now."

Jess nodded. "Do you want to meet up next Saturday? I have some stuff I can drop off real quick and you can look it over. Then maybe we could meet again later to go over everything in detail if you want?"

"Really?"

"Yeah, I mean, if you want to."

She swore she could almost immediately feel a fraction of the stress melt from her shoulders. "Yeah, that's perfect."

Liz, who had resumed scrolling on her phone, suddenly perked up. "Wait," she interjected, her brows furrowing as she looked at Jess. "You can't on Saturday. You're coming to my soccer game, remember?"

"Oh," Jess muttered, her expression shifting as a flicker of remorse crossed her face. "Yeah, sorry. I completely forgot."

She turned back to Sam, her gaze apologetic. "Can you fit it in on another day?"

Sam offered a small, understanding smile. "You're the one doing me a favor, so just let me know when you can, and I'll make it work."

The tension in Jess' shoulders eased, her lips curving into a softer smile. "How about early tomorrow? I can swing by your apartment and drop it off."

"That's perfect," Sam replied with a nod.

"Great," Jess said, her smile widening as a hint of warmth returned to her voice. "Send me your address, and I'll be there in the morning."

Sam immediately pulled out her phone, quickly typing out the address before hitting send.

Then she peered back up at Liz. "You still play soccer?"

"Of course," she replied with a look that made the question seem insane. "It's a rec league, but it's mostly ex college players, so it's super competitive."

Sam hummed as she nodded once. "Sounds fun."

"It is," Liz gushed, finally brightening up for the first time since they'd arrived. "Playing in college was the best. This makes it feel like it never really ended."

Sam brought the drink to her lips, taking a sip.

"Hey, you should come play with us next Saturday!" Liz exclaimed.

The idea was tempting—being back on the field sounded incredible—but her schedule was already crammed with work and the endless wedding tasks Scarlett kept roping her into. Adding something else, even something fun, probably wasn't the smartest move.

"I don't know," Sam muttered. "I'm pretty busy with everything going on."

Liz frowned, although the look didn't hold all that much disappointment. "Right. I understand." She reached forward, taking a sip of her drink. Then a small, challenging smirk formed on her lips as she glanced back up at her from behind her glass. "I understand you being too scared you'd lose against me."

Sam caught the glint in her eyes, a spark that instantly reminded her of the childhood best friend who never backed down from a challenge. The one who would push until she had no choice but to take her on.

And she loved it.

The corners of her lips curled upward before she could stop them.

"Ugh," Tiana groaned beside her, rolling her eyes. "You're so easy to get to. It's ridiculous."

Sam broke out into a grin as she said, "We both know I'd run circles around you, just like when we were kids."

Liz's eyes tightened a fraction, an edge of seriousness seeping in behind the teasing smile. "Means nothing if you can't prove it."

Sam caught the amused, but also slightly weary, look in Jess' eyes as she looked at Liz.

"Fine," Sam replied. "I'm in."

Liz's grin widened, showing all of her teeth. Then she threw a glance at Tiana. "You're right. She's always been this easy to get to."

"Wow, this place is packed."

Sam looked up to see Scarlett approaching the table.

"Hey," she called out, shooting Scarlett a smile.

Scarlett rounded the table, slipping an arm around Sam for a quick side hug before turning her attention to Tiana with an easy grin. "You must be Tiana. I've heard a lot about you."

Tiana beamed back, standing and throwing her arms around her in a tight hug. "If it's from Sam, then I know it has to be all good things."

Scarlett laughed, squeezing her back before stepping away. "I like her already," she said, throwing Sam a playful, pointed smile over her shoulder.

Sam leaned back, watching as Scarlett and Tiana fell into effortless conversation, their animated voices blending together as though they'd known each other for years.

With a knowing smirk, Sam slid a little closer to Jess, her voice quiet. "I knew they'd be best friends right off the bat."

Jess chuckled, shaking her head as she lifted her drink. "You were right," she said before taking a slow sip.

Across the table, Scarlett frowned, her eyes narrowing at her phone screen.

"What is it?" Sam asked, her brow furrowing as she leaned forward slightly.

Scarlett hesitated, her thumb hovering over the screen before she finally set the phone down on the table with a sigh. "Terrence just texted me," she said.

"His sister's gonna come to the bachelorette weekend next month."

"That's a good thing, right?" Jess asked carefully. "Didn't you invite her?"

"I did," Scarlett admitted, blowing out a long breath. "But now I'll spend the whole weekend stressing over whether she likes me or not."

Sam's brow furrowed. "His sister doesn't like you?"

Scarlett gave a small shrug. "It's not that she doesn't like me—or at least, I don't think that's it," she said with a sigh. "Our personalities just don't mesh. I've tried, but it's always felt—forced."

"That's surprising," Sam said, tilting her head. "Everyone loves you."

Scarlett scoffed, shooting her a look. "No. Everyone loves *you*." Then her expression shifted, her hazel eyes lighting up with sudden excitement. "Wait—oh my gosh, you should come with us!" She clapped her hands together as if the idea had struck like lightning. "It'd be perfect! You could totally get her to loosen up and have fun!"

Sam frowned, apprehension washing over her.

"You guys should all come!" Scarlett continued, her excitement bubbling over as she turned to Liz and Tiana.

"Are you sure?" Sam asked carefully. "I thought you were excited to have a weekend with just you guys," she added, nodding between her and Jess.

Scarlett waved her hand dismissively, as if that thought was already far behind her. "I was, but I think it'd be so fun if you were all there, too."

"Well, you don't have to convince me," Liz said with a grin. "A weekend at a resort is exactly what I need right now. Send me the dates. I'll add them to my list of dates and addresses I already have marked down for your other wedding stuff."

Scarlett beamed, her enthusiasm doubling as she swung her hopeful gaze back to Sam.

"I don't know," Sam muttered, frowning at her. "I can't really travel right now with everything going on."

Scarlett shook her head. "We're not traveling. We were just gonna stay at a hotel on the beach for the weekend. It's barely even a thirty-minute drive from the city."

"Well, that sounds perfect. I'm in," Tiana said, her wide grin practically daring Sam to argue. She scooted in closer to her, wrapping an arm around her shoulders. "Come on," she said, squeezing her arm. "It's useless saying no, anyway. You know I'll talk you into it."

Sam frowned slightly, before blowing out an exhale. "Okay," she muttered. "Yeah, sure."

"Yes!" Scarlett exclaimed, clapping. "I'll call the hotel tomorrow and see if we can reserve a couple more rooms on the same floor."

"Great, now that that's settled," Tiana said, tipping her glass back and finishing her drink in one smooth motion. She stood, grabbing Sam's hand. "Let's dance."

Sam blinked but didn't resist as Tiana tugged her out of the booth. With a resigned smile, she downed the last of her drink and slid out from behind the table.

Scarlett took a sip from her own glass, her gaze shifting to Jess. "You guys coming?"

Jess nodded, sliding out of the booth with her usual easy smile before glancing over at Liz.

Liz wrinkled her nose, her scowl mild but firm. "I'm good. Not exactly in the mood to get elbowed by sweaty strangers."

Sam waited as Jess slipped past her, following behind Scarlett and Tiana toward the pulsing lights of the dance floor.

The music hit like a wave, thudding through the floor and reverberating in her chest. The space was packed, bodies swaying and bouncing to the beat, the crowd pressing in tight on all sides. Sam could hardly move without brushing against someone else.

And yet, none of it mattered. Not the chaos, the crush of people, or the way her shoes stuck faintly to the floor.

Because as her gaze lingered on Jess, her cheeks faintly pink beneath the shifting lights, and Scarlett laughing at something Tiana whispered, Sam felt a rare lightness settle in her chest.

It felt good—better than it should—to just be there, letting go for once.

Sam laughed, the sound bubbling out of her unexpectedly as she caught Jess' eye. Jess grinned back, laughing along with her.

A moment later, Sam felt someone move beside her, close enough to grab her attention. She turned her head just as a woman began swaying in time with her, then smoothly shifted to press her back against Sam's front.

The woman shot a playful, coy smile over her shoulder.

Sam hesitated for half a second, but with the last drink finally settling warm in her veins, she let herself fall into the rhythm. She wasn't looking for anything, but she didn't mind the easy, thoughtless contact, either. They moved together, bodies naturally syncing to the beat.

As they turned, her eyes swept over the dance floor and landed on Jess and Tiana. Both of them were watching, but in entirely different ways.

Tiana's expression was predictable. Obvious jealousy that Sam had seen a dozen times before.

But Jess didn't look jealous—not even a flicker of it. Instead, her gaze lingered, sharp and focused, as if she were carefully assessing the contact between them. There was a quiet intensity in her expression, her blue eyes steady and searching. Then, after a beat, she glanced away, her posture softening, as though whatever she'd seen had given her an answer.

"You guys want another drink?" Tiana called out over the music.

"I'm good." Scarlett said, her long dark curls shifting as she shook her head.

Jess tilted her head in agreement. "Yeah. I'll get one."

"Me too," Sam added, stepping back.

The woman she'd been dancing with gave her a questioning, faintly disappointed look before sauntering off into the crowd. But Sam barely noticed. She was already trailing after Jess and Tiana as they weaved toward the bar, slipping between groups of people clustered near the edge of the dance floor.

When they reached the bar, Tiana leaned in, catching the bartender's attention. "Tequila shots?" she asked, a mischievous gleam in her eyes.

Sam chuckled, resting her elbows on the counter. It wasn't what she'd planned to order, but it also didn't sound half bad. "Sure. Why not?"

Jess flashed a grin. "Let's do it."

"Three tequila shots, please," Tiana called out, raised her hand to the bartender.

He nodded and turned away, grabbing glasses from beneath the counter.

Before he could return, a woman appeared behind Tiana, her voice low and confident. "Can I buy you a drink?"

Tiana glanced over her shoulder, her lips curving into a polite, sweet smile. "I just ordered one."

The woman stepped closer, undeterred. "Maybe I can get your next one, then?"

Sam bit back a smirk, watching the interaction unfold. That was the usual with Tiana—she never failed to attract attention wherever they went.

Tiana chuckled lightly, her eyes flicking toward the crowd, already distancing herself from the conversation. "Not tonight. Thanks, though."

The woman hesitated for a beat before nodding and walking off, her smile fading as she melted back into the sea of people.

"Not your type?" Jess asked from the other side of where Sam stood.

Tiana smirked, her teasing eyes instantly meeting Sam's. "There's only one woman I'm trying to take home tonight."

Sam snorted, shaking her head as her gaze darted away, but it wasn't quick enough to miss the flicker of surprise that crossed Jess' face.

Tiana's relentless teasing was something Sam had long grown used to. Most of the time, it was just that—

teasing. A way to push her buttons and get a rise out of her, nothing more.

But Jess didn't know that.

And even if she and Jess were just friends, it still didn't feel right. Because if their positions were reversed, she wasn't sure she'd want to hear someone say something like that about her.

Actually—she was positive she wouldn't.

Maybe someday she'd get there. She hoped she would. But not yet. Not now.

"She's joking," Sam said to Jess with a laugh.

"Am I?" Tiana asked, the flirtatious smile still firmly planted on her lips as she cocked her head and leaned back against the bar.

"Here you go," the bartender said, sliding three shot glasses with lime slices toward them.

"Thanks," Sam replied before giving him the name of her open tab.

She slid one of the shots in front of Jess while Tiana grabbed the other.

Sam picked hers up carefully, grimacing when a few drops of liquid sloshed over the side and dripped down her fingers. She shook her hand lightly, swiping the liquid onto her jeans.

And as she turned, she noticed the woman from the dance floor strolling past. Her gaze lingered just long enough to flash Sam a coy smile before disappearing into the crowd.

A dry chuckle sounded from Jess beside her.

Sam turned, her brows furrowing. "What?"

She shook her head softly, looking away as she picked up the lime wedge. "Just brings back memories."

Tiana leaned forward, resting one arm against the bar. "The tequila shots? Or the girls drooling over her?" she deadpanned.

Jess released a puff of air, throwing Tiana a knowing look before picking up the lime wedge with her free hand. "Both."

Tiana hummed, matching Jess' demeanor as she raised her glass in the air. "Well cheers to," she paused, making a disgusted face, "*not* that."

Sam laughed to herself, shaking her head at the two of them as they clinked glasses and pour the shots back.

She followed suit, taking the shot. It'd been a long time since she'd really gone out. And even longer since she'd taken a straight shot of alcohol. She'd almost forgotten the horrible taste that now scorched her throat as she forced it down.

Her cheeks clenched in revulsion as she quickly sucked on the lime wedge.

A glass clinked on the left beside her where Tiana set hers down, sliding it forward to the opposite edge of the bar.

"So," Tiana started, wiping the back of her hand against her mouth, "how did you and Liz meet?" She leaned forward, peering past Sam to where Jess stood on her other side.

Sam tried to even out her expression.

It wasn't that she *didn't* want to hear about Jess and Liz's relationship. That wouldn't be fair. Especially after Jess had to deal with Tiana's overt flirtation just a minute before. Besides, if they were really going to make it as friends, then that would be part of it. Getting used to hearing the details of her with someone else.

And it was fine. She could do it. Although, it probably would've been a thousand times easier if she was dating just about anyone else.

The corners of Jess' lips quirked up in a small smile.

"We met a while ago, when I first started working with her company."

Tiana nodded. "Love at first sight?"

Jess tilted her head back in a snort of laughter. "Not exactly. We talked off and on when we ran into each other at work. Then one day, she asked me to go out with her and her friends. And things just went from there."

"So you guys have been together for a while, then?" Tiana asked.

The smile fell slightly from Jess' face as she shrugged. "It's been sort of off and on since then."

Her eyes flicked to Sam for just a moment before bouncing back to Tiana.

"We ended things a few times," Jess clarified, her eyes falling back down to where she fiddled with her empty glass.

Sam hated that those words reminded her of them. The way they'd never really officially been something, but still seemed to bounce back and forth, nonetheless.

Tiana gave her a sympathetic quirk of her lips. "Well, you're together now. And that's what matters."

Jess nodded once as some of the warmth seeped back into her features.

Tiana glanced between Sam and Jess, her grin widening. "One more?" she asked, eyebrows bouncing in a playful challenge.

Sam smirked, shaking her head slightly before giving in. "Why not?"

Tiana flagged down the bartender with a quick wave, and within moments, another round of tequila shots was set before them.

"Cheers," Tiana declared, lifting her glass with a triumphant grin.

Sam tapped her shot against Tiana's, then tossed it back. The sharp burn hit her throat immediately, and her eyes watered as she set the glass back on the counter. At least the tequila was doing its job, helping to dull the sting of the previous conversation.

"I'm gonna go check on Liz," Jess called, her voice cutting through the music as she gestured toward the booth. Without waiting for a response, she disappeared into the crowd, leaving them alone at the bar.

Tiana turned to Sam with a grin. "Ready to go back out there?"

Sam hesitated, glancing toward the mass of people on the dance floor. Something about the energy wasn't quite the same anymore, but she pushed the thought aside. "Yeah, let's go."

Tiana grabbed her hand, pulling her into the thrumming crowd. The music pounded through her chest as they wove their way back into the chaos. People swayed and spun around them, the room a blur of colored lights and motion.

The woman who'd been dancing with her before returned at some point, but Tiana subtly shoved her out of the way, taking her place instead. But even then, Sam barely noticed.

Her eyes kept floating across the room, catching glimpses of Jess every so often. Watching her smile, the way she laughed with Scarlett where they sat beside Liz in the booth.

She pulled her gaze away as she leaned in toward Tiana. "I'm gonna go sit for a sec."

Tiana continued dancing as she stepped away in the opposite direction. "I'll grab a couple more drinks and bring them back to the table."

Sam nodded, then made her way through the crowd back to the booth.

"I was just about to make Jess get back up so we could dance with you guys," Scarlett said with a frown as she returned.

"Sorry," Sam said with an apologetic smile. "Just give me a few minutes and I'll go back out with you."

Sam watched as Liz shot Jess a disappointed look, one of those tight smiles that said more than words. And she knew Jess' answering expression. It was the one she used when things felt off. The one that told her she wanted something more.

Scarlett leaned over to Jess. "Wanna get a drink with me real quick before?" she asked with a wide grin.

For a moment, it seemed like Jess might actually stay. That they might have a few more moments in that hazy, alcohol-laced night together. But then Jess caught Liz's hopeful look, and Sam saw the quiet resignation in her eyes.

Jess shook her head, forcing a smile. "Yeah, no, you're right," she said to Liz. "It's getting late."

Tiana appeared, setting four shots on the table with a triumphant grin, breaking the brief silence. "Here we go," she said, sliding them one-by-one to Sam, Scarlett, and Jess.

"Oh," Jess muttered with a small frown, glancing at Liz. "Actually—I think we're about to head out."

Tiana's smile faded into mild disappointment, but she quickly recovered, shrugging with a playful grin. "Alright, then," she said, nudging the extra shot toward Sam. "Two for you."

Sam raised an eyebrow as she glanced down at the two glasses lined up in front of her. "Trying to make up for lost time?"

"Something like that," Tiana muttered with a teasing smile. "Cheers!" She clinked her glass with Scarlett's before downing her shot.

Sam followed, the liquor thick in her throat as she glanced over at Jess, who still hadn't moved.

"Sure you don't wanna stay?" Sam asked, her voice softer than she'd intended.

"No," Liz interjected before Jess could respond, pulling her phone from her purse. "I'm calling the Uber now."

Tiana immediately wrapped an arm around Sam's shoulders, leaning in with a smirk. "Don't worry, I'll stay as long as you want. Maybe we can keep the fun going after we leave, too."

Sam felt the heat of Jess's gaze, and glanced over at her, catching her even expression.

"Well, I'm glad you guys came out tonight," Sam said, leaning back in the booth as she turned to her. "We need to do this more often. I can't remember the last time I had this much fun."

Jess smiled softly. "Me too."

Tiana nudged Sam's arm, breaking the moment as she leaned close, kissing her cheek. "Then maybe you should listen to me more often," she said. "Less work, more play."

Sam snorted a laugh as she nodded. "Yeah, yeah." But as she glanced back at Jess, a flicker of memory hit her—another night, another crowded, where she'd felt that same pull, that same ache when Jess had been just out of reach. When another girl had been draped over her.

Another night that had ended very differently.

"Uber will be here in a couple minutes." Liz announced, standing from the booth with her phone in hand. "We should go wait outside."

Sam's gaze flicked to Jess, catching the way her eyes lingered on her for just a beat too long. Then Jess turned to Scarlett, leaning in for a hug.

She whispered something into Scarlett's ear, the words too quiet to catch over the hum of the bar.

Scarlett let out a soft chuckle as they pulled apart, her gaze drifting to Sam with an almost knowing look.

"Yeah," Scarlett said with a nod. "I'll make sure she gets home okay."

***

Sam danced until her legs burned, and the hours blurred together. It wasn't until Scarlett finally declared she was ready to head out that she realized how late it had gotten.

"You ready?" Tiana yelled over the music, leaning close enough for Sam to hear.

"Yeah," Sam answered, swiping a hand through her hair. The ache in her legs from the long day and night was impossible to ignore now.

They filtered off the dance floor, exiting the bar onto the bustling sidewalk outside, where the city was still alive with late-night energy. Strangers shuffled around them, laughing and calling for rides of their own.

Sam pulled out her phone, squinting at the screen as she opened her ride app. "You wanna share one?" she asked Tiana.

Tiana tilted her head, a playful smile spreading across her face. "Actually, do you wanna hang out at your place for a little while? I'm not ready to end the night yet."

Scarlett huffed a laugh from beside them, muttering something under her breath, though Sam only caught the word 'subtle'. She glanced up in time to see the knowing smirk Tiana shot her, nudging her shoulder lightly.

"Yeah, sure," Sam replied with a faint chuckle. "Just don't expect much. I've barely unpacked."

Tiana shrugged, her flirtatious grin firmly in place. "I don't mind."

Scarlett waved them off with a grin, climbing into her Uber. A minute later, their own ride pulled up, and Sam and Tiana slipped inside.

By the time they arrived, the streets were quieter, and the hum of the city felt like it was winding down. Sam led Tiana into the building, the soft ding of the elevator cutting through the silence as they stepped inside.

When they reached her apartment, Sam unlocked the door, flipping on the lights as they stepped in.

"Man," Tiana muttered, "you're some big tech geek, and you didn't even try to get a penthouse?"

Sam chuckled, tossing her keys on the marble island in the small kitchen. "I don't like having a lot of space."

Tiana hummed. "I'm surprised. You'd think you'd be dying for space after being stuck in some of those homes we had to deal with when we were kids."

Sam went to the fridge, grabbing two water bottles. She handed one to Tiana before taking a large gulp of her own.

"I had fun tonight," Tiana said, taking a sip. "I like your friends."

Sam smiled, taking another gulp. "Yeah, they're great."

"I like Jess," Tiana said slowly, giving her a small, pointed smile. "She's—" she paused, tilting her head back in thought, "*protective* of you."

Sam shook her head. "She's not protective. She's just a good friend."

Tiana nodded slowly as she set the water bottle down, then stepped away, looking around the apartment. She glanced down the short hallway to the bedroom.

Then she ambled back there, pushing the door open. Sam stayed put, leaning against the counter as she tilted the water bottle up, draining what was left in one long gulp

"You haven't changed at all," Tiana called out to her with a boisterous laugh. "Everything is in the exact same place as you've always set up your rooms."

Sam smiled to herself. It felt good having someone around that had known her for so long. Most of the time, it felt like she was moving farther and farther away from her past. Whether it was intentional or not. But having Tiana there felt like the only good reminder of those years.

Sam heard the faint rustle of movement coming from the bedroom. She pushed off the counter, ready to head back and see what Tiana was up to, but before she could take a step, Tiana appeared in the doorway.

A wide grin stretched across her face.

Sam's gaze dropped to her hand, and the moment she saw what Tiana was holding, the reason for that grin became painfully clear.

"You still keep it on the right side of your dresser drawer," Tiana said with a chuckle, holding up a strap on. "I guess old habits die hard, huh?"

Sam laughed, shaking her head as she looked away. "And you still go through all my stuff like it's yours."

Tiana shrugged, casually tossing the strap onto the couch as she sauntered back toward Sam. She stopped just shy of closing the distance between them. Then she looked up at Sam with a familiar smile.

Tiana's hand slid easily around her back, her touch as natural as if they'd done this a hundred times before—which, in truth, they had.

It felt normal—good, even. Being close to someone she trusted. Someone who really knew her.

But even though it felt good, something about it didn't feel *right*.

As Tiana leaned in, Sam instinctively pulled her head back.

"Not tonight," she murmured, her voice soft but firm.

Tiana hesitated for a moment before nodding and stepping back with a small, disappointed smile. "Guess some things *do* change then, huh?"

Chapter seven

Sam looked up from her computer to the window of her apartment, where the morning sun streamed through the glass, casting golden stripes across the hardwood floor.

She glanced down at the time glowing on the corner of her monitor, sitting atop the wide white desk cluttered with notebooks and pens. Even after working for a couple of hours, it was still relatively early in the morning.

She stifled a yawn, lifting one hand to rub at her tired eyes while the other hovered over her keyboard.

A knock at the door broke through the quiet. Sam frowned, glancing up. It was too early to be expecting anyone.

Stretching her neck, she pushed back from the desk and trudged toward the door.

Sam pulled it open and blinked in surprise. Then, slowly, a smile spread across her face.

"Hey," she said, her voice hoarse from hours of quiet. The headphones bobbed around her neck as she shifted in the doorway.

Jess smiled back. "Sorry, I know it's early. I just—couldn't sleep. Figured you'd be up, too."

Sam smiled softly. "It's fine." She stepped aside, letting Jess in.

"I brought coffee," Jess said, holding out the cup like a lifeline.

Sam groaned, taking the cup from her quickly, like it was the last drop of liquid left on earth. "You're the best," she muttered, taking a sip, the bitter edge pulling her out of her fog.

As Jess wandered past her into the small space of the living room, Sam made a beeline for the kitchen, navigating around the mess of papers, boxes, and everything else she hadn't gotten to in the past few days.

"Sorry," she called over her shoulder, setting the cup down by the sink as she tried to quickly organize the chaos. "Got sucked into work this morning. Thought I'd have more time to clean up before you got here."

The second Jess froze near the couch, Sam knew exactly what she'd walked into. She didn't even need to look. Her gut twisted, a wave of embarrassment surging through her before she even spotted it—the strap-on, sitting there in plain view.

"Shit," Sam muttered under her breath, crossing the room in two long strides. She snatched it up, quick but not quick enough to erase the awkwardness choking the air. "Sorry. I—uh, forgot she left this out."

Jess' face flushed, her eyes darting everywhere but the couch. "It's fine," Jess muttered, her voice too high, too tight.

Sam could see it, how Jess' mind was probably working overtime, piecing together whatever thoughts about Tiana she'd been avoiding. Hell, it wasn't like Sam wanted to think about it either, at least not in that moment.

Without another word, Sam disappeared down the hall, dumping it onto her bed before she could overthink it. The apology fumbled out of her mouth as she came back. "I'm sorry, that wasn't—"

"No, no, it's fine," Jess cut her off, her voice hitting that painfully awkward tone, followed by a laugh that was obviously more nerves than humor. "Really. You don't have to explain anything."

Sam knew that laugh, and more than that, she knew Jess didn't want an explanation. The tension between them was so thick it was suffocating, but when their eyes met, Sam couldn't hold it anymore. The ridiculousness of it all cracked her, and before she could stop herself, she was laughing.

Jess' eyes widened in surprise, but a second later, she was laughing, too. Not just a nervous chuckle, but a deep, genuine laugh. The kind that made her shoulders shake and her cheeks flush.

And just like that, the tension shattered.

Sam ambled to the kitchen, still chuckling, as she grabbed her coffee and returned. She stepped around the couch, dropping onto the gray cushions.

Jess wrinkled her brow, looking down at the couch with apprehension.

Sam looked at her curiously for a moment before realization dawned on her face, and she burst into another laugh.

"It's clean," she said, taking a sip of the coffee. "I promise."

Jess hummed, moving around the arm of the couch to sit on the opposite side before setting her drink down on the small black coffee table.

"So," she began, leaning back into the cushions, her gaze flicking to Sam, "what happened to taking the morning off?"

Sam pressed her lips together, giving a small shrug. "I tried, but couldn't really sleep in even though I'm tired from last night."

Jess smiled, her features softening. "Last night was fun. Really fun. It's been too long since I've had a night like that."

Sam turned, resting an arm along the back of the couch as she angled her body toward Jess. "Why? You have your best friend here."

Jess gave a light shrug. "Scarletts settled down more since she met Terrence."

Sam snorted, raising an eyebrow. "She seems exactly the same as always to me."

Jess smirked, taking a sip of her coffee before setting it back on the coffee table. "I think that has more to do with you being back here than anything."

Sam cocked her head. "Really?"

"Don't act so surprised," Jess said with a light laugh.

Sam's lips curved into a faint smile as she brought the cup to her mouth. "You and Liz don't go out a lot?"

Jess glanced away, thinking. "I go out with her and her friends sometimes," she replied. "But it's just different, I guess."

Sam watched her intently, waiting for the deeper explanation.

"I mean—don't get me wrong," Jess added quickly, "They're great, and Liz is too, obviously."

Sam nodded slowly, adjusting the cup in her hands. "Well, she's a lot better than some of those other girls you dated. Better than that one girl from college."

Jess' face scrunched in confusion. "Which girl?"

Sam shot her a pointed look.

Jess' eyebrows tugged together as she cocked her head. Then a look of realization dawned on her. "Tess?" she asked with a laugh.

Sam groaned. "To this day, every time I meet a 'Tess', I instantly can't stand them."

Jess burst into laughter, shaking her head.

"I thought I could get along with almost anyone, but man, that girl," Sam muttered, a grimace pulling across her lips.

"Oh stop. You like everyone." Jess said, reaching forward to grab her coffee. "Besides, she wasn't that bad. You were just jealous."

The words landed hard, like a small bomb dropped between them. For a heartbeat, Sam just stared at her, caught off guard. And she saw it in Jess too. The momentary pause, like she hadn't meant to say it aloud.

And that realization filled her with a quiet satisfaction.

"Whatever," she muttered, a smirk ghosting across her lips.

Silence hung between them, and she let it stretch for a moment longer, savoring the rare crack in Jess' composure. It was good to know she wasn't the only one having trouble with what to say and what not to say. But before she could press further, Jess cleared her throat, reaching into her bag for the stack of papers she'd brought.

"I brought a few mock-ups for the PR campaign idea I told you about," Jess said, her tone shifting to business. "Figured we could go through them and pick what you want to send out to new clients about the possible acquisition."

Sam leaned forward, taking the thick stack from her hands and flipping through the pages. They were good. Better than she'd expected, actually. But she wasn't surprised. Jess had an eye for that kind of thing— making hard tasks look polished and effortless.

She set the papers down and met Jess' gaze with an impressed smile. "These look great."

Jess nodded, her tense expression melting into one of satisfaction. "Good. And once you get me the rest of the details, I can finalize them. Then we can get to work on a release for next month."

Sam nodded slowly. "Sorry. I was planning to get the rest of the details together for you last night, but—I couldn't really focus on it."

Jess hummed, glancing away as her lips formed a tight line across her face. "Yeah, I bet."

Sam snorted a laugh. "No, I mean—nothing like that. I tried to work. Just had too much on my mind, I guess, with everything from last night."

She opened her mouth to say more, but the words dried up when she caught Jess glancing at her like she was weighing whether to bring up something heavier.

"Yeah," Jess started, her voice softer now, hesitant. "How do you feel? I mean—after seeing Liz's parents again."

Sam's grip tightened on the edge of the papers, knuckles paling. She'd known it was coming—of course Jess would ask. But it still felt like the floor tilted beneath her, just for a second.

Talking about her mother had always been easy, in a way. It wasn't a complicated situation. A woman with a drug problem left a child behind.

It was a story told many times before. A one sentence explanation that everyone understood. Sure, it was sad. But it was also *simple*.

The other parts, however, were anything but. How could she explain the other adults in her life not wanting her when she needed it most? When it all finally came to its inevitable end, and none of them thought she was worth taking in.

There was no simple way to explain that. No neat and clean words to describe that humiliating realization. The painful moment she discovered that it wasn't just an addict who didn't love her enough to stick around.

But that none of them did.

She forced herself to exhale slowly, leaning back into the couch as she rubbed the back of her neck.

"It was—weird," Sam admitted. Her voice was rougher now, like it was raking out against old, scarred memories.

Jess was quiet for a few moments, waiting for an explanation that Sam didn't know how to give. Then finally she asked, "So, private school? You never told me about that."

Sam shrugged. "My first grade teacher said I needed more of a challenge than what I could get in public school. She applied for me and got me into the scholarship program at the private school down the road." She cleared her throat, rolling her shoulders. "That's uh—that's how I met Liz."

Jess nodded, looking down. "Liz said you guys went to school together. But she didn't mention any of the other stuff."

That wasn't a surprise. To her, that time was completely life altering. Her entire world crumbled in just a few days. But to Liz, nothing changed. Sure, she lost her best friend. But she kept everything else. The same parents. Same school. Same soccer team.

The same *life.*

While Sam was left picking up the pieces of hers.

"Yeah," she breathed. "I wouldn't expect her to."

Jess' gaze softened. It was the way she'd looked at her from the very beginning. The same way she'd looked at her the first time they'd really ever talked about it. One rainy night in the diner. One night that seemed to alter things between them.

Even now, eight years later, she could still feel the warmth from Jess' hand on her own. The way every one of her nerve endings had ignited when Jess wrapped her arms around her as they rode home that night.

The way her body ached—*begged*—to feel it again the moment it was gone.

"Last night was fine, though." Sam swallowed, her throat tight. "I mean, they were fine. It was just— weird."

Jess' brow furrowed, and she leaned forward, resting her elbows on her knees. "Maybe they think pretending everything's fine is easier."

Their faces flashed in her mind. The way Mrs. Jacobs had hugged her so tight it almost hurt, like she was still the little girl they'd known. And maybe she had been, for a brief moment, until the reality of it all came crashing back in. The memory played on repeat—the look in Mr. Jacobs' eyes when he asked her why she hadn't played soccer in college, the way he'd lit up talking about the old days, like he'd completely forgotten what had come after.

"It was like they didn't even remember what happened." The words ghosted past Sam's lips in little more than a whisper. "Like none of that was real."

Jess' expression softened even more. "Just because they wanted to act like it didn't happen, that doesn't mean you have to do the same."

"Yeah," Sam muttered, her voice rougher now, and tinged with something bitter.

She cleared her throat, forcing an uncomfortable smile, trying to break away from the unpleasant feelings. "Either way, it's not a big deal. It just threw me off, I guess."

Jess' face evened out with something Sam couldn't quite place. Maybe pity. Maybe something more.

"Well, if it *does* feel like a big deal, that's okay, too," Jess said quietly.

Sam's jaw clenched, the muscles ticking beneath her skin. Then she cleared her throat, looking for anything that would change the subject. That would bring back the easy, happy air they'd had before.

She smiled again, running a hand over the back of her neck. "Yeah, well, it helped having you there last night. Thanks for—all of that."

Jess's gaze softened, her shoulders slumping slightly as if she'd just lost a small, private battle. "Of course," she said, almost whispering. "You know I'm always here for you."

Sam looked away. It was too much, the way Jess said it, like she meant every word.

"Thanks," she muttered, finally meeting Jess's gaze.

Then she rolled her shoulders, settling back into the couch, glad to let that conversation pass.

"Okay, what's next?"

Chapter eight

The dress boutique was tucked away on a quiet street, the kind of place that oozed sophistication with its polished hardwood floors and the faint scent of lavender hanging in the air.

Sam had barely managed to snag a coffee on the way over after a restless night. Scarlett's bachelorette weekend was coming up fast, and between work, wedding prep, and the company's acquisition, her brain felt like it had been running a marathon.

Scarlett, however, was completely in her element. She moved through the boutique with purpose, a clipboard in hand and her eyes scanning every rack like she was planning a military operation.

"Okay," Scarlett said, turning to Jess. "The Maid of Honor dresses are over there." She nodded to some smaller, colorful dresses in the corner. "But I already called ahead to have them put aside some of the ones you said you liked on their website so you could try them on."

"Oh," Jess mumbled with a clearly forced smile.

Sam shot her an amused smirk, knowing how much she probably wanted to avoid that.

"Wanna look at what they have, though?" Scarlett asked, rifling through a nearby rack. "They might have more stuff here in person."

Jess shook her head. "No, that's okay. I'll start with those and look at the rest if they don't work out."

Scarlett muttered something absentmindedly as she directed each of them toward some racks with dresses that fit the style she was going for.

"So," Sam muttered, her eyes drifting over the racks of dresses that seemed to stretch endlessly, "do you have anything in mind yet?"

"I think I want something with lace," Scarlett answered as she circled a new rack. "Something classy and timeless, but also modern."

Sam nodded, having absolutely no idea what that meant. She turned to Jess, arching her brows in question.

Jess smirked as she pointed her toward one of the walls. "Start with those."

They fell into a quiet rhythm, searching through the racks. Every so often, one of them would hold up a dress for inspection, eliciting nods, cringes, or half-laughs depending on how wildly off the mark the pick was. Scarlett turned a lace dress in her hands, frowning at it like it had personally offended her, while Jess hummed as she thumbed through a line of options.

"Hi, ladies," a cheerful voice cut through the low hum of their activity. They all turned to see a saleswoman with a warm, practiced smile. "Amber's tied up with another client, but I'm here if you need anything. Just flag me down when you're ready to try something on. I'm Tess."

Sam immediately turned to Jess, whose head whipped around to her at the same time. Their eyes locked, and Jess's mouth twitched at the corners, already fighting back laughter.

Sam snorted, unable to help herself. Jess clapped a hand over her mouth, her shoulders shaking as silent laughter rippled through her.

"Okay," Scarlett answered, shooting Sam a questioning glance. "Thanks."

Tess began walking away, and as she did, Scarlett looked between them. "What?"

"Nothing," Sam said quickly, but the grin splitting her face made it impossible to sound convincing.

"Absolutely nothing," Jess echoed, her voice muffled by her hand. But when her eyes darted back to Sam, her laughter doubled.

Scarlett's gaze bounced back and forth between them, growing impatient.

Jess' laughter finally died off as she shook her head. "Remember that girl I dated in college?"

Scarlett cocked her head to the side, eyes glazing over in thought. Then, after a moment, she jerked her head back and said, "The one Sam was like super jealous of?"

"What?" Sam asked, glaring at Scarlett. "I wasn't jealous!"

Jess laughed hard again, and Sam couldn't help the way it infected her, pulling the smile back across her own lips.

Scarlett gave her a pointed look, arching one brow. "Really? Because I distinctly remember you drunk-calling me from that sorority party just to rant about how their names were too similar."

Sam's face flushed as she sputtered, "That's not—"

"What?" Jess interrupted, her wide eyes darting between them as her grin morphed into something deeply entertained. "You never told me about that!"

Scarlett shrugged, turning back to the dresses in front of her.

Sam opened her mouth in a desperate attempt to form some response. But any attempt at rebuttal failed entirely. Instead, she shook her head, looking down with an embarrassed smile.

When she looked up again, Jess was watching her with fresh amusement.

"Don't," Sam groaned in warning, although she couldn't keep the smile off her lips for long.

Jess chuckled, lifting her palms in the air. "I'm not saying anything."

Scarlett picked up a new dress, turning around to hold it up in front of her. "What about this one?"

Sam pulled her eyes from Jess, humming softly as she looked over the new dress. "It could work, I guess."

Scarlett frowned, turning back to hang it where she found it. "Definitely not that one, then."

Jess smirked knowingly, her fingers trailing lightly down the intricate white lace of a long gown hanging on the rack. The glint in her eyes told Sam she was already gearing up to tease her about something, but before she could speak, Scarlett's voice broke in.

"Okay, what about this one?" Scarlett asked behind them.

They both turned around at the same time.

"Oh yeah," Sam said immediately with a grin. "I like that one."

Jess nodded in agreement. "It definitely looks more like you."

Scarlett gave one satisfactory nod, hanging it on the empty fitting room rack beside her.

"What about this one?" Sam muttered, pulling another dress out from the rack in front of them. "You said you want something with lace, right?"

Scarlett's eyes went wide, striding toward them. "Holy shit, it's gorgeous!"

"Well, that sounds promising," Tess called out, ambling toward them with a polite smile. "Are you ready to try some on?"

As Scarlett took the woman around, pointing out each dress she'd found, Sam made her way to a set of chairs placed outside the dressing room.

She dropped into one of the plush seats, letting out a small sigh as she leaned back. A moment later, Jess followed, sitting in the second chair beside her.

"And which of you is trying on the Maid of Honor gowns?" the saleswoman asked, closing the door to Scarlett's fitting room before turning toward them.

Jess grimaced as she answered, "Me."

The woman smiled, nodding as she waved her into the fitting room beside Scarlett's. "Right this way."

"Have fun," Sam called out behind her with a teasing grin.

Once Jess was out of sight, she began scrolling through her phone, checking for new emails as they changed. Caleb had sent her a couple of updates from their most recent client. But luckily, nothing seemed urgent enough to require immediate attention.

Scarlett's door swung open first, and she stepped out, wearing one of the dresses she'd found.

"What do you think?" she asked, turning in front of the mirror.

"It's nice," Sam answered, placing her phone in her lap. "Do you like it?"

"Well, I want it to be better than *nice*," she muttered, smoothing the fabric down.

She turned to Jess' dressing room door, knocking hard against it. "Are you dressed?" she called. "Come out. I need you to look at the one I have on."

Jess stepped out a moment later, one arm twisted awkwardly behind her back as she held a dark green ruffled dress in place.

"What do you think?" Scarlett asked, twirling her dress from side to side. "Sam's not a fan."

"Hey, I didn't say that," Sam said, leaning back in her chair. "It just doesn't seem like what you said you wanted."

Jess hummed as she studied it. "I agree. Doesn't match your style."

Scarlett looked at herself in the mirror for a moment before turning back to Jess.

"That looks great on you!" she said, nodding toward her. "Is that the one I picked out?"

Jess frowned, tugging at the ruffles that flared out from her hips. "Yeah. If you like it, I'll get this one."

"Well, do *you* like it?"

Sam smirked, letting out a light snort of laughter. "She hates it."

Jess looked up at her, as if ready to disagree. But then she broke out into laughter, nodding. "I hate it."

Scarlett rolled her eyes, waving her back into the dressing room. "Okay, try the next one."

Sam chuckled, looking at her phone as they both disappeared back into the dressing rooms. She continued through the unread email chains, reading through updates from the developers on the most recent changes they'd pushed to the production version of the software.

After another minute, both the dressing room doors opened at the same time. She looked up at Scarlett, seeing a new dress that paired much better with her features.

She smiled up at her. "I love that one."

"That's beautiful," Jess said from beside her, and Sam turned to look at her.

The moment her gaze landed on Jess, she faltered. Jess wore a dark blue satin gown with a low neckline. It trailed to the floor, leaving one open slit running up the length of her thigh.

She swallowed, suddenly feeling as if she should look away.

"I know, right," Scarlett gushed, posing in front of the mirror. "I love this one."

Sam nodded slowly, working to keep her gaze pinned on Scarlett.

Scarlett turned once more, then peered at Jess, breaking into a wide smile. "Oh my gosh, I love that one on you!"

Jess turned to the mirror, smiling. "I like this one," she said before her eyes flitted to the side, meeting Sam's in the reflection.

Sam pulled her eyes away to look back at Scarlett. "You guys both look great."

"You wanna try some on?" Scarlett asked, throwing Sam a teasing look.

Sam huffed a laugh. "You mean I can't just wear this to the wedding?" she asked, waving a hand down at her plain white t-shirt and jeans.

"Wear whatever you want," Scarlett replied with a light shrug as she turned back to the mirror. "But you might stand out a little."

"Fine by me," Sam muttered as her phone buzzed in her lap with a new text from Caleb.

She swiped it open to see a message asking her to call him.

Scarlett groaned. "I have way too many dresses to try on. I'm gonna be here for hours."

"So?" Jess muttered, smoothing down the front of her dress. "This is like your favorite thing to do."

"Yeah, but I have a million other things to do today. Can you try some on for me?" Scarlett asked. "I just want to at least see them on someone in person."

Sam stood up from the cushioned chair. "Hey, I gotta step out for a sec," she mumbled, reading a second, more urgent sounding text from Caleb. "Be right back."

Sam stepped out into the main area as she clicked the call button on Caleb's contact.

He picked up on the first ring, immediately launching into the latest problem arising with their new client.

She listened intently as he continued, taking her through each and every detail of what he viewed as another new major road bump. Luckily, she'd listened to enough of these panic filled rants from him to be able to quickly decipher what was actually a big problem, and what was mostly just his own stress.

And in this particular case, it seemed to be the latter.

She listened to him rant for another minute before realizing it would take more than a phone call to settle his stress.

"Alright," she said, cutting him off. "I'll be back at the office in a bit and I'll take a look at everything."

Sam hung up and checked the messages on her phone one last time, scrolling through the most recent emails as she rounded the corner back to the dressing room area. The bottom of a wedding dress fluttered in the corner of her vision.

"Hey Scar," she muttered, closing out a message thread as she slipped the phone back into her pocket. "Sorry, I have to—"

She stared ahead, freezing mid-step. She blinked once, her mouth parted with the unfinished words.

Jess' eyes met hers in the reflection, and she somehow looked just as frozen in place. She turned slightly, away from the mirror, and Sam could see then which dress she was wearing. It was the one she'd picked out. The one that somehow now seemed a thousand times more stunning.

Jess glanced down, running her fingers across the trail of lace on the front of the dress. "She needed me to try some on for her."

Sam just stood there, unable to stop herself from staring as her mind went blank.

Jess looked like she was about to say something more, but then she stopped. And the way she stared

155

back at her in that moment—the cautious intensity—sent some long-lost feeling coursing within her.

A feeling that definitely shouldn't belong to her.

And with that feeling came a warning.

"Uh—I," Sam stammered, shaking her head and looking anywhere else. "I have to go."

Jess might've nodded her head or given her some type of questioning look. Sam knew her well enough to imagine the exact way her eyes would've tightened around the edges, waiting for an explanation.

But still, Sam refused to look. Refused to let herself take even one more small glance.

It wasn't right. She might not have known exactly what that feeling meant. But she did know she had no right to feel it. Whatever it was.

"Scar," Sam called, turning toward the closed dressing room door. "I have to go. Something came up at work."

Scarlett's muffled groan came from the other side. "Fine," she grumbled. "You better pick up though if I FaceTime you."

Sam hummed, half turning away, her eyes trained on the ground. "Yeah," she mumbled. "Okay."

"Did you still want to meet later this week?" Jess asked softly. "About the PR stuff."

Something in her voice sounded careful, as if she was speaking to a skittish animal, afraid it would dart away at the first wrong word.

Sam cleared her throat, rubbing a hand over the back of her neck. "Yeah." She glanced up at Jess, seeing the timid but gentle look in her eyes. A look that made her want to both stay and go at the same time.

She glanced away again, forcing a painful smile. "I'll text you later, about a day and time." Then she turned, mustering every ounce of will she had to break the tension. She nodded toward the back of the shop. "You might need to call Tess back to help, so you're not here all night."

Jess gave one slow nod, her lips pursing slightly.

Sam cleared her throat once more as she walked away. "I'll see you later," she called over her shoulder.

Chapter nine

Sam stepped onto the edge of the field, the faint scent of freshly cut grass mixing with the earthy tang of the dirt beneath her shoes. The wide expanse of green stretched out beneath the mid-morning sun, its rays casting long shadows from the goalposts at either end.

A handful of women were scattered across the field, some jogging and kicking a ball back and forth, while others stood nearby in clusters, chatting and laughing.

Liz was easy to spot, with her bright red ponytail bobbing back and forth as she jogged after a ball.

"I don't get the appeal," Tiana muttered as she ambled up beside Sam, one hand raised to shield her eyes from the blinding sunlight. "Why would anyone want to run around chasing balls in this heat?"

Sam smirked as they walked toward the sidelines where a row of bags, water bottles, and spare gear lay strewn across the grass. "Maybe you'd get it if you had even a single ounce of coordination."

"Oh, I'm coordinated," Tiana mumbled. "Just not with—balls." She made a disgusted face, and Sam burst into laughter.

When she looked up, she saw Jess looking at them from the sidelines, offering a small wave.

"Hey," Sam said with a smile as they approached.

Jess smiled back at Sam before her gaze moved to Tiana. "Are you playing too?"

"Mm definitely not," Tiana replied, scanning the field. "I'm just here for the free and—" Her gaze trailed over a woman with tattoos and short cropped hair as she walked by. "Very—*hot*—entertainment."

Jess shot Sam a mildly surprised look.

Sam smirked, shrugging as she dropped to sit in the grass beside her.

"Hey," Liz called, jogging toward them with a wide grin. "Was wondering if you'd actually show. I thought maybe you'd wuss out."

Sam gave her a half-hearted glare as she began lacing up her cleats. "Someone had to come keep you humble."

Liz's grin grew, and she could almost see that same twelve-year-old best friend in her once again. And for the first time since they'd seen each other, it felt good. A reminder of the good times they'd shared.

And that, maybe, they could have those good times again. Eventually.

"You wanna play mid or forward?" Liz asked, leaning forward in a deep stretch.

"What are you playing?"

Liz lifted her head, and Sam immediately recognized the competitive glint in her eyes. "Whichever one will be defending you."

Sam smirked to herself. That was the answer she'd been hoping for. "Midfield."

Liz nodded once as she rose out of her stretch, rolling her shoulders back. "Hope you kept up your cardio. It won't be fun if I can outrun you."

"Even if I hadn't," Sam said as she stood, brushing the grass off her shorts, "you'd still never be able to outrun me."

Liz hummed, the edges of her eyes tightening. "We'll see."

Sam grabbed her water off the ground. She took a long, steady sip, feeling the anticipation settle into her chest. It had been years since she'd played, but just being out there—the smell of fresh-cut grass, the sounds of cleats scraping turf—already brought everything rushing back.

Liz waved her to follow, leading her toward the others gathered near the center of the field. After quick introductions and handshakes, they split up into teams, falling easily into position.

Although it had been years since she'd last touched a soccer ball, everything came back to her at lightning speed. Within minutes, she adjusted to their faster pace and more physical style. And by the time they hit the half hour mark, every bit of rust had worn off.

"You sure you didn't play in college?" One woman called out to her from a few feet away after she blocked one of Liz's pass attempts and launched the ball down the field.

Sam grinned as Liz ran beside her, shoving her in the shoulder.

"I let you have that one," she grumbled, the competitive playfulness clear in her tone.

With every play, Liz pushed harder, her movements sharp and unrelenting as they grappled for control of the ball. The tension between them escalated, each tackle becoming more aggressive than the last. And when the ball came sailing their way again, Liz grabbed a fistful of Sam's jersey, yanking her sideways as she surged forward.

Sam stumbled, her footing slipping for just a second before she caught herself and bolted after her. Liz reached the ball first, but Sam was close behind.

Their hips collided hard as Sam leaned in. Liz grunted, throwing her weight against her, but Sam held her ground, refusing to give even an inch.

The ball sprang loose, rolling a few precious inches ahead.

And then Sam saw her opening.

She stepped forward, cutting across Liz's path. But just as she moved, Liz shoved backwards, swinging an arm wildly as she tried to regain control.

Sam barely registered what happened before Liz's elbow smashed into her brow with a sickening thud.

The pain was instant—sharp and blinding. It radiated through her face as her vision went white for a split second.

She staggered, instinctively lifting a hand to her right eye as she squeezed it shut against the sting.

"Shit," she hissed as the dull throb rippled beneath her skin.

She heard a woman's muffled yell somewhere nearby. "What the hell, Jacobs?"

Sam let herself pause for a moment, although she could see everyone around her continuing the play, with Liz running down the field after the ball.

She pulled her hand away, glancing at the smear of red stained against her fingertips. Luckily, it was less than she'd expected, which probably meant it was just a minor gash and wouldn't need stitches.

She lifted her shirt, wiping the blood and sweat from her brow before jogging forward to rejoin the game.

Liz cut a quick pass to a teammate, the ball gliding seamlessly across the field as they started to connect a series of sharp, clean touches. Sam followed closely, shadowing Liz's movements, her eye narrowing as the opposing player lined up for a shot.

The ball sailed through the air, a little too high, cutting an arc a few feet above the crossbar.

The play halted as one of the defenders broke off to chase the ball down. Sam slowed to a stop, exhaling through her nose as she wiped her face again.

"Halftime?" one person called out to the rest of the players on the field, and they all nodded or offered breathless, mumbled responses.

Sam braced her hands on her knees, breathing hard. A light tickle traced her cheek, and she swiped a hand up to brush away the thin line of blood trailing down toward her jaw.

She straightened up, ignoring the sting as she turned and ambled off the field to where she'd left her backpack and water bottle.

As she neared the sideline, she caught sight of Jess striding toward her.

"Let me see," she commanded, her face set in a stony expression.

Sam resisted the urge to laugh at her intensity. "It's nothing," she said, grabbing her water off the ground.

Jess stepped up to her, lifting a hand. Then it paused in midair, as she seemed to catch herself before dropping it back down to her side.

Instead, she moved to Sam's side, leaning in to inspect her brow.

"Sorry," Liz's voice cut through the moment, jogging toward them with an unapologetic grin. "I forgot you're not used to the way we play."

Sam hummed, taking a sip of her water.

She didn't mind the hard play. If anything, she actually preferred it. She enjoyed having a clear goal and fighting brutally to get it. And she enjoyed having Liz to play against. Someone who wouldn't give her any easy breaks.

"If that's the most you learned playing in college," Sam said, "then I don't think I missed out on much."

Liz laughed as she sprayed water into her mouth. "Oh, that's nothing. I was just warming up."

Sam smirked, taking another drink of her water as Jess looked back and forth between them, not one ounce of amusement adorning her face.

She crossed her arms over her chest. "You wanna sit out the second half?"

Sam shot her a flat look.

"Just saying," Jess mumbled, although her tone still held a sharp edge. "That's not gonna stop bleeding if you keep running around out there."

Sam grunted a laugh. "Don't try to pretend like you wouldn't keep playing if that happened to you."

Jess' mouth pressed into a firm line as she glanced out at the field. "You could have a concussion."

This time, it was Liz who laughed. "If she did, it wouldn't be anything new."

Jess looked back at her, eyes questioning.

Liz swallowed down another gulp of water before continuing. "You think *I'm* too physical when I play, but you should've seen this one," she threw a nod at Sam, "when we were kids."

Sam averted her gaze, already knowing which memories Liz was recalling. And they weren't the ones she was particularly keen on sharing.

Liz laughed again, shaking her head. "Wasn't just on the field either. Man, I can't even count how many times she picked fights with the kids at the school down the street from ours." Liz snorted another laugh that grated on her nerves. "My mom would get so pissed at us every time we got home and Sam had some new injury that was bad enough she'd have to take her to urgent care to get checked out."

Sam swallowed, heat rising in her cheeks.

She'd more or less blocked out those particular memories. The ones that would've probably made her hard for any parent to want.

Liz was right. Maybe she really could understand why her parents hadn't wanted to take her in after her mom died.

"Guess that's one thing that's changed," Liz said with a dry chuckle. "You don't seem as pissed off as you were back then."

Sam looked up finally, forcing a small smile of acknowledgment on her lips. "Guess so."

She avoided looking at Jess as Liz stepped away, talking to some of the other players. A few yards behind her stood Tiana, completely absorbed in conversation with the woman who'd walked by them before the game.

"Looks like she's having fun," Sam muttered with a chuckle, trying to break through the leftover air of the prior conversation.

Jess hummed in acknowledgment, but kept her serious demeanor.

A twinge of anxiety ran through Sam's chest, and she shifted the weight on her feet as a distraction. The thought of Jess imagining her as some rage-filled burden of a kid—the worst version of herself—was enough to send her brain reeling for a distraction.

She scratched the back of her neck, opening her mouth to say something—anything. But Jess beat her to it.

"I have something for you," she said, her face completely neutral as she turned, stepping toward a backpack on the ground.

Sam waited as Jess unzipped it and pulled a manilla folder out of the pocket before turning back around.

She held it out, nodding once. "I can email this all to you too, if that's easier."

Sam took the folder and flipped it open, scanning over the neatly organized pages inside.

"It's a more detailed breakdown of some of the stuff we went over last week."

She skimmed over the first page, quickly reading the headings.

"Look it over whenever you have time," Jess continued. "Then when you're ready, let me know and we can meet about it and finalize everything."

Sam nodded, raising her shirt to wipe away a trickle of blood that rolled down onto her cheek.

"Ready, Hayes?" a woman on her team called out. She looked up to see her walking back out onto the field, along with most of the others.

She nodded, then turned back to Jess with an appreciative smile. "Thank you for doing this."

Jess gave her a tight nod, her eyes locking once more on the cut on her brow.

Sam crouched, tucking the folder carefully into her backpack before dropping her water bottle beside it. She swiped a hand over her face, wiping away the last trace of blood and sweat.

Jess cleared her throat beside her. "Try not to get hurt in the second half," she said, not meeting her eyes. "Otherwise the bloods gonna stain your shirt."

Chapter ten

Sam stared down at the laptop, the movements of the people in the coffee shop blurring around her.

She'd needed to get away from the office that day. And her apartment too. She just needed somewhere separate. Somewhere she wouldn't feel the sense of crushing stress, but also didn't feel entirely alone.

So, she'd settled for the coffee shop a few blocks from her apartment.

It hadn't been a terrible choice. At least not at first. But as the day progressed, the stress did too.

She typed out a line of code, headphones blasting music so loudly she could barely make out the lyrics.

She deleted the line, immediately retyping a few more before releasing a frustrated breath. Then she punched a finger down on the delete key, erasing all the work she'd completed over the last thirty minutes.

Her phone buzzed in her lap with yet another text from Caleb, directly followed by one from a developer with some new changes for her to approve.

The words on the screen blurred together as she blinked away the tired haze covering her eyes.

More than anything, she wished she could just shut her laptop, take her motorcycle, and ride for hours on some empty road far away from it all. She imagined the nip of the wind whipping against her—the road whirring by so fast she couldn't think about anything else, even if she wanted to.

The phone buzzed in her lap again.

This time with an email. Another developer. The first few words of a question filled the notification preview.

She sighed, leaning back in the chair as she swiped the phone open.

Texts were usually the most urgent, so it would be best to reply to those first.

She glanced at the first few unopened conversations, but her eyes didn't stop. They continued downward. All the way down to the thread with Jess where she'd sent her the address to her apartment.

She stared at it for a moment, her thumb hovering above.

They hadn't spoken since the soccer game. And maybe if she was really honest with herself, she'd admit that she sort of wished Jess would reach out.

Even if it was just to follow up on the PR packet she'd given her.

But she hadn't.

Sam slowly tapped on the message thread, watching as it expanded across the screen.

She stared at it for a moment, ready to click back out and resume the endless list of things she had to do. But the very thought of doing that brought on a sense of dread so strong it bordered on nausea.

She stared down at Jess' name, swallowing as she clicked on her contact.

And then, as if moving on its own, her finger tapped the call button.

She blinked once, snapping back to reality for a split second as she held the phone up to her ear.

It barely finished the first ring before Jess' voice came through.

"Hey," she said, somehow sounding both exuberant and soft all in one.

And just the sound of it was enough to quell the dread within her.

It took a second before she remembered she had to say something back.

"Uh—hey," she said, clearing her throat and straightening up in the cushioned leather chair.

Jess was quiet for a moment, as if waiting for her to say more—to explain why she'd called. But she didn't know what else to say. Actually, she had no idea why she'd called in the first place.

She cleared her throat again, rubbing a rough hand against the back of her neck. "Sorry—uh—hope I'm not interrupting you at work or anything."

She cringed, hating herself for not having thought this through more.

Voices murmured in the background, and she could hear the phone shuffling around before Jess said, "No. Perfect timing, actually. I just got out of my last meeting."

Sam nodded, wracking her brain for words that refused to come.

"Oh," she muttered. "Good. That's—good."

She squeezed her eyes shut, wishing she could hang up and Jess would forget she ever called.

"So you looked over the packet I dropped off?" Jess asked.

Sam blinked. "What?"

More shifting crackled through the phone, along with more murmuring voices. "The PR stuff," Jess answered. "You're ready to go over it?"

"Oh—yeah," Sam said, the words tumbling out. "Yeah, of course." She shifted, changing the phone to her other hand. "That's why I called."

"Great," Jess said, not missing a beat. "Do you want to text me some days and times that work? Your schedule is probably busier than mine, so just let me know what's best for you."

Sam swallowed, staring down at the laptop in front of her as a new string of emails appeared. They kept coming, like a swarm of bees attacking from every angle. Different words jumped out at her, each with their own version of some new urgent problem she couldn't ignore.

"Sam?" Jess' soft voice came through the phone.

She shook her head, promptly shutting the laptop.

"Yeah. Sorry."

Jess was quiet for a moment before she finally spoke again. "Actually, are you free now?"

"Yes," Sam breathed, the word shooting from her mouth like water expelling from half drowned lungs.

***

Jess took a sip of her coffee as her eyes trailed over the papers splayed across the table before them.

"So," she started, setting the cup down. "These give an overview of some different strategies we could use, if you wanted to."

Sam glanced down at the papers, each word blurring together. She nodded slowly, feeling Jess' lingering gaze.

"Or," Jess said softly, leaning back in her chair, "we don't have to go over these right now. We could talk about something else first."

Sam looked up at her, head cocking to the side in question.

Jess shot her a pointed look, tapping her finger lightly against the arm of the chair.

"I'm sorry," Sam mumbled, shaking her head. She ran both hands over the front of her face, rubbing her palms roughly against her eyes. "I'm just—distracted—I guess."

"With?" Jess prodded gently.

Sam sighed, falling back into the chair. "Everything."

Jess nodded slowly. "The clients? Or the buyout?"

"Both," Sam breathed, finally feeling a small ounce of relief in the dam that had built up within her over the last few weeks. "The buyout mainly."

She could feel Jess' eyes on her, watching—deciphering. "Has it been hard working with Liz?" she asked quietly.

"No," Sam said immediately, shaking her head. And it was true. Although it was weird being around Liz again, especially while she was dating Jess, it wasn't bad. Or at least, not entirely bad. "It's fine. She's—fine."

Jess snorted a dry laugh. "That doesn't sound super convincing."

Sam smirked. "She's—competitive." She glanced up at Jess. "But I guess you already know that."

Jess hummed, looking away. "Seems like she's more competitive with you than anyone else."

It was true. It had always been like that, ever since they were kids. Something about it did feel different now, though. Some undertone of seriousness, or added stakes, that had never been there before.

She didn't want to think about that, though. She didn't want to think about work, or Liz, or any of it.

Sam forced it all away, letting every thought fall away until all that remained was the present moment, and what was right in front of her.

"So," she started, an amused smile tugging on her lips, "how'd things go the other day with the dresses? Did you need *Tess'* help?"

Jess smirked, her eyes holding challenging amusement. But she stayed silent.

Sam's smile only grew beneath the weight of Jess' gaze. "What?" she asked with a laugh.

"You always do that when something's bothering you."

The edges of Sam's smile faltered. "Do what?"

"Put all your focus on something." Jess ran a hand through her hair, brushing the long blonde locks over her shoulder.

"What am I focused on now?" Sam asked quietly, the rest of the smile falling from her lips.

Jess looked at her for a long moment before finally glancing away, her throat bobbing as she swallowed. "Me."

The word hung in the air.

Sam looked down at the table, letting a weighted silence fall between them.

After a long moment, Jess finally spoke again.

"You know, you could've just told me you wanted to hang out and talk," she said quietly. "We're friends. You don't need an excuse to call me."

Sam's eyes flitted up, finding Jess' once again. A memory floated into her mind. One she'd pushed down, far away.

And even though she knew she shouldn't say it aloud—that bringing up their past wasn't a good idea—she couldn't help herself.

"I called you once."

Jess stilled, but Sam could tell by the look in her eyes that she knew exactly what she was referring to. Still, she felt the need to continue.

"A year after—" Sam paused, swallowing. "After I left New York."

A muscle flickered in Jess' jaw, and her eyes fell to her lap as she whispered, "I know."

She knew why Jess hadn't answered. She hadn't even really expected her to. But still, she just needed to say it out loud and know once and for all that Jess knew she'd at least tried. Even if it was just one phone call.

"You didn't pick up," Sam said, barely above a whisper.

Jess sighed, closing her eyes. "I know."

Silence fell between them once more, and after a few moments, Sam knew that Jess wouldn't say anything more.

"I'm sorry," Sam said, releasing a deep breath. "I know I should've just called and asked to talk. It's just—" She paused, shaking her head slightly. "I guess I still don't really know how to navigate this whole *friends* thing while you're—" She swallowed, the next words feeling odd in her mouth. "With someone."

"I know the feeling," Jess muttered. Sam waited for her to elaborate, not exactly knowing what she meant by that. But instead, Jess just shook her head lightly before continuing. "But it's the same as it always was."

Sam smirked, shooting her a look. "Well, I wouldn't say it's exactly like it was."

Jess broke out into a laugh, her cheeks turning a light pink. "You know what I mean."

Sam chuckled, grinning as the weight of the words she'd spoken a few moments before began to ease.

"I'm glad we can be friends again though," she said, the wide grin on her lips relaxing into a soft smile.

"Even if it's hard to get used to with things being—different."

Jess looked back at her, a serious expression pulling through her gaze. "Did you not think we would ever be friends again?"

Sam held her gaze.

It'd taken her so long to even allow herself to think about Jess after they'd ended things in New York. And then, in those rare moments when she finally had, those thoughts held no speck of optimism. They couldn't. It almost felt like a matter of survival. Because if she did let herself think—or believe—that they could be something to each other again, then she'd question the choices she'd made that led her to leaving in the first place.

And she couldn't afford that. She couldn't afford for any seeds of doubt to seep in.

Doubt is the enemy to success. The enemy of everything she'd worked for.

"I don't know," she answered honestly.

Jess' gaze flicked away, her expression shifting ever so slightly—just enough for Sam to see the answer she'd given wasn't satisfactory in some way.

But before she could ask why, Jess' phone vibrated on the table, pulling their attention away.

Jess glanced down, her brows pinching together as she picked it up, swiping the screen with a small frown.

Sam looked away, taking a slow sip of her coffee while she waited.

"I'll be back in a minute," Jess muttered, already rising from her seat.

She stood from the seat, raising the phone to her ear as she walked toward the front door and out onto the sidewalk.

Sam watched her for a moment before opening her laptop. A handful of new messages had come through in the short time they'd been talking. She released a deep exhale through her nose, opening the most recent one.

As she read through, making notes on the latest developments around an issue they'd been working through, Jess trudged back toward the table.

"Sorry," she muttered, sitting back down in the chair, her eyes still fixed on her phone as she typed something out.

Sam watched her for a moment before closing her laptop. "Everything okay?"

Jess continued typing, her brow furrowed. Then finally, she sighed, setting the phone back on the table, faced down. "Yeah. Just something with Liz."

Sam nodded slowly, waiting for the frown to leave Jess' face.

It didn't.

"Do you need to go?" Sam finally asked, hating the disappointment she felt just at saying those words aloud.

Jess looked down at her phone, biting her lip as if contemplating. Then, eventually, she blew out a deep breath. "No."

A beat passed before Jess looked up at her. Apprehension laced her features, like she was trying to decide whether or not to elaborate.

"We just—" Jess started, before pausing. "Liz wanted to go look at an apartment today."

Sam remained quiet, trying to figure out why that would've been a problem.

"For us," Jess continued slowly.

"Oh," Sam blurted, the realization catching her off guard. "I thought you liked your apartment, though? Didn't you just move in?"

Jess sighed, some of the tension leaving her face as she slouched back in the chair. "I do. And yeah, I did."

Sam's brow furrowed. "But you want to move somewhere else?"

"No," Jess replied, irritation lacing the word. "I told her I didn't want to go look at it. But I guess she made the appointment, anyway."

"Ah," Sam muttered with a slow nod, as everything finally fell into place.

Jess pursed her lips, glancing off to the side. "Yeah."

She knew she might not enjoy hearing the details of their relationship, but still, there were questions she wanted to ask. Questions to help Jess talk out whatever was upsetting her. Although, given their past, she might not have been the most appropriate person to ask.

But that's what they were to each other now—friends. And if she wanted that to work out, then that was something she'd need to work through.

"So you guys are moving in together?" Sam asked, mustering the best smile she could.

Jess gave her an almost appreciative half smile that made it clear she knew what she was trying to do.

Then the smile fell as she replied, "No. We're not."

Sam's brows knitted together as the small understanding she thought she'd gained faded back into confusion.

Jess looked away again, like she was deciding what she should or shouldn't say.

"Sorry," Sam said. "I didn't mean to ask—"

"No," Jess cut in, shaking her head. "No, it's okay."

The phone buzzed on the table, and Jess' eyes flicked down for a split second before looking back up and giving her a tight smile. "You didn't do anything wrong. I just—I'm not sure it'd be fair to Liz to talk about our issues with.."

"Me?" Sam finished as Jess left the unspoken word hanging in the air.

Jess frowned. "Anyone." She let out a deep sigh, running a hand through her hair. "But yeah."

Sam smiled softly. "You're a good girlfriend. She's lucky to have you."

Jess' lips quirked upward in a teasing smile. "See, and you're biased. You'd probably just take my side regardless and make me think I'm right about everything."

Sam tilted her head back, laughing. "Oh, I don't know about that," she lied. "I could probably find a few things if you really wanted me to."

Jess' eyes narrowed as she shot her a teasing glare. "I doubt it."

The phone buzzed again, this time continuing in an incessant rhythm.

Jess looked down at it, the previous amusement in her eyes fading. She loosed a breath as she plucked it off the table, glancing at the screen.

She pressed the side button, muting the vibration, then looked back up at Sam with an apologetic smile. "I better go."

Sam nodded, offering her a small, reassuring smile. "Yeah. I understand."

Jess stood, reaching for her large black purse that hung on the back of her chair. "Sorry I couldn't stay longer to go over everything."

"That's okay," Sam replied, shaking her head.

"Do you have time to meet tomorrow? Maybe over lunch or something?" Jess asked, flipping her hair over her shoulder.

Sam hummed, tilting her head back as she mentally ran through her schedule—the meetings, the deadlines, and the stretches of time she'd carved out to focus.

"Yeah," she said after a beat. "That should work."

"Great," Jess said with a nod, the smile just barely touching the edges of her eyes. "I'll come by your office around then."

Chapter eleven

Sam pushed back from her desk, standing and rolling her stiff neck with a quiet groan. She glanced at her phone, tapping the screen again to check the time.

Jess was supposed to have arrived a while before. And when that time had passed, she'd texted her asking if they were still on to meet.

But now a full hour had gone by and—nothing.

Sam swiped her phone open, tapping on their message thread. She opened her contact and clicked the call button, holding the phone up to her ear.

It rang a handful of times before playing the automated voicemail.

Sam let out a breath, pulling the phone away to end the call.

Although Jess had mentioned how busy she'd been with work that week, it still wasn't like her to bail on plans. Especially without saying anything.

She clicked the call button once more, holding it back up to her ear as she tried to quell the slight unease in her chest.

The phone rang a few times, and just as she was about to hang up, the ringing stopped.

Sam paused, waiting. "Jess?"

The line was silent for another moment before Jess cleared her throat on the other end.

"Yeah," she answered, her voice quiet. "Hey. Sorry."

The worry in her chest eased slightly with the sound of her voice, but it was instantly replaced with fresh concern.

"Hey," Sam said. "Are we still meeting today?"

"What?" She could hear a shuffling on the other end of the line before Jess muttered, "Shit. I didn't realize what time it was."

Sam nodded to herself as she leaned back against the edge of the desk. That worked out. She'd felt out of it all day, her body aching with exhaustion. Even just spending the day at the office had left her completely drained.

At least now she'd have more time to work on finishing up some of the last minute tasks on her list for that day. Maybe she wouldn't have to be up half the night working and could go to bed at a decent hour for the first time that week.

"Sorry," Jess continued, clearing her throat again. "I was going to text you. I—" She paused, as if hesitant. "I'm not feeling that great. Can we reschedule?"

Sam swallowed against the slightly aching rawness in her throat. Maybe she'd picked up whatever Jess had gotten.

"Yeah, of course," she answered. "What's wrong? Do you need anything?"

Jess fell quiet on the other end before she said, "No. That's okay. Thanks though."

"Are you sure?" Sam asked, hoping she would change her mind. Even if it wasn't her place, she couldn't imagine not helping her when she needed it.

"Yeah," Jess said, her voice finally sounding a little softer. "I'm okay."

Sam nodded, tapping her thumb against the side of the desk. "Well, call me if you change your mind, okay? Is—" She paused, chewing on the next words as they left her mouth. "Liz going to bring you food or something? She probably already knows, but there's a place off Fourth street that has good soup and stuff for when you're sick."

Jess was quiet for a long moment. Long enough that Sam pulled the phone away to make sure the call hadn't ended.

"Thanks. Maybe I'll check it out," Jess answered softly. Then she cleared her throat. "And—sorry about missing the meeting."

Sam shook her head, walking to the other side of the desk and sitting down in the chair. "Don't worry about it," she said, having already forgotten. "Just make sure you get enough rest and all that."

Jess fell quiet again before she mumbled. "Yeah. I'll call you later, okay?"

"Kay," Sam answered. "Bye."

"Bye."

She pulled the phone away, setting it on the desk beside her open laptop. It was just barely past lunchtime, so there were still a few hours left where the offices would be open. If she hurried over to Liz's office, she could probably catch her before she left for the day and they could finish up the last of the project. Which would work out better, anyway. Then they'd have everything finished ahead of schedule, which would definitely impress Howard.

It might even impress him enough that he'd want to give the final green light and send over an official offer.

Sam packed her bag up, shooting Liz a text to let her know she was on her way.

***

"Hey," Sam said, knocking lightly on the edge of Liz's door as she stepped into her open office.

Liz glanced up at her, and right away she could make out the slight redness in her eyes. She sniffled lightly, rubbing a hand across her nose.

"Hey, come in."

Maybe Liz had picked up whatever sickness Jess had.

Sam ambled in, keeping a few feet between them, just in case. The last thing she needed was to get sick and miss out on a few days of work.

"Are you sick too?" Sam asked, setting her backpack on the floor as she sat down in the chair across from her.

Liz looked up at her, brows wrinkling. "What?"

"Whatever Jess has. She said she wasn't feeling good. Had to cancel our meeting earlier."

Liz's lips pressed into a thin line. She let out a small, unimpressed hum. "Surprised she didn't tell you, with you guys being such good friends and all."

Sam stiffened slightly at her tone. "Tell me what?"

Liz looked up at her with a hard stare. "We broke up."

Sam blinked, cocking her head. "What? Why?"

Liz shook her head with an exasperated sigh. "Same stuff that made us break up the last time." She paused, rolling her eyes. "And the time before that."

Sam nodded slowly. She knew things between them hadn't been perfect, but they also didn't seem bad. Or at least, not from the outside.

"I'm sorry," she said quietly.

"It's fine," Liz said dismissively, wiping a hand across her nose. "Its happened before and we got back together. We just need another break to realize how much we want to be together."

Sam nodded, but kept quiet. Hearing things like that from the person Jess was dating—or *had* been dating—felt wrong. Even if she and Liz were friends in the past, Jess was more than that to her. Jess would always have her loyalty. No matter how much time had passed.

Liz's phone buzzed on her desk. She reached for it, holding it up to her ear. "Hey," she said, leaning back in her chair.

Sam pulled her laptop out of her bag, flipping it open in her lap.

"Yeah," Liz mumbled into the phone. "Jess and I broke up. *Again*."

Sam glanced up in time to see her roll her eyes.

"Let's go out. I want fun and drinks. *Lots* of drinks."

Sam pulled up the string of notes on her computer as she tried and failed to tune out the conversation.

"That's perfect," Liz said, smiling into the phone. "Okay, I'll meet you there."

Liz released a heavy breath as she hung up and set the phone back on the desk. "So, this is the last of it, right?"

Sam cleared her throat. "Yeah. Shouldn't take too long."

"Good," Liz muttered. "No offense, but I'll be happy when this is all over."

Sam gave her a tight smile. "Me too."

Chapter twelve

Sam rubbed her burning eyes, blinking against the fluorescent lights as she picked up her phone. The day had bled into a haze, just like the one before had after she'd left Liz's office. It was all blurring together.

"Hello?" she mumbled into her phone, barely aware of the people she passed in the office lobby. Leaving for the day should've felt like freedom, but this time it felt more like surrender.

"What're you doing right now?" Scarlett's joyful voice rang through the speaker in her ear.

Sam groaned, stretching her throbbing neck and shoulders. "Leaving the office. Why?"

She stepped through the glass-paned doors and into the chilled night air where people ambled past on the sidewalk.

"Come bowling with us."

Sam stepped back beneath the overhang of the building as a chill ran through her body. She'd felt out of it all day, even after getting an extra hour of sleep that morning.

"I don't think I'm up for bowling," she mumbled, wishing she'd ridden her bike to the office instead of walking the few blocks. At least then she wouldn't be standing there, freezing, waiting for her feet to move.

"Oh, come on. Don't be lame," Scarlett said, a playful edge to her words. "Terrence will be there, and it's been forever since you guys hung out. He's excited to see you."

Sam frowned. She'd already cancelled on her once that week when they were supposed to get dinner. So even if she didn't feel up to it, she owed it to her to go.

"Okay," Sam breathed. "Sure. Send me the address."

***

The bowling alley hummed with the low thrum of background music and the rhythmic clatter of pins being struck. The faint smell of oil and fried food filled the air, mingling with the bursts of laughter and cheers from nearby lanes.

Sam tried to keep her focus despite the endless fog of exhaustion that hung over her.

"Sam! Over here!"

Scarlett's voice pulled her attention, and she spotted her waving from their lane, where Jess and Terrence were already seated. She forced her legs to move, trying to look presentable and not like she'd just spent the entire day feeling like her body was fighting a losing battle.

"Sam!" Terrence exclaimed, rising to his full towering height as she approached. His dark, muscular frame gave him a commanding presence, but the warmth of his boyish smile softened the intensity.

"Hey," she said, mustering a smile as he pulled her into a crushing hug.

"It's been forever," he said, stepping back and giving her a once-over with a playful grin that made him seem much younger than he was. "Scar said you'd be here, but I didn't believe her. How've you been?"

Sam chuckled dryly. "Busy. You know how it is."

"I'll bet," he replied with a laugh. "We've got a lot of catching up to do."

"Hey," Jess said, her voice drawing Sam's attention as she shifted on the bench to make room.

"Hey," Sam replied, exhaling the first real smile she'd managed all day as she slid onto the seat next to her.

They settled into a rhythm, easy conversation flowing around her, though Sam barely registered most of it. She nodded along, forcing herself to laugh at the right moments, but her mind was elsewhere—floating, fading in and out.

Scarlett had just bowled a spare when her phone buzzed on the scoring table. She glanced at the screen and let out a small groan.

"Shit," she muttered, standing up and grabbing her drink. "I forgot I was supposed to call my mom tonight. She's been hounding me for days about the schedule for the rehearsal dinner."

Terrence chuckled where he stood beside her. "Want me to handle it? I can charm my way out of it for you."

Scarlett raised an eyebrow at him. "Oh, you think so?" she teased, then sighed, glancing at Sam and Jess apologetically. "Sorry, I should go take this before she starts blowing up my phone."

"Its fine," Jess said with a wave of her hand. "Take your time."

Terrence grabbed his jacket and placed a hand on Scarlett's lower back. "I'll come with you." He turned back to Sam and Jess, flashing a quick grin. "Don't cheat while we're gone."

Scarlett rolled her eyes affectionately as she led the way toward the exit, already dialing her phone.

Terrence followed, throwing a quick wink over his shoulder before they disappeared into the crowd.

Jess' voice cut through the fog. "Tired?"

Sam shrugged, picking up her ice water. She took a sip, the cold biting against the soreness in her throat. "Long work days. Not feeling too great today," she admitted.

Jess frowned, concern darkening her eyes.

"How are you feeling, though?" Sam asked. "You sound a lot better than yesterday."

Jess glanced away, clearing her throat. "Yeah," she drawled. "I wasn't sick, just—not in the mood to do much."

Sam watched her, waiting to see if she would tell her what she already knew.

Jess' throat bobbed as she swallowed, eyes still fixed on the scoring monitor. "Liz and I broke up."

Sam waited a beat to see if she would say anything else, but she didn't.

"I'm sorry," Sam said softly.

Jess' eyes flicked up to hers as her head cocked slightly to the side, eyes narrowing. "You don't sound surprised."

An apologetic frown pulled across her face. "I saw Liz at the office yesterday."

Jess gave a knowing nod, her lips pressing together in a hard line. "Great," she muttered. "I'm sure she just couldn't wait to tell you all about it."

Sam shook her head. "We had work to do. We didn't really talk about it all that much."

Jess gave one small nod.

"I really am sorry, though."

Jess glanced at her, a faint smile tugging at her lips. "You know," she began, her voice casual, "it feels weirdly—fine. Not great, obviously. But it's not the end of the world either."

Sam raised an eyebrow, surprised but relieved to see Jess handling it that way. "Yeah?"

Jess shrugged, tracing the edge of her cup. "I mean, it's not like I didn't see it coming. We were just drifting for a while. I kept thinking we'd get back on track, but—" She shrugged, her expression light. "It just wasn't there anymore."

Sam nodded slowly, letting Jess's words sink in. "So, you're okay with it?"

Jess stared off for a moment before nodding slowly. "Yeah," she said, looking back at her. "I think I am.

I'm sad it didn't work out, but we were—going in circles, you know?"

Sam watched her, searching for anything hidden behind the words. "Makes sense. Sometimes it's better to just let go."

"Exactly." Jess leaned back, exhaling deeply, as if breathing out the last remnants of the relationship.

A flicker of relief filled her chest. The last thing she'd wanted was to see Jess hurt, and hearing her talk about it with such clarity made Sam's own shoulders relax.

"Plus," Jess added with a smirk, "now I don't have to pretend to love those late-night war documentaries she was always so into."

Sam let out a laugh, shaking her head. "Gonna go back to late night horror instead?"

Jess groaned, but her eyes gleamed with a playful glint. "Probably not."

Sam smirked. "So what, you only pull out the horror movies when you're trying to make a move on someone?"

Jess' eyes narrowed as she grinned. "You know, it turns out most girls aren't that terrified when it comes to jump scares. So that move only ever worked on you."

Sam chuckled, feeling the mood shift back to their usual ease. Jess seemed brighter than she had the last few times she'd seen her, like she'd shed a layer that had been weighing her down.

"What did we miss?" Scarlett asked, as they returned. She dropped her phone on the table, sliding into the seat after Terrence.

"Just Jess admitting her hatred of war documentaries," Sam replied with a grin, nudging Jess' shoulder. Jess shot her a mock glare, but the amusement in her eyes was unmistakable.

"Good," Scarlett declared, lifting her drink. "Here's to more fun and zero war documentaries."

Chapter thirteen

A harsh cough wheezed from her throat as she blinked at the computer screen in front of her.

Sam had awoken that morning to chills and aches all over her body. So, as much as she hated it, she'd cancelled her meetings for the day and started work from her apartment instead.

Although, after just a couple of hours, it was a struggle to even sit upright, much less focus on work.

Her phone buzzed, and she picked it up, seeing Scarlett's picture fill the screen.

"Hey," she said, her voice rasping into the phone.

"Well, you sound like shit."

Sam groaned. "I *feel* like shit."

Scarlett snorted a laugh. "So I guess you don't want to grab coffee, then?"

As much as she wanted to get an energy boost to power through a few more hours of work, she knew that was probably the last thing her body really needed.

"I wish," she grumbled, closing her eyes as she leaned her head back against the chair. "But I don't think so."

She heard Scarlett say something to someone else before she said, "Alright rain check. Get some sleep or something. You need to feel better for the trip next weekend."

Sam hummed. In the craziness of work, she'd almost entirely forgotten about the bachelorette weekend she'd agreed to.

"Yeah. I'm on it," she mumbled.

Scarlett said something else she couldn't really make out before the phone went dead.

And right as she was about to set it back down, it buzzed again, this time with a new text.

Jess' name popped up.

Jess Miller: Are you home?

She typed out a quick answer.

Yeah. Why?

She waited a few moments, watching as the typing bubble appeared, then disappeared again. She waited another few moments without another text popping up, then set the phone back down.

Thirty minutes later, a light knock on the door pulled her from her daze.

She walked to it, each step an immense effort.

The foggy thought floated through her head that Caleb must've needed to drop off some work documents and forgot to let her know.

She pulled the door open, only half aware as the person on the other side came into view.

"Oh," she rasped, surprised.

Jess looked back at her with a pained smile. "Scar was right. You do sound bad."

Sam let out a weak laugh, the sound catching in her throat. "I've been better."

Jess held up a plastic bag tied at the top. "I went to that place you mentioned the other day. Brought some soup, in case you were hungry."

Sam grimaced, pressing a knuckle to her temple to dull the pounding ache behind her eyes. "Thanks," she mumbled, stepping back to let Jess in. "I don't really have an appetite, though."

Jess stepped around her, heading straight to the small kitchen area.

Sam shuffled back to the couch, sinking into the cushions with a low groan as Jess opened the fridge.

"Do you really have no food here?" Jess asked with a laugh.

Sam shrugged, the slight movement sending aches up her shoulders and into her pounding forehead. "Doesn't make sense to," she mumbled. "I'm never home."

"So what would you do if you got hungry today?" Jess asked, coming around the side of the couch and giving her a pointed look. "Starve?"

The corner of Sam's lip tugged upward into a smirk. "I'd wait for my amazing friend to surprise me with food."

Jess bit back a grin, rolling her eyes. "Right." She glanced away, eyes trailing through the apartment. "Tiana didn't come to bring you anything?"

Sam watched her for a moment, wondering why she would've expected her to do that. But maybe that's the kind of thing a friend like Scarlett would've done. Not Tiana, though. It wasn't her style.

"No," Sam breathed, closing her eyes. "She avoids sickness at all costs."

Jess nodded, still looking around the apartment.

"You probably shouldn't be in here either," Sam muttered. "You might get sick."

"I doubt it," Jess said dryly. "Unlike you, I get more than four hours of sleep a night, so my immune system is still intact."

Sam smirked, keeping her eyes closed.

Jess was quiet for a moment before she asked, "Do you want me to go?"

Sam opened her eyes, turning her head towards her. She didn't, even if she really should be focusing on work. It felt nice to have someone there. She couldn't remember the last time someone had come to check on her when she wasn't feeling well.

"No," Sam said softly.

Jess's small smile wavered as her gaze caught on something behind Sam. Her expression shifted as she looked back at her with an incredulous glare. "Were you seriously working before I got here?"

Sam followed her line of sight to the glowing computer screens, casting a faint, blue-tinged light across the room. "I had stuff to do," she muttered as a cough clawed its way up from her chest.

She bent forward, the cough rattling through her lungs like it had been waiting for its chance. By the time it finally subsided, her body felt impossibly heavy. A shiver rolled through her, and she crossed her arms over her chest for warmth.

Jess didn't say anything, but Sam could feel her watching. A moment later, Jess leaned forward, reaching out to rest the back of her hand gently against her forehead.

Sam's eyes fluttered closed as she leaned into the cool touch.

"You have a fever," Jess stated, pulling her hand away. "You should be sleeping."

Sam let out a sigh. "I already tried."

The couch dipped, and she opened her eyes to find Jess sitting beside her, brows drawn into that same familiar crease of concern. It was the look Jess always wore when she cared more than she let on.

"Want to watch a movie, then?" Jess asked softly.

A small smirk formed on Sam's lips. "Yeah, but I swear, if you put on a scary movie, I'll get right back up and start working again."

Jess chuckled, reaching forward to grab the remote off the coffee table in front of them. "No scary movies." She clicked the power button on the remote. "I can't deal with you squealing every five seconds."

Sam smiled to herself, closing her eyes once again as she turned her body and settled further into the couch. Her shoulders shook lightly as another round of chills moved through her body.

"Do you have blankets somewhere?"

Sam hummed. "On the bed."

Jess' footsteps padded away on the hardwood floor, then returned a moment later.

Warm fabric draped down gently over her legs, and she opened her eyes again when she felt Jess sit back down beside her.

She watched her, too tired to care that she was blatantly staring as Jess clicked through the TV.

And it struck her how lucky she was to have someone like her in her life. Actually, she couldn't quite imagine how she'd gone so many years without her. It hadn't felt like a long time when it was happening, but now that they were in each other's lives again, it felt impossible to have ever gone without her. Or anyone that truly cared about her in that way.

Jess set the remote down on the couch beside her as something began playing. Then she pulled her knees up to her chest, leaning back into the couch.

After a moment, she turned, looking back at her. "What?" she asked with a curious half-smile.

There was so much she wanted to say. So much that built up inside her. But it was just a feeling. And she didn't know which words would do it justice.

"I'm just—" Sam paused, the fogginess of the fever making it near impossible to think coherently. She blinked, letting out a breath. "Thank you for being here." She swallowed against the raw burning in her throat. "Thanks for being such a good friend. Even after all this time."

Jess gave her a small smile before looking back at the TV. "You don't need to thank me."

"Yeah I do," Sam whispered.

Jess' smile fell from her face slightly. "Would you really expect me to not show up when you need help?"

Sam stayed silent, watching the way the light of the TV flickered across her face.

"You were going to do the same for me the other day," Jess said, still looking straight ahead. "It's no different."

But it *was* different. It didn't feel like it meant anything when she offered.

And maybe that was the difference. Maybe to Jess, it was no big deal.

But Jess showing up felt like—something.

"Why didn't you tell me you guys broke up that day?" Sam asked quietly.

The muscle in Jess' jaw shifted, the light from the TV flickering across it.

"You think I wanted to immediately tell—" She paused, as if contemplating her next words carefully. "My *ex*—about my freshly failed relationship?"

Sam blinked, absorbing her choice of words. Her mind clung to them, unable to process the rest. And she couldn't help the smile that formed around the edges of her lips.

Jess gave her a sideways glance, instantly rolling her eyes. "Don't—"

"That's the first time you've called me that," Sam said, laughter bubbling through her lips.

Maybe it should've made her feel bad in some way. It probably would have for most people—being reminded that they were the person of the past. But really, it did the opposite for her. It made what they had finally feel real. Like even though they'd never officially declared anything about what they were to each other, at least Jess felt like it was as serious as she did. As serious as what she had with Liz.

Jess groaned, but her own laughter came through with it. "I knew you wouldn't let that slide."

Sam's grin widened, but she forced it down, relaxing her head back onto the couch. "You still could've told me."

Jess snorted a dry laugh. "It was bad enough finding out I was dating your childhood best friend," she muttered. "You guys comparing notes on the breakup and failed relationship would've been even worse."

Sam pursed her lips, the words stirring uncomfortably within her. "You and I never broke up."

Jess gave her a sidelong, pointed look. "Right."

Sam's brows pulled together as she shifted, sitting up straighter. "We didn't," she repeated, mustering whatever energy she could. "We never—"

Failed.

She stopped herself as that word entered her mind. It probably wasn't important to Jess. The ending was the same. And maybe to her it was all the same as what she'd just gone through with Liz.

But for some reason, she didn't want her to think of it that way. She wanted her to realize that they'd never really fully tried in the first place.

So how could she think they'd ever failed?

"We never really tried," Sam whispered, more to herself. "So we never really—" Sam paused, swallowing. "Failed."

Jess looked back at her, but her eyes held an unreadable look. Something careful—almost guarded.

And after a long moment, she finally turned, looking back at the TV.

At some point, Sam felt her eyelids begin to flutter closed. She couldn't tell how long it had been, but the fever seemed to be taking over, pulling her from consciousness.

Her head bobbed, and she caught herself, tugging it upward as she blinked, trying to stay awake.

"Wanna try to sleep now?" Jess asked softly.

"No," Sam said quickly, straightening up. Now that she'd had Jess there with her, the thought of her leaving felt lonely.

"I'm good," she said, the words tumbling out in a muffled rasp. "Not tired."

Jess cocked one eyebrow. "You're lying."

Sam smirked, letting her eyes close as she pulled the blanket up around her chest.

And when she heard Jess' footsteps moving through the apartment a moment later, she couldn't muster the energy to open her eyes to see what she was doing.

"Put this between your arms," Jess' soft voice said a few moments later.

Sam cracked her heavy eyes open, seeing Jess standing in front of her, holding two pillows.

She smiled, her eyes blinking lazily. "You still remember that?"

A look of something resembling hurt flashed through Jess' eyes. And maybe if she felt better, she'd be able to figure out what she'd said that was wrong. But even then, she wasn't sure she'd be able to figure it out.

"Of course I do," Jess answered, holding one of the pillows out.

Sam pulled her legs up and turned her body until she was laying across the couch. Jess placed one of the pillows between her open arms, then motioned at her knees.

Sam spread them, taking the second pillow and placing it between them. "You forgot the third one," she mumbled. And even through the thick feverish fog, those words felt familiar. Some memory they might have shared in a different lifetime.

"You don't need it. Just lean your back into the couch," Jess replied, her eyes trailing over the setup. After a moment, she nodded with a satisfied look, then sat down in the small space that was left.

Sam let her body sink into the couch, every inch of her aching and heavy, but something about Jess being there took the edge off the fever's grip. She pressed her cheek into the cool pillow, Jess' leg resting lightly against her own.

For a few minutes, they stayed like that, the sound of the movie a low hum in the background. Sam's thoughts swam in and out of focus. But she kept herself awake—aware enough to still feel Jess' presence beside her.

"Sam?" Jess's voice cut through the haze, soft but steady.

"Hmm?" Sam mumbled, eyelids fluttering open.

"I'll still stay if you want, but you really need to sleep," Jess said, her voice dropping to a near whisper.

Sam exhaled slowly, letting those words sink in. She hadn't realized until now how much she needed to hear them. That she didn't have to keep pushing herself. That someone would be there. And that she wasn't alone.

She shifted, settling deeper into the couch, the weight of the blankets and pillows a welcome pressure on her sore body. "Kay," she mumbled.

Jess shifted beside her, adjusting her position on the couch, but Sam felt the warmth of her still there, still close. And that was enough. More than enough.

Sam's breathing slowed, her body finally surrendering to the exhaustion that had been clawing at her for days. But this time, as she drifted off, she didn't feel the usual isolation pressing down on her.

Sam cracked her eyes open, watching her for a long moment, not having enough energy to tear her eyes away from the one thing that brought her some sense of calm relief.

Jess glanced down, a soft smile tugging at the corners of her lips. "I'm not going anywhere."

Chapter fourteen

The front of the resort slowly came into view, its grand windows gleaming under the late afternoon sun. Sleek glass doors reflected the lush palm trees that lined the entrance, and the faint sound of water trickling from a nearby fountain mingled with the low hum of cars idling in the drop-off area.

"Fancy," Tiana crooned from the seat beside her, leaning her head out the open window to get a better look.

The car slowed to a stop under the large canopy, and Sam leaned forward from the back seat, thanking the driver.

She hopped out of the car, meeting Tiana at the back to grab their bags. Sam pulled out her one small backpack before helping Tiana with her two large suitcases.

"You know we're only here for the weekend, right?" she mumbled, struggling to pull the second suitcase out.

"Yes," Tiana answered, rolling her eyes. "But some of us like to have more options than the same plain t-shirts every day."

Sam huffed as the second suitcase finally slid free, landing on the ground with a dull thud.

"Careful," Tiana scolded.

"Maybe pack lighter next time," Sam shot back as she handed Tiana the handle of the bag.

They shut the trunk and made their way toward the resort's entrance, where tall glass doors glided open automatically. The cool air-conditioning was a sharp contrast to the warm breeze outside.

"Checking in?" A woman asked from behind a tall black marble desk.

"Yeah," Sam answered with a smile, pulling her wallet out of her back pocket.

A few moments into the check-in process, a familiar voice called out from behind them with a squeal. "You're here!"

Sam glanced behind them to see Scarlett running up, with Jess laughing a few feet behind. Trailing a little farther back was another woman, shorter and more reserved, her dark mid-length hair brushing her shoulders as she moved. She had a delicate resemblance to Terrence—the same dark rich skin tone and almond-shaped eyes—but the shy, tentative way she took in her surroundings was a stark contrast to her brother's bold, easygoing presence.

Tiana grinned as Scarlett pulled her into a tight hug, as if they'd been best friends for years.

"This is really nice," Sam said, as Scarlett pulled her in for the next hug.

"I know, right," Scarlett gushed, waving a hand around the lobby. "My man has good taste."

Jess smiled as Tiana hugged her, mumbling something that Sam couldn't quite make out. But Jess laughed at it, shooting her an amused look.

Then Jess stepped toward her.

"Hey," she said softly, wrapping her arms around her torso in a gentle hug.

Sam hugged her back, the familiar comfort making her chest flutter in a way she didn't quite want to name.

Scarlett stepped back, motioning to the woman behind them. "This is Terrence's sister, Jasmine."

Jasmine hovered near the edge of the group, hands clasped in front of her as she gave a small, polite nod.

"Jasmine, Sam—and Tiana," she said, waving a hand at each of them.

Sam smiled warmly at her. "Nice to meet you."

Jasmine nodded again, her tight smile faltering for a moment before she managed a quiet, "You too."

Tiana wasted no time as she stepped forward, wrapping her in a big hug.

Sam choked back a laugh at the way Jasmine's mouth fell open in surprise. But luckily, after a moment, she seemed to relax into it, letting out her own soft chuckle.

"Good to meet you guys," Jasmine muttered, her smile slowly brightening.

"Okay ladies," the woman behind the front desk cut in. "Your room is all ready," she said, handing a key to Sam, then Tiana.

"Oh, you guys are in the same room?" Scarlett asked.

Tiana nodded, then narrowed her gaze on Sam. "But if you wake me up at the crack of dawn with your loud ass typing, I'm kicking you out into the lobby."

Sam snorted a laugh. "You sleep through anything. Pretty sure I could start a motorcycle up in there and you still wouldn't wake up."

Tiana waved her off, grabbing the handle of one suitcase while Sam took the other one for her.

"Okay," Scarlett started, checking her phone. "We have a boat picking us up in like thirty minutes, so drop off your stuff real quick and get your bathing suits on, then meet us out there at the docks."

"Oh, fun," Tiana said, clapping her hands.

"What's the boat for?" Sam asked, adjusting the backpack on her shoulder.

"Terrence booked it for us. It's gonna take us to some little beach where they have cliff jumping and jet skis we can ride."

Sam's smile grew as Tiana frowned beside her. It'd been too long since she'd been able to go for one of her late night rides to relax. Especially with all the stress of work. But the jet skis sounded like a perfect alternative.

Jess chuckled, giving Sam a knowing look. "I knew you'd be excited once you heard that."

"Yeah," Tiana muttered, "I'll leave the jumping and fast things to you while I lay out and relax."

"Okay, okay," Scarlett cut in, "hurry and drop your stuff off! The boat's gonna be here soon."

***

The midday sun warmed the side of her face as the boat slowed, the hum of the motor softening to a gentle purr. Ahead, the beach stretched in a crescent of golden sand, bordered on one side by a towering rock wall.

The driver tossed out the anchor, then gestured toward the beach, pointing out the rock wall and the three jet skis parked in the sand.

Sam hopped off the side of the boat, landing with a splash into the calf deep water. She turned, watching as the driver slowly helped Scarlett step off the boat, with Tiana and Jasmine waiting behind.

Jess approached the edge of the boat where Sam had jumped off, pausing as she eyed the water below. Sam reached up, offering her hand. Jess immediately took it, her fingers curling around Sam's as she stepped carefully down into the shallow water.

They waited a moment until the others were all off, then waded up onto the sand.

"The reservations for dinner tonight are at seven," Scarlett said, pushing her sunglasses up onto the top of her head as they laid their towels out. "I figured we could just take it easy and have an early night. But tomorrow, I wanna go up to the rooftop bar and club they have at the resort. I saw some videos, and it looked super fun."

Sam sat down on the towel beside Scarlett, listening to the plans.

Then, after a few minutes, Scarlett stood, brushing the sand off of her hands. "I'm taking a jet ski out. Who's in?" She looked between them, and Sam waited to see if the others would want to take them out first. "Jess?"

"I'll go," Jess said, taking a quick sip from her water bottle before tucking it back into her bag.

"Jasmine?" Scarlett asked, turning to her with a smile.

Jasmine shifted where she sat, giving her a timid look. "I don't know," she muttered. "I want to, but I've never driven one before."

"Want me to go with you?" Sam asked. "It's really easy. I can show you."

"Oh," Jasmine muttered, hands fidgeting in her lap. "Um—yeah, okay."

Sam stood, and they all walked over to where the jet skis lined the edge of the sand.

Jess and Scarlett easily pushed theirs into the water, while Sam tugged her shirt off, quickly replacing it with one of the life jackets.

She pushed the last jet ski off into the water, helping Jasmine up onto the front while she climbed on behind her.

"Okay," Sam said over the soft rumble of the engine. "Just use this to speed up, and don't take the turns too sharp."

"Like this—"

Jasmine hit the throttle before Sam could brace herself, the jet ski jerking forward with a sudden burst of speed. Sam's hands shot to the sides of the seat, gripping it tightly as they shot across the water.

Jasmine let out a startled squeal that quickly turned into an exhilarated laugh, her hair whipping wildly in the wind.

Sam couldn't help but laugh with her, adjusting her balance as the spray of saltwater misted against her skin. "See!" she shouted over the rushing wind. "Easy!"

The jet ski cut cleanly across the waves, carving a path toward Scarlett and Jess, who were further ahead.

Within moments, they were soaring alongside them, Jasmine pressing the throttle just a little harder.

"Well, that didn't take long," Scarlett called out as she circled back around them. "You like it?"

Instead of answering, Jasmine shot them forward once again, laughter bubbling from her throat. Within moments, they were all speeding ahead, weaving in and out around each other.

And the moment Sam saw Scarlett making sharp turns, splashing water high up into the air, she knew Jasmine would want to do the same. She braced herself as the jet ski shot ahead near where Jess had slowed to a stop.

Then, right as she'd expected, Jasmine took a hard turn, cutting too sharply.

Sam squeezed her eyes shut as she felt her body rip off the jet ski, tumbling out into the water.

The world spun in a chaotic blur of cold, rushing waves. For a split second, everything was quiet, muffled beneath the surface of the water as she clawed her way up. She broke through, immediately wiping the water from her eyes.

"Oh my gosh," she heard Jasmine's frantic voice from somewhere far off. "I'm—I'm so sorry—I didn't—"

Sam let out a laugh, shoving the soaked hair back from her face. "It's fine!" she called, grinning despite the chill biting at her skin. "It happens!"

A low hum grew louder behind her, and Sam turned just as Jess pulled up on her own jet ski, stopping beside her with a smug, amused look. "Guess you're not as strong as you used to be."

Sam barked out a laugh, shivering as the cold sank deeper into her bones. "I wasn't ready," she lied.

Jess smirked, shaking her head as she extended a hand. Sam grabbed it, pulling herself up and settling into the seat behind her.

Looking back over her shoulder, Sam spotted Jasmine slowly circling back toward them, her expression a mix of guilt and embarrassment.

"You good to ride on your own?" Sam called out.

Jasmine gave her a sheepish, apologetic look. "Yeah. Probably safer that way."

Sam smiled, wrapping one arm loosely around Jess' waist in front of her.

And by the slight smirk she caught on Jess' face, she knew what she was about to do.

The jet ski lurched forward, sending her body backward as she clung with one arm to Jess. Then it immediately slowed, sending her slamming forward.

"Shit," she muttered, her body tensing as she threw her second arm around Jess, holding her tightly.

Jess glanced back over her shoulder, a wide grin stretching across her face. "Now you know how I felt the first time I rode on your bike."

Sam snorted a laugh. "Yeah, right," she muttered, relaxing her arms around her waist. "I'm a much better driver than you."

They rode for a while longer, cutting through the sparkling waves as the sun inched higher, warm against their backs. The rhythm of the jet ski and the wind against her skin made it easy to lose track of time until Sam spotted Scarlett and Jasmine heading back to shore, their figures small against the bright sand.

"Ready to go back?" Jess called over her shoulder.

"If you are."

Jess turned the jet ski toward the beach, slowing as they neared the shallows. Once they were close enough, Sam hopped off, landing with a splash as the water lapped against her legs. They secured the jet ski on the sand, the sound of waves crashing gently filling the surrounding quiet.

They made their way across the beach, the sun drying their damp skin as they trudged through the warm, uneven sand.

"Why are you the only one that's wet?" Tiana asked from where she laid on her back, blocking the sun with one hand.

Jess chuckled as she sat down, and Sam caught the slightly embarrassed look on Jasmine's face.

"Slipped," Sam said, shivering as water dripped down from the life jacket onto her bare thighs. She glanced down, realizing she'd forgotten to take it off and leave it with the jet ski.

She unzipped the front, pulling it off her shoulders and dropping it into the sand at her feet.

"Thought you were supposed to be the athletic one," Tiana muttered.

Sam shot her a half-hearted glare, and when she looked up, she caught Scarlett staring at her chest and ribs, lips parted slightly.

Sam followed her eyes, peering down at the angry scars cascading across her body. In the cold of the water, they'd taken on a deep purple hue, making them stand out much more than usual against her skin.

Scarlett blinked, slowly closing her mouth, but her eyes remained on the scars. And that's when she realized that Scarlett was probably the only one in that group who hadn't seen the full extent of them. She couldn't blame the reaction.

She remembered the way Tiana had frozen up the first time she'd seen her without a shirt after the accident.

And she couldn't even bring herself to think about the day Jess had first seen them.

After a moment, Scarlett seemed to snap out of it, catching herself. But she didn't look away the way everyone else usually did.

Instead, she met her eyes with an intense look, giving her a small genuine smile.

It reminded her of one other smile she'd given her in the past. The first time they'd seen each other after her and Jess stopped speaking.

Not a look of pity. But of understanding. Of caring.

Sam sat down on the towel beside her, and Scarlett immediately put an arm around her waist, leaning her head against her shoulder.

And Sam became all too aware of the way the rest of the group had clearly caught on to what had happened. Tiana and Jess both watched them, each with an entirely different look.

"Sorry," Scarlett whispered beside her. "I guess I didn't realize how much—"

"It's okay," Sam cut in, wanting nothing more than for the conversation to change to something else.

She took a drink from her bottle, looking off into the distant water.

"I think they make you look badass," Tiana said nonchalantly. "They make you seem mysterious or something."

Sam grimaced, twisting the cap back onto her water.

And when she looked back up, she caught the way Jess' jaw flickered. The look on her face that said she had something to say and was trying desperately to hold it back.

Scarlett seemed to be watching her too, and quickly cut in, asking Jasmine something about her extended family that was attending the wedding.

Some of the tension seeped out of her shoulders as they went back and forth, discussing different family members and how long it'd been since they'd all been together.

And soon enough, Jess seemed to relax back to normal as well, joining in the conversation.

They laid out, talking and enjoying the midday warmth.

But eventually, Sam sat up, ready for the next thing. Laying out had never been her thing. She needed something to do.

"Anyone ready to jump off the rocks?" she asked, blocking out the sun with one hand as she peered up at them.

Jess smirked as she leaned up on her elbows. "I was wondering how long you'd last just laying here."

"Not me," Tiana muttered, sitting up and pulling out her phone. "I'll take pictures though."

"I'm ready," Jasmine said, quickly standing.

Scarlett grinned up at her, clearly pleased with how she'd relaxed into the day. "Me too."

Sam stood, then took Scarlett's hand, pulling her up.

"You coming?" Sam asked as she trudged through the thick sand past Jess.

Jess looked back and forth between her and the cliff with a slight frown. "I don't know."

"She's scared of heights," Scarlett called back over her shoulder as she followed Jasmine to the base of the cliff.

"No, I'm not," Jess shot back, although her face told a different story. Still, she stood, joining in beside Sam.

"You sure?" Sam asked with a chuckle as they approached the area where the guide had told them would be the easiest to climb. "You look scared."

"I'm not scared," Jess muttered, as if working to convince herself.

They all climbed up the rock wall to the first ledge, where the guide had shown them to go.

"Who wants to go—"

Jasmine suddenly leapt off, arms swinging wildly in the air as a high-pitched yelp escaped her throat.

Scarlett burst into laughter, along with Tiana, who stood on the beach off to the side, phone held high in the air, pointed at them.

Sam laughed, leaning over the edge to peer down at where she'd landed in the water. "I guess the adrenaline of the jet skis really got her going."

"I'm next," Scarlett said with a wide grin. Then she called down to Tiana, "Make sure you get this!"

Tiana gave her a thumbs up. Then Scarlett took a few steps back before running and launching herself off the edge. She screamed, dropping into the water with a splash.

Sam leaned over the edge again, checking the foamy white water Scarlett had disappeared into. Then a moment later, her head popped up, and she instantly laughed, swimming off to the side where the sand met the water.

Sam turned back, looking up to the next highest rock ledge. It was probably only a few feet higher, and she could spot an easy way to climb up.

"You're up," Sam said to Jess as she began climbing up the wall to the next jumping point.

"Where are you going?" Jess asked, standing with her back flat against the wall, at the point farthest from the edge.

Sam grunted, hoisting herself up onto it. "I'm jumping from here."

"What—*Sam*," Jess snapped, her tone sharp with a deadly seriousness that only made Sam's grin widen.

She chuckled, stepping up onto the last part of the rock and planting herself on the edge of the cliff. The wind whipped at her damp hair as she glanced over her shoulder.

"Sam," Jess commanded again, her voice edged with frustration. "Come back down here."

Sam turned back toward the drop, hands resting casually on her hips. "You know, it's fine if you're too scared to jump," she called over the edge with a teasing smile. "You can climb back down."

Jess glared up at her, but Sam only laughed, thoroughly entertained.

Then a moment later, Jess began climbing up toward her.

Her brow lifted as she watched her. "What are you doing?" Sam asked, cocking her head as Jess closed the distance, each hand and foot finding the rocks with ease.

Jess breathed heavily as she pulled herself up each part of the rock wall. And when she neared the top, Sam put a hand out, helping her up the last few feet.

"If you're gonna be stubborn and do it," Jess started, her breathing slightly labored, "then I am, too."

Sam watched her, unable to stop herself as she held a protective arm out between Jess and the nearby edge. "Okay, fine. I'll go back down with you."

Jess glared at her again, but this time, it looked more like a challenge. "No."

Sam watched her, the amusement falling from her eyes as a slight anxiety entered her chest at how high up Jess was from the ground.

She frowned, peering over the edge into the water once more, checking for the clear, rockless area below.

"What? You only care how safe it is once I'm up here with you?" Jess asked.

"Come on, what's taking so long!" Tiana called from below, the phone still pointed up at them.

Sam pursed her lips, checking the water once again to ensure there was nothing they could hit.

"Okay," Sam muttered. "I'll go first. Watch where I go, so you know where to land."

Jess scoffed. "Absolutely not." Then she stepped forward, her shoulder brushing against Sam's back.

Sam glanced over her shoulder, frowning. "Same time?"

Jess didn't answer. Instead, her warm fingers slid into Sam's, lacing around her hand.

Sam glanced down, smiling slightly at the familiar feeling. Then she looked away, clearing her throat.

"On three?" Jess asked, inching farther out.

Sam nodded once, peering out into the water below. "One. Two. Three—"

They jumped.

The air rushed past in a split second of weightless silence, and even as they plummeted toward the water, Jess' grip on her hand didn't falter.

The crash into the water knocked the wind from her lungs, but Sam surfaced a moment later. Her free hand shot out instinctively, tugging Jess up with her.

Jess emerged sputtering, hair plastered to her face as she reached blindly for Sam's shoulder to steady herself.

"You okay?" Sam asked breathlessly, keeping them both afloat.

Jess pushed the wet strands out of her eyes, blinking wildly as she looked at Sam—and then she laughed. It started small but grew louder, rippling across the water between them.

Sam's own laughter followed, the sound blending with Jess' in a way that made the cold water and aching muscles completely irrelevant.

Jess finally caught her breath, still grinning as she clung to Sam's shoulder. "You're insane."

"Lets do it again—"

"No way," Jess cut her off, laughing as she splashed a handful of water at Sam's face.

They swam to the side until Sam felt the soft sandy bottom beneath her feet. She ambled up onto the dry beach, bending over to shake her wet hair out.

"Let me see the pictures," Scarlett said to Tiana as they approached.

She took the phone, swiping through. "Oh my god," she gushed. "These are so good."

Scarlett reached out, handing the phone to Jess as she shook her wet hands off.

Sam came up behind Jess, looking over her shoulder at the pictures. She swiped through, laughing at the few of Scarlett screaming in midair. Then she swiped to the next and stopped.

It was a picture of them, standing at the top ledge, hand in hand, with Sam turned, smiling at her.

She hadn't seen many pictures of herself in recent years. Or actually—ever. The only photos she'd had were either taken for official school things, or for business functions as she'd gotten older. And in the only candid photos she had as a child, she never seemed to be smiling.

Sam swallowed, realizing for the first time that she'd never really seen herself that happy. At least not in a photo.

Jess' thumb hovered over the picture, as if she was having some realization of her own. Or maybe she was thinking something entirely different.

Jess cleared her throat softly. "Um—do you—do you guys want one together?" she asked, looking between her and Tiana.

"Yes!" Tiana said immediately. She crossed the few feet to her, engulfing her in a tight embrace. "We don't have any good pictures together."

Sam wrapped one arm around her as Tiana struck different poses before ending with one kissing her cheek.

She chuckled as Tiana pulled her head down, laughing into her neck.

Then finally, Tiana released her to retrieve her phone from Jess.

"So cute," she squealed, swiping through them.

They made their way back down the beach as Tiana continued through the photos.

"I'm surprised you jumped from up there," Scarlett said to Jess. "I didn't even think you'd make it from the smaller one."

Jess grunted. "Me either. Can't let this one show me up, though," she muttered, nodding her head at Sam.

Tiana snorted a laugh, glancing up from her phone. "You'll drive yourself crazy trying to follow that. Trust me, she can't help it. Danger attracts her like a moth to a flame."

Sam shot her a look, her brows crinkling together. "No, it doesn't."

Tiana gave her a pointed look, then rolled her eyes. "Yes, it does. You've always been like this."

Sam frowned, not ready to give up the argument.

But Tiana waved her off. "It's fine. I'm not saying it's your fault. Think about the other kids in the foster home with us whose parents were addicts," she continued nonchalantly. And the mention made something tighten in Sam's chest. "You guys all did it—or—" she paused, thinking. "At least some version of it."

Sam looked away, an icy wall building up within her by the second. "That's not true."

Tiana seemed to grow serious then, as if she'd been forcing herself to act like she didn't care. And now, she was letting that facade finally drop.

She gave her a challenging, almost angry look that Sam hadn't seen in years. "Right," she muttered. "So then, why do you still go for midnight rides on your bike?"

Then her eyes flicked down the scar across her neck and chest. They lingered there for a moment before meeting her eyes again. And then, Sam knew. At least some of that carefree attitude toward the whole thing was a front for how much she cared.

Sam softened slightly, releasing a breath.

And she noticed then that while Jasmine and Scarlett had continued walking up the beach, Jess had lingered there with them, hearing every word.

Sam's eyes flicked to her, and Jess seemed to be watching her with a weary, but curious, look. As if she was turning over some puzzle in her mind.

The sound of an approaching boat caught her attention, and she looked up to see the guide approaching.

"You guys ready to go back?" Scarlett called out to them. "I'm hungry."

Sam cleared her throat. "Yeah. Me too."

Jess continued walking, leaving her and Tiana standing there in silence.

"Sorry," Tiana muttered, although she held a hard look that offered no real apology. "I didn't mean to say all that."

Sam shook her head slightly. "It's fine," she muttered, draping her arm over Tiana's shoulders as they walked back to the rest of the group.

Chapter fifteen

The restaurant was winding down, the noise level dropping to a dull murmur as the last of the dinner crowd paid their checks. Scarlett and Jasmine had just left, excusing themselves after the long day, but Sam had stayed with Jess and Tiana while they finished the last of their meals.

After a moment, Sam noticed Tiana's gaze kept drifting toward the bar, where a handsome woman was laughing with a friend.

Tiana caught Sam's eye with a sly grin. "I'm gonna go say hi," she declared, already on her feet and sauntering toward the bar.

"That doesn't bother you?" Jess asked, nodding her head toward where Tiana now stood looking at the attractive woman beside her with a coy smile.

Sam cocked her head, looking back at Jess. "Does what bother me?"

Jess shifted in her chair with a hesitant look. "You know," she muttered. "Tiana—flirting—like that."

Sam's eyebrows tugged together. "No?" she drawled. "Why would that bother me?"

Now Jess was the one who looked confused. She opened her mouth, then paused, shaking her head before closing it again. "Aren't you guys.."

It took Sam a moment to realize what she was getting at. And when she did, she broke into a laugh. "We're not like that."

Jess hummed, her eyes narrowing slightly like she wasn't entirely convinced. "I mean," she continued, throwing another glance toward Tiana before looking back at her, "I know you guys aren't officially together or anything, but—" She paused, hesitating. "You and I weren't either and.."

Sam understood then. And she also understood why Jess might have viewed them so differently than how Sam did.

"It's not like that," Sam answered. Then she cleared her throat, scratching a hand over the back of her neck. "I mean, it's not like—us." Jess' eyes flickered to hers. "Or," Sam continued, feeling the need to clarify. "It's not like us—*before*."

Jess' eyes immediately left hers again, and she wondered whether the clarification should've been left unsaid.

"We're just friends," Sam said quickly, filling the silence.

Jess' eyes fell to the table, and she reached forward, swirling the small bit of wine left in her glass. Then a dry smile ghosted over her lips as she said quietly, "Friends who sleep together aren't really *just friends.*"

Sam snorted a laugh. "Well, it's been like two years since the last time, so I don't know if it really counts still."

Jess' eyes flicked back up to hers, a look of surprise filling them. But she said nothing.

"What?" Sam asked.

"Didn't you—" She paused, clearing her throat. "What about that night? After the club?"

Sam chuckled, shaking her head as she remembered what Jess had seen on the couch the morning after. "No. Nothing happened."

Jess nodded slowly, her eyes losing the somewhat guarded confusion they'd held over the last minute.

"You really thought we were together this whole time?"

Jess loosed a breath, some part of her demeanor softening as she lifted her wineglass and poured the last of it into her mouth.

"Are you tired?" Jess asked, setting the glass down and turning her body toward her.

Sam smiled softly, her eyes crinkling in amusement at the sudden change. "A little. Why?"

Jess pushed back her chair, then stood, dropping her napkin on the table. Her blonde hair flowed in the breeze, a stark contrast against the night sky.

"Walk with me?"

Sam chuckled as she stood. "Like a walk on the beach?"

Jess walked around the table, probably knowing just as well as Sam did that the answer was already 'yes'.

Sam followed her to the edge of the restaurant patio, where the concrete hit the sand. She squinted off into the darkness that enveloped the water line.

Jess let out a small, uncertain hum. "Yeah, maybe no beach walk. I'm not trying to end up in a horror movie."

Sam chuckled. "Well, you've watched enough of them to know what to do. You'd definitely be the main character that survives 'til the end."

Jess looked back at her as she continued up the cement path, leading somewhere off into the resort. "Yeah, but you'd be the one that does something stupid, and I'd end up getting killed trying to save you."

Sam smirked, following her up the winding path that was covered with trees on both sides. "You're probably right."

A light breeze blew through, rustling the leaves of the surrounding foliage.

"Scarlett had fun today," Jess said, running a hand through her hair.

"Yeah?"

Jess' head bobbed as she nodded. "You know, she always has more fun when you're there."

Sam gave her a sidelong look. "You think?"

Jess hummed, the corner of her lips tilting upward. "Don't act like it's the first time you've heard that. Everyone has more fun with you around."

She wasn't exactly wrong. It was something that she'd heard every so often. But still, hearing it from Jess felt different somehow.

"Do *you* have more fun with me around?" Sam asked, shooting her a playful smile.

Jess rolled her eyes as she chuckled. "If I say yes, are you gonna tease me about it all night?"

Sam grinned. "Maybe."

"Then no," Jess replied, eyes narrowing in a half-hearted glare.

"Very convincing," Sam smirked. She gazed up at the starry night sky, letting out a deep sigh. "I still can't believe she's getting married."

"Why not?"

Sam shrugged. "Guess I'm just surprised I know anyone that's getting married. I feel like we're all still so young."

Jess nodded faintly, but said nothing.

Sam turned, studying her expression. "You don't think so?"

Jess lifted one shoulder in a small shrug. "I don't think it's about the time. It's about the person."

Sam watched her, feeling the sudden urge to ask if she thought Liz was the right person at any point. But she also wasn't sure she wanted to hear the answer.

"You've really never thought about it?" Jess asked.

"Thought about what? Getting married?"

Jess nodded, her eyes still fixed on the path in front of them.

Sam snorted a laugh. "In order to do that, I'd need time to think about anything beyond work. And I don't see that happening anytime soon."

Jess hummed softly. "What about kids?"

Sam turned to her, brows tugging together. "What about them?"

"Do you want them?" Jess asked so casually it was like she was asking what she wanted for dinner.

Sam blew out a breath, chuckling. "Uh—yeah. Yeah, I do. Definitely."

The corner of Jess' lips turned upward as she looked at her. "So marriage sounds like a totally foreign concept, but kids is a no brainer?"

Sam tilted her head back in a laugh. "Okay wait," she started, putting up a hand. "I didn't say it was a foreign concept. Just that I've never really thought about it."

Jess turned away, but amusement still danced in her eyes. "Right."

They continued up the path until it wrapped around to a corner of the building. Sam followed behind her until she turned the corner and stopped.

Sam burst into laughter, looking out into the back parking lot area filled with dumpsters where the path had ended.

"Maybe we should've taken our chances with the creepy beach walk after all."

Jess shook her head, laughing along with her. "Yeah, maybe."

"Wanna head back?" Sam asked, eyes drifting over the dingy yellow lighting of the mostly empty lot.

Jess' laughter died off as she let out a long exhale. "Not really."

Sam looked at her, watching the way her eyes stared off into the distance. Like she needed that night. That time alone—or—alone with just them.

Sam stepped ahead, stopping at a spot on the curb in front of the bushes. Then she sat down, nodding beside her for Jess to do the same.

Jess arched one brow, her eyes flicking to the curb once before bouncing back to meet Sam's stare.

"We're at a beautiful resort and you're fine with just sitting in the back on the ground by the dumpsters?" she asked with an amused smirk, but even before half the question had left her mouth, she'd already dropped down, sitting beside her.

Sam shrugged. "You said you didn't want to go back. So unless you changed your mind about taking our chances with the dark beach, then.." she trailed off, waving her hand in the air around them.

"I'm not sure this is any less creepy than the beach," Jess muttered, her nose wrinkling as her gaze drifted over the parking lot.

Sam rested her hands on the ground behind her, leaning back until she peered up at the star filled sky.

"How many cities did you move to after New York?" Jess asked suddenly.

Sam turned to her with a curious smile. "What's with all the questions tonight?"

Jess shrugged nonchalantly. "I don't know," she muttered. "I guess I just keep thinking about all the stuff we never talked about." Her throat bobbed as she swallowed, eyes flickering down at her lap. "Things I never had a chance to ask."

Sam frowned, feeling a pang of guilt twist in her gut. She knew what Jess meant—there were entire years of silence between them, a chasm filled with all the things left unsaid. And now it seemed like Jess was trying to bridge that gap all at once.

Sam let out a soft sigh, her gaze drifting across the yellow light of the parking lot. Her eyes landed on a discarded styrofoam cup near the base of the dumpster. She had an idea. A way to ease the tension and turn that conversation into something lighter.

She walked toward the cup, plucking it off the ground, then turned it over, emptying the small bit of remaining liquid onto the ground.

"Thirsty?" Jess mumbled, her face contorting in disgust.

Sam set the cup down on the asphalt, then made her way back to the curb.

"Let's play a game."

Jess raised an eyebrow, the curiosity in her eyes replacing some of the unease. "A game?"

Sam nodded, bending down to scoop up a handful of small pebbles from the planter behind them. "Yeah," she said, grinning as she held one out to Jess. "Make a shot. You get to ask a question."

Jess' lips quirked up into a smile, amusement dancing in her eyes. "And if I miss?"

"Then it's my turn," Sam replied, settling back onto the curb.

Jess glanced at the cup, then back at Sam. "You're making this up as you go, aren't you?"

"Obviously," Sam said with a laugh. "But you wanted to ask questions, so here's your chance."

She held one pebble out to Jess, then nodded toward the cup. "Lets see if you still have those beer pong skills."

The corner of Jess' lips quirked up in a small smile.

She tossed the pebble. It skittered across the ground, missing the cup by a few inches.

"Guess not," Sam mumbled through a smirk, bracing herself as Jess shoved a playful hand against her arm.

Sam took one from the pile, tilting her head as she lined it up.

She tossed it, watching as it hit the inside of the rim, knocking the cup over.

"I go first," Sam said, standing and walking toward the cup.

"What, that doesn't count," Jess protested.

Sam glanced back at her with a pointed look as she sat the cup up again, placing it up against the brick wall lining the outside of the dumpster.

"That definitely counts."

Jess reached out, grabbing another pebble from the pile and lining up a shot.

"Hey," Sam said, dropping down beside her. "I haven't asked my question yet."

"I'm just getting ready," Jess mumbled, that all too familiar competitive look gleaming in her eyes.

Sam chuckled, watching her.

"What's the question?" Jess asked, not taking her eyes off the cup as she moved her arm in a practice throwing motion.

Sam hummed, tilting her head back as she thought. "What was your favorite part of today?"

Jess shot her a teasing smile. "Watching you fall off the jet ski."

Sam threw her head back in laughter. "You know you talk a big game for someone who barely made it jumping off a six-foot cliff."

Jess narrowed her eyes in a mock glare before turning and lining up her own shot. She released, and the pebble flew through the air, landing perfectly inside the cup.

Her head spun toward Sam with a victorious smile.

Sam grinned as she rolled her eyes. "You're hands down the most competitive person I've ever met."

Jess smiled wider before looking back straight ahead.

"Alright, what's your question?" Sam asked, tossing a rock in the air and catching it in the other hand.

Jess bit her lip, eyes narrowing in thought. "Have you been back home since that last time? When I graduated."

"No," Sam answered immediately. Then she paused as one specific memory forced its way into her mind. "Well—" She cleared her throat. "Yeah. Once."

Jess glanced at her, a question in her eyes.

But before she could ask, Sam tossed a rock. It ricocheted off the back of the bricks and into the cup with a thud.

She smiled slightly, leaning back once more. "Do you see your dad a lot now that you're closer to home?"

Jess let out a soft sigh. "Probably not as much as I should."

Sam nodded slowly, watching her.

"We talk every week, though. Phone calls and stuff." Jess paused, looking down at the new pebble in her hand. "He, um—he has a girlfriend now."

Sam's head pulled back in surprise. "Oh."

She could hardly imagine him talking to anyone enough to even have friends. Thinking about him forming a romantic relationship sounded nearly impossible.

"Yeah," Jess drawled, giving her a look that said she probably thought the same. "So that's—different."

"Have you met her?"

Jess shook her head. "No. He just told me about it a couple months ago." She let out a soft chuckle. "And it's a good thing he told me over the phone because I probably would've looked as shocked as you did just now."

"Yeah, that's—" Sam paused, searching for the right words. "Hard to imagine."

Jess laughed as she tossed another rock, easily making it in.

She opened her mouth, then paused. Her throat bobbed as she swallowed, then she asked, "What did you really think that day we ran into each other?"

Sam blinked, thinking back to that day and how she felt. How shocked she'd been. But also the other things she'd felt. Anxiety, maybe even panic. But also something else. Some sense of relief. As if she'd been waiting for that moment for a long time without realizing it.

Jess turned slightly, looking at her.

Sam cleared her throat, pulling her knees up in front of her and resting her elbows against them. "That it had been way too long." She let out a breath. "And that I wished it had happened sooner."

It was the truth. She hadn't really thought about it that deeply when it happened, or at all since. But that was it. For some reason, it felt like regret. Like she hadn't realized until the moment she'd seen her that she'd made a mistake in letting so much time pass.

Jess' eyes flicked down as Sam plucked another pebble from the pile. She threw it, and it bounced off the edge, skittering across the ground. Sam frowned, resting her elbows back on her knees.

Jess chuckled as she picked up the next rock. "Wishing you'd picked a different game now?"

Sam snorted a laugh. "I'm just warming up."

Jess tossed the next one, easily landing it in the cup.

"Did you date anyone in the last four years?"

She thought for a moment. "What do you define as 'dated'?"

Jess rolled her eyes, leaning past her to grab another pebble. "That's the only answer I need."

Sam laughed, turning to look at her. Jess shivered, shifting slightly closer to her. Their arms brushed against each other, and Sam suddenly wished she'd brought a jacket that night so she could've given it to her.

Without a word, Sam leaned down and picked up a pebble, angling her body slightly toward Jess to keep the subtle contact between them. Her eyes flicked to the cup in the distance, narrowing with focus before tossing the pebble with a quick flick of her wrist.

It landed perfectly.

"Did you date anyone?" she asked, turning to Jess. "I mean, before Liz."

Jess shrugged lightly. "There was one girl," she said. "It wasn't that serious, though."

Sam nodded, wondering how serious she and Liz really had been. From the outside, they'd seemed serious enough. Especially if Jess had met her parents.

Jess threw the pebble and missed.

Sam picked one up and tossed it, making it in. "Were you and Liz serious?"

Jess pursed her lips, eyes dropping to the ground in front of them. She was quiet for a long while, and Sam began to wonder if it was too soon to ask that question.

Finally, Jess replied, "Yes."

Some small uncomfortable feeling tugged at her gut.

"And no," Jess breathed. She shook her head slightly. "I don't know. It was—complicated." Sam watched her carefully, taking in every detail in the way she crinkled her eyes and chewed her lip.

"It just felt like there was always *something*," she continued. "Like, for some reason, we could never just be—happy—or okay."

Sam watched her, wondering what she would've said about them. Wondering if she would've said something similar.

But the thing was, they were *always* happy. Even when there was *something*—they'd always been happy when they were together.

Jess stayed quiet for another moment before throwing the next rock. It landed in the cup with a thud.

And still, she stayed quiet, watching it for a long moment.

"All out of questions?" Sam asked in a teasing tone, trying to break whatever seemed to be plaguing Jess at that moment.

But still, Jess stared at the cup, an intensity filling her features.

Then finally, she turned to her.

"Why didn't you call again after that first time?"

Sam stared at her, her heartbeat quickening in her chest.

There were so many things that flowed through her mind. So many potential answers, but none of them fit. None of them really seemed to answer the question. And maybe, still, after all these years, she didn't know what that answer was.

"I don't know," Sam said softly.

Jess stared at her with more intensity than she'd seen since the moment they'd first run into each other again.

Then, finally, she turned away.

Sam wanted to say something else. Something that would let Jess know how complicated the answer was. That it wasn't just something she'd never thought about or never considered. But she didn't know how to say it.

She turned, picking up another rock.

She threw it, landing in the cup.

And before she could second guess it, she asked the first question that came to mind.

"Did you want me to call you again?"

Jess didn't look at her. She didn't even move a muscle as she said, "I don't know."

She'd halfway expected that answer. It was what she deserved after having just given her the same. But still, she couldn't let it go.

"Did you?" she asked again, watching her.

Jess reached past her, grabbing another pebble. "One question only," she muttered. "Those are the rules, right?"

She threw the rock immediately, easily landing it in the cup.

But Sam couldn't focus on anything else. Some long-buried feeling had surfaced, gripping her attention and refusing to let go.

"Did you want me to call you again?"

Jess turned to her, something resembling challenging anger in her eyes. "Why should I have to answer that if you didn't?"

Sam's jaw tightened. "I *did* answer."

Jess pursed her lips, shaking her head as she looked away. "That wasn't an answer."

"Did you want me to call you—"

"What do you want me to say, Sam?" Jess asked, whipping her head back to look at her, anger flaring in her eyes. "You want me to tell you that I waited for you? That, for days, I was disappointed every time someone called and the name on the screen wasn't yours?"

Sam swallowed, a mix of feelings bubbling into her chest.

"You want me to tell you how bad it hurt to know I wasn't even worth a second phone call? That after weeks of waiting, I—" Jess' voice cracked slightly, and Sam resisted the urge to take her hand. "I cried myself to sleep because it felt like I'd lost you all over again. For the millionth time in my life, I—"

She stopped as her voice broke. The side of her body moved against Sam's arm with a heavy breath.

"I'm sorry—"

Jess shook her head. "It doesn't matter," she said, looking at her with that burning gaze. "Because you *didn't* call again." She choked out a dry laugh that made Sam's heart ache in her chest. "And maybe you really don't know why. And if you don't know, then it's probably a good thing you never called again."

Sam swallowed, shifting closer as she felt Jess' body shiver.

"I thought—" Sam started, her own voice sounding more fragile than she'd expected. "I thought that if you wanted to talk, you would've called me back."

Jess shook her head slightly, staring off into the distance.

"You weren't the only one waiting," Sam continued. "And yeah, when I saw you that day. When I saw you with Liz, I—" She swallowed as Jess turned, looking at her. She searched for any word she could find, forcing herself to say how she felt—what she wanted. "I wanted—"

Her phone began ringing in her pocket, and she paused. Jess' eyes flicked down, looking at it before looking back up at her.

Sam sighed, reaching a hand in her pocket and pulling it out.

Tiana's name filled the screen.

She swiped it open, holding it up to her ear. "What's up?"

"Where are you guys?" Tiana asked, a soft murmur of voices in the background.

"We went for a walk," Sam answered. "It's not really a good time—"

"Do you have the room key?"

Sam pursed her lips, running a hand over her face. "Yeah. Why?"

"I didn't bring mine. I need you to let me into the room."

Sam loosed a breath, tilting her head back as she stared up into the dark sky.

"I mean, if you're busy or something, though, I could ask someone at the front desk to help me get in," Tiana muttered.

Sam closed her eyes, shaking her head. "No, it's fine. I'll come back and let you in."

She caught the look on Jess' face, her lips pressed into a firm line as she pushed up off the curb to stand.

"I'll meet you at the room in a few minutes," she said before hanging up.

Sam stood, pushing the phone into her back pocket. "Sorry," she muttered. "Tiana needs the room key—"

"It's fine," Jess said, brushing her off as she started walking back down the path they'd come from.

Chapter sixteen

The club pulsed with energy, lights flickering over the crowd in rhythmic waves. Sam sat on the edge of the booth, trying to ignore the way tension sat heavy in the air between her and Jess. It had been like that since the previous night. They'd barely spoken all day, exchanging only a handful of clipped words, mostly for the benefit of the others.

Sam leaned her elbows against the crowded table at the club, tilting the rest of her drink back.

Scarlett suddenly broke off mid-sentence, her gaze shifting over Jess' shoulder toward the bar. "Jess, that girl over there is totally checking you out."

Jess turned, following where Scarlett was looking. She stared for a moment before turning back, swirling the last of the liquid in her glass.

"Maybe you should go talk to her?" Scarlett urged gently. "You know, flirt a little. Help yourself move on from the breakup."

Jess lifted one brow. "I don't need help moving on."

Scarlett frowned. "Well, you seemed off this morning. Thought maybe it was bothering you."

"I'm fine. Seriously." She swallowed, and as Sam watched the interaction, it felt like Jess was purposely avoiding her gaze. "It wasn't—that." Jess said slowly. "I was just out of it. I'm fine though." She loosed a breath, tugging what looked like a forced smile onto her face.

"I'm gonna grab a drink," Tiana said, standing up and smoothing down her tight dress. "You all good with another?"

They all nodded, and Tiana slipped away toward the bar, leaving Scarlett and Jasmine to dive back into wedding plans. Sam sat still, her eyes tracking Jess, feeling the unease simmering beneath her own skin.

She cleared her throat, leaning forward slightly. "Hey," she said softly, keeping her voice low enough that the others wouldn't hear. "About last night…"

Jess' eyes flicked to her, a flash of something passing over her face.

"I'm sorry," Sam continued, swallowing the lump in her throat. "I didn't mean for things to get so—tense."

Jess' expression softened, but only slightly. "It's fine," she said, brushing it off. "Really."

Sam pressed her lips together, nodding, though she didn't fully believe it. There was still something between them—something left hanging from the night before—but it wasn't the time to push.

Before the silence could stretch too long, Tiana returned, a playful grin lighting up her face. Behind her was the woman Scarlett had pointed out earlier, the one who'd been checking Jess out from across the bar.

"Hey guys, this is Joanna," Tiana said, introducing the woman. Joanna smiled, but her attention immediately zeroed in on Jess.

Sam forced a polite smile as the woman settled into their group, her interest in Jess painfully obvious. Jess, to her credit, was polite, nodding along as she chatted with her, though her responses stayed clipped and reserved.

The drinks arrived shortly after, and Sam downed hers quickly, hoping to ease the awkwardness settling in her chest.

"Alright, I need to dance," Scarlett announced suddenly, pulling Jasmine to her feet.

Sam hesitated, but followed the group as they moved toward the dance floor. The music was louder there, the lights more erratic, casting flashes of neon across their faces. And Sam couldn't help but notice the way

Joanna stuck close to Jess, still talking—pressing for every bit of her attention.

Before long, Jess and Joanna were dancing together, the space between them shrinking with every beat of the music. She watched Jess' hands find the other woman's waist, the two of them moving in sync.

Tiana pulled Sam closer as she danced beside her. "You okay?"

Sam nodded quickly. "Yeah. All good."

But even as she said it, she couldn't tear her eyes away from them.

Tiana pulled back, looking first at her, then following her gaze across the dance floor. And when she looked back at Sam, she wore an intrigued expression.

Sam stared at her, waiting. But Tiana just kept looking at her like she'd done something completely out of the ordinary.

"What?" Sam finally muttered.

Tiana blinked, cocking her head as the look morphed into an entertained grin. "Are you *jealous*?"

"What?" Sam asked, yanking her head back in surprise. "No, of course not."

Tiana spit out a laugh as her eyes widened. "Oh my god, you are! You're totally jealous!"

Sam set her jaw, evening out her expression as she continued dancing, looking anywhere but at Jess and the woman.

"Wow," Tiana said, shaking her head as she glanced back to where Jess was dancing. "Guess there's a first time for everything."

"I'm not jealous."

"Right," Tiana mumbled, rolling her eyes. "If you want her, why don't you do something about it?"

Sam continued moving distractedly to the beat of the music.

"I don't," she muttered, hearing the lie in her own voice. "And even if I did, she just got out of a relationship. Trust me, she needs a friend right now. She doesn't want.." She trailed off as she glanced back at Jess. "She doesn't want that."

Tiana looked back at her, all the teasing amusement replaced with a serious look. "What about what *you* want?" she asked. "You always put everyone else's needs first. And I love you for that, but—" She paused, releasing a breath. "You're gonna drive yourself crazy. You have to go after what you want sometimes, too."

Sam swallowed, her eyes flicking back up to Jess. She watched as the woman moved closer, wrapping one arm around Jess' waist as she turned them.

Sam looked back at Tiana, shaking her head. "She doesn't want that."

"Oh please," Tiana scoffed. "She looks like she wants to kill me every time I touch you."

Sam shot her a look, brows tugging together. "That's not true."

"It's not?" Tiana asked, quirking one eyebrow up in challenge. "How about we test that and see who's right?"

"What do you—"

Before Sam could finish the sentence, Tiana stepped closer to her, sliding one hand around her lower back. She pulled their bodies closer, then turned until her back was flush against Sam's front.

Sam stiffened slightly as Tiana swayed her hips. She ground purposely against her, the curves of her back rolling over every intimate spot.

And she let Tiana take her hands, gently wrapping them around her hips. Then she reached one hand up, wrapping it around Sam's neck and pulling her head down slightly.

Sam gave her a cautious, curious look as Tiana gazed deeply into her eyes.

Then, right when she thought Tiana might try to kiss her, she turned her head slightly, kissing her neck instead in a slow, much too intimate way.

Sam swallowed thickly, waiting a beat before pulling her head away.

She barely caught the split-second where Tiana glanced at some spot ahead of them on the dance floor. And after she did, she turned her body back to Sam, twisting in her arms.

Tiana's hands slid around her in an embrace, still swaying to the beat of the music. Then she chuckled near her ear as she whispered, "I win."

Sam glanced up to where Tiana had looked a moment before. And sure enough, she was right.

Jess stood there, a foot or so of space now firmly placed between her and the woman she'd been dancing with.

She stared at them, not meeting Sam's eyes, but instead, her eyes seemed to meticulously trail over their entwined bodies. Her mouth was set, lips slightly pursed together, but her eyes held an intensity that was oddly familiar. Although she couldn't quite place the memory in which she'd seen it last.

"Or do you need me to prove it again?" Tiana muttered, shooting her a mischievous smirk before letting her lips drift over her neck once more.

Sam pulled away as she snorted a dry laugh. "No. You made your point."

She removed her hands from Tiana's hips, stepping back slightly.

"That doesn't mean she wants me, though. I already know it's weird for her to see me with someone else like—that."

Tiana rolled her eyes exaggeratedly, shaking her head. "You're so oblivious sometimes."

Sam frowned, scratching a hand over the back of her neck.

"Come on," Tiana nodded, leading them off the dance floor

They made their way to the bar, squeezing in between a group of people. Tiana leaned against the counter, still catching her breath from the dance floor.

Tiana's smirk softened into something more sincere as she glanced back at Sam. "You know, I think I've done enough meddling for one night," she said, raising her voice over the music. "I'm gonna head back early."

Sam blinked, surprised. "Already? It's not even midnight."

Tiana shrugged, but there was a glint of something playful in her eyes. "Yeah, well, I'm tired from the weekend," she leaned in, lowering her voice, "Besides, the best girl in here is already spending all night thinking about someone else."

Sam felt the flush creep up her neck. "I'm not—"

"Yeah, yeah," Tiana cut her off with a dismissive wave. "Anyway, can you give me your key card? I forgot mine in the room."

Sam hesitated for a second, her hand instinctively patting the pocket where she'd stashed it earlier. "You sure you don't want me to go with you?"

Tiana smirked, letting out a low chuckle. "Not unless you really want to give Jess another reason to be jealous."

Sam frowned as Tiana held out her hand expectantly, wiggling her fingers. With a sigh, Sam pulled out the card and placed it in her hand.

Then Tiana leaned in, pressing a quick, friendly kiss to her cheek. "Good luck, babe. And remember what I said. Go get what you want."

Before Sam could respond, Tiana slipped away, weaving her way through the crowd with that effortless confidence she always had. Sam watched her go, a strange mix of relief and anticipation settling in her chest.

"Where's she going?" Scarlett's voice came from behind her, and Sam turned to find her standing there, with Jasmine following close behind.

"Heading up early," Sam replied, nodding toward her retreating figure. "Said she was tired."

They lingered by the bar a while longer, conversation ebbing and flowing as they sipped on their drinks. The club had reached its peak. Every foot of the dance floor was filled with people.

Sam glanced back every so often, catching glimpses of Jess still talking with Joanna. The woman was leaning in close, but Jess' smile looked tight and strained.

Sam forced her attention back to Scarlett, who was animatedly telling a story about her latest work drama.

"And then she told *me* how to do my job," Scarlett said, rolling her eyes dramatically.

Jasmine snorted, hiding her smile behind the rim of her glass. "I'm surprised you didn't say anything back."

"Oh, I wanted to," Scarlett replied with a scoff. "But I'm trying this new thing called 'professionalism.' It's exhausting."

Sam chuckled along, but her gaze drifted back to Jess once more. Tiana's words flowed back through her mind as she watched Jess lean away from the woman's touch.

"So what happened between you two last night that put her in such a bad mood this morning?" Scarlett asked, giving Sam a pointed look.

Sam arched one brow as she took a sip of her beer. "What happened to *Jess tells me everything*?"

Scarlett shrugged lightly. "She didn't wanna talk about it."

Sam nodded, swirling the drink in her hand. "Then I guess nothing happened."

Scarlett rolled her eyes as she looked out to where Sam had been staring. "Well, I'm glad she's putting herself out there again."

Sam turned away, taking a swig of her beer.

"Even if she does kinda look like she's dying to get away now," Scarlett continued with an amused chuckle.

Sam looked back over her shoulder once more, catching the obviously fake smile Jess had on her lips.

Scarlett sighed, setting her empty glass on the bar. "Well, I'm ready to head back," she said, looking between Sam and Jasmine. "But I don't want to leave Jess here by herself."

"I'll stay," Sam said immediately.

"You sure?" Scarlett asked, although she knew she wasn't surprised by the offer.

Sam nodded with a reassuring smile. "Yeah. I'll hang out until she's ready to leave. Make sure she gets back okay."

"I think I'm gonna go with you," Jasmine added, stifling a yawn. "I'm not really used to these late nights."

Scarlett smiled at her, then turned, squeezing Sam's arm. "We'll see you in the morning at checkout."

She turned to Jasmine, giving her a gentle tug on the arm. "Come on, let's get out of here before I start falling asleep at the bar."

Jasmine gave a small, sleepy smile as she followed Scarlett toward the exit. "Goodnight, Sam," she called over her shoulder.

"Night," Sam replied, watching them disappear into the crowd. She blew out a breath, turning back to the bar and signaling for another drink. She wasn't sure how long she'd have to wait, but she wasn't planning on leaving until Jess was ready.

Sam took a slow sip from her glass, letting the cool liquid slip down her throat. Her eyes found Jess again, and this time, she could see it clearly—the way Jess subtly shifted her body away, the slight wince when Joanna's hand landed on her arm. It was enough to make Sam's decision for her.

With a deep breath, Sam pushed away from the bar and made her way toward them.

She weaved through the array of people, stopping beside Jess.

"Hey," she said with a soft smile.

"Oh, hey," Jess replied, taking a small step closer to her.

Joanna didn't bother even glancing toward her, her eyes still clinging to Jess. In reality, she actually kind of felt bad for her. Maybe on another night, she would've had a fair chance. But Sam knew better than she did. That night wasn't it.

"Where'd everyone go?" Jess asked, craning her neck past Sam to scan the crowd.

"Back to the rooms," Sam answered, throwing a nod over her shoulder.

"Oh," Jess muttered, disappointment painting her face. Then she looked back at Sam. "You didn't want to go?"

Sam shrugged lightly. "Figured I'd hang out a little longer."

Jess nodded, opening her mouth to say something before Joanna cut her off.

"Let me buy you another drink?" she asked with a wide grin.

Jess frowned, giving her a semi-apologetic smile. "That's okay. I think I'm at my max for the night."

The woman's smile dropped for a moment before she quickly recovered. "Oh, yeah, I probably I am too," she said with a chuckle. "I can definitely keep dancing, though."

She took a step toward Jess, her hand outstretched. But Jess pulled back slightly. And that was all it took.

Sam shifted behind Jess, sliding one arm around her waist, resting her hand on her hip. Jess stiffened for a split second before she completely relaxed into the front of her body.

Sam rested her chin lightly against her shoulder. Then said in a low voice, but loud enough for Joanna to hear, "Dance with me?"

The way Jess turned to look at her left their faces only inches apart. And the look in her eyes was intense with surprise and curiosity. She swallowed, then nodded.

"Oh," Joanna muttered, her eyes flicking between them. "I—sorry—I didn't realize you two—"

She knew what she was asking. And yes, leaving it unsaid would be a lie. But at that moment, she didn't care.

Jess stayed quiet too, and Sam felt her hand drift over her own, where it rested on her hip. Jess ran her thumb lightly over her wrist, and Sam instantly had to remind herself of why she was doing this in the first place. That it wasn't real.

She held Joanna's stare, offering a small smile she knew would give her the answer she needed to see.

Joanna looked between them once more, then gave Jess a tight smile. "Well, it was nice meeting you. Have a good night."

Sam watched her walk away, waiting until she was far enough into the crowd that she wouldn't be able to see them anymore. Then she loosened her grip on Jess, immediately pulling her arm away and stepping back. It was like a switch had flipped off, her boldness evaporating as quickly as it had come.

"There," Sam said with a forced grin. "Problem solved."

Jess didn't respond right away. She just stared at her, eyes searching, the intensity of her gaze making Sam feel exposed in a way she hadn't expected.

"You were just doing that because she was here," Jess said finally, her voice soft but edged.

Sam opened her mouth, ready with a quick denial, but the words stuck in her throat. She looked away, her gaze fixed on the row of liquor bottles behind the bar. "You looked like you needed an out," she muttered.

Jess' expression softened, but there was a flicker of disappointment in her eyes. "Right," she said, her voice losing its edge. She looked down at the space between them, flexing her fingers like she was trying to release the tension. "Well, thanks. It worked."

Sam's heart twisted at the way she said it, the flatness of her tone. "I—"

"I think I'm ready to leave," Jess interrupted, crossing her arms over her chest.

Sam nodded, swallowing against the tightness in her throat. "Yeah. Me too."

***

Sam yawned as they walked through the lobby.

Jess slowed, stopping halfway to the elevator. "Actually," she said, turning halfway, "I'm gonna see if the shop is still open and grab a couple water bottles."

Sam stopped, ready to follow her.

"It's okay," Jess said with a small smile. "You don't need to come with me."

"You sure?" Sam asked, glancing around the empty lobby.

"Yeah," Jess said with a wave of her hand. "I'm fine."

"Okay," Sam said with a nod, scanning the area once more. "I'll see you in the morning, then?"

Jess nodded. "Yeah. I'll see you guys before we all head out."

"Alright," Sam said, turning for the elevators.

She took the elevator up, yawning again as the exhaustion clouded her vision. When the elevator dinged, coming to a stop at her floor, she trudged out, making her way to the door of their room.

She knocked lightly, trying not to make too much noise. A few moments passed with no response.

"Tiana," she called through the door, knocking again.

A minute went by, but again, no answer. She let out a sigh, rubbing a tired hand over her eyes. In hindsight, giving an incredibly heavy sleeper the only key probably hadn't been the best idea.

She pulled her phone out, clicking the call button on Tiana's contact.

It rang a handful of times before going to voicemail.

She sighed as the faint ding of the elevator rang out down the hall. Light footsteps padded toward her as she knocked again.

"Can't get in?" Jess' soft voice asked from a few feet away.

She turned, seeing her approach with two water bottles tucked under her arm.

"No," she answered with a frown.

Jess stopped beside her, adjusting the bottles in her hands. "What're you gonna do?"

Sam tucked the phone back into her pocket, then shrugged. "Guess I'll head back down and see if someone at the front desk can get me another key."

She yawned again, her eyes blurring with teary exhaustion.

Jess opened her mouth, then paused, as if apprehensive.

Sam watched her for a moment. "What?"

"Well," Jess started, shifting the bottles in her hands again, "I was gonna say, you could stay in my room, but—" Her eyes bounced away for a moment. "There's only one bed."

"Oh," Sam said, slightly surprised by the offer.

"I mean," Jess continued quickly, "that's fine with me. I just meant—I don't know if you're okay with that."

Sam scratched a hand over the back of her neck, thinking it over. She glanced back at her locked hotel door. It probably wouldn't take too much time to get a new key from the front desk downstairs. But it was already late, and they had to get up early the next morning for check out.

But was it a good idea to sleep in a bed with Jess? Her brain said yes, that it would be totally fine. They were just friends. Sleeping in a bed together meant nothing.

But there was also another part of her—something much deeper—that said it was a bad idea.

"You look like you're making a life or death decision," Jess said, the corner of her mouth tilted up in slight amusement.

Sam chuckled, letting out a breath as her shoulders relaxed. "Sorry—no. I'm just tired. Can't think straight."

"I can go back down to the lobby with you to get another key," Jess offered. "I'll just drop these off real quick," she said, nodding down at the water bottles.

"No," Sam said, shaking her head. "No, that's okay."

She was overthinking things. Jess was right. It wasn't some gigantic decision. She was just letting what Tiana said earlier get in her head.

"Are you sure it's okay if I crash with you?" she asked. "I don't want to take up your space. I know how you like to take up the whole bed."

A smile cracked over Jess' lips as she rolled her eyes. "I think I can deal with sharing for one night."

"Right," Sam mumbled with a smirk as Jess pushed past her down the hall.

She followed her to the end as she stopped in front of the last door on the left.

Jess switched the bottles to her other arm as she pulled her key card out and held it up to the door. The lock box beeped, and Jess pushed the door open, holding it as Sam walked through after her.

Cold air swept over her.

"Think you have the AC blasting high enough?" Sam muttered as she switched on the main light.

"I love the air conditioning in hotels," Jess replied, placing her things down on the dresser below the TV. "If it's really cold in the hotel room, it makes the bed feel so much better when you go to sleep."

Sam hummed, sitting down on the edge of the perfectly made bed.

"I have some clothes you can wear, if you want."

"Oh," Sam mumbled as she stifled a yawn. She hadn't even considered the fact that she didn't have any of her stuff with her. "Yeah. Thanks."

She pulled her phone out, checking her latest emails as Jess went through her suitcase on the floor in the corner of the room.

She typed out a few replies, answering assorted questions from the development team before Jess stood back up.

She tossed a couple items beside her on the bed. "Are those okay?"

Sam picked up the large black t-shirt and sweat shorts, turning them over. The corner of her lip tugged upward when she saw the familiar college lacrosse logo on the front. She'd worn that shirt before. More times than she could even count.

"Yeah. Thanks."

Jess walked to the bathroom with another set of clothes in her hands, then called back over her shoulder, "I'm gonna shower real quick."

Sam waited until she heard the water running. Then she stood, pulling each item of clothing off before quickly replacing them with the shirt and shorts Jess had given her. She folded her clothes neatly and set them on the chair beside the small table in the corner of the room below the window.

A shower sounded nice, but she didn't have enough energy to stay up. So instead, she went to the other side of the bed and set her phone down before pulling back the comforter.

The more responsible part of her said that she should take the next few minutes to finish replying to emails and missed messages from work. But the other part of her just wanted to lie there, enjoying the peaceful feel of the bed. And even with the lights still on, the rhythm of the running water was enough to almost lull her to sleep.

She let her mind replay the events of the weekend until it came to the conversation they'd had the night before. Jess' words. The look in her eyes. Then it skipped to a different look. The one she'd seen that night at the club when Tiana was dancing on her.

She blinked, opening her eyes to end the memory right as the water shut off.

A few moments later, the bathroom door clicked open, and Jess walked out, clothed in a t-shirt and sweatpants. She glanced over at Sam as she ran a towel through her wet hair, squeezing water from the ends.

Her eyes seemed to catch for a moment on the shirt she was wearing.

"Want a water?" she asked, looking away as she draped the towel over the back of the chair

Sam cleared her throat. "Yeah," she said as Jess took the bottles from the dresser and handed her one. "Thanks."

She downed a few big gulps before setting it on the nightstand beside her phone.

Jess set her own things on the other nightstand, then went to shut the main light off, leaving the bathroom light still on.

She returned, pulling her side of the comforter back and sliding into bed.

Silence fell between them for a moment, the only sound, the light hum of the air conditioning still running.

Jess shifted, and without needing to look, Sam knew she'd turned toward her.

Sam turned her head, looking at her in the dim yellow light of the room. Wet hair draped over her shoulders and across the white pillow. It was a sight she'd seen so many times before. It almost seemed normal. Like sleeping beside her, even as friends, was the most natural thing in the world.

"What?" Jess asked, her nose crinkling slightly as her eyes squinted through the darkness.

Sam couldn't help the wide grin that broke out over her face. "I'm pretty sure I've worn this shirt more times than you have."

Jess' expression faltered for a moment, like those were the last words she'd been expecting. Then she broke out into a laugh.

"It's basically more mine now than yours," Sam continued.

Jess adjusted the pillow beneath her, still laughing. "Well, then I guess it's nice of you to have let me keep it all this time."

Sam smiled, turning her head toward the ceiling again.

"Did you have fun tonight?" Jess mumbled through a yawn.

"Yeah. It was a good night," Sam answered. "Scarlett and Jasmine seemed like they had fun."

"They did."

"You looked like you were having fun, too," Sam muttered, the image of her dancing with the woman floating back into her mind.

"Did I?" Jess asked. Sam picked up on the somewhat daring tone in her voice. As if silently challenging her to elaborate.

Sam hummed, closing her eyes. That was one challenge that was probably best left untouched. Especially when they were mere feet away from each other in bed.

Jess was quiet for a moment before she continued. "Tiana looked like she was having a lot of fun, too."

Sam opened her eyes, turning to Jess once more. The corner of her lip tilted upward, unable to stop herself. "Did she?"

A semi-annoyed, but also amused, look passed over Jess' face. "You know, you keep saying she's just a friend, but I've never seen *friends* dance like that."

Sam snorted a laugh. "*You've* danced on me like that."

"Exactly," Jess shot back, "and afterwards we'd end up in bed together."

The words sparked a certain burn in her stomach, but she pushed it away, ignoring it as fast as it had come.

She cleared her throat, forcing a light laugh as she said, "well I guess we still end up in bed together even without the dancing."

Jess chuckled, and Sam was grateful for the small pause to calm whatever feeling had begun to work itself up inside her.

She shifted again, pulling her arm out from under her head and replacing it with the other one.

A few beats of silence passed, and Sam wondered if that would be the end of the conversation. Really, that would probably be for the best. It seemed that the more they talked, in any situation, much less in bed beside each other, it always led back to something that made her feel a burning anticipation.

And she'd felt enough toward Jess in the past that she knew that feeling was something she needed to be careful with.

She closed her eyes, letting out a slow breath, trying to will away the thoughts creeping up, trying to keep things simple.

They were friends. Nothing more.

Chapter seventeen

"I'm happy with how smoothly things are going so far," Michelle said from beside her as the elevator doors closed.

Sam had spent the better part of the morning at Michelle's office, working on setting up the integration for their new client. And she was right. Everything was going much better than they'd anticipated.

"Yeah, me too," Sam answered as she pulled out her phone and saw a text from Jess with the address to her apartment.

They'd planned to meet there that day to go over some more PR stuff. Although, the last meeting with Michelle had run longer than expected.

Right as she was about to type out a quick text to let her know she'd be a little late, the phone began buzzing in her hand, filled with Jess' name on the screen.

"Hey," she said, holding the phone up to her ear. "Sorry, I was just about to text you."

"That's okay," she replied, her voice cutting in and out. "I just wanted to make sure we were still on to meet up?"

"Yeah," Sam answered. "I was with a client, but I'm all done now."

The phone went silent for a moment, before Jess' broken words crackled through. "Okay—sent—did you—"

Sam glanced down at the screen as the elevator whirred on its descent.

"I have my bike, so I'm gonna ride over now," she said, placing the phone back against her ear. "Should be there in like twenty."

She thought she could make out Jess' muffled, suddenly louder voice as it crackled in and out. But as the phone cut out again, she couldn't make out what she was saying.

"I'm in an elevator, so the reception is bad," Sam continued. "But I'll see you in a bit."

She ended the call and stuffed her phone into her backpack just as the elevator chimed softly at the ground floor.

When the doors slid open, she followed Michelle into the expansive lobby, where the sound of rain immediately met her ears. Sheets of water streamed down the towering floor-to-ceiling glass windows, distorting the view outside.

She frowned, adjusting the motorcycle helmet in her hands. At least her bike was in the parking garage.

"It's really coming down," Michelle said beside her.

"Yeah," Sam murmured, her gaze fixed on the relentless rain. "Guess I'll get an Uber then."

That was one big con of being back in Seattle. The rain was an almost constant surprise.

"Where are you headed?" Michelle asked, turning to her as she pulled her keys out of her purse.

Sam relayed the cross streets of the address to Jess' apartment.

"I'm going that way," Michelle said. "You want a ride?"

"Are you sure?" Sam asked hesitantly. "It's not out of your way?"

"Not at all," Michelle replied with a dismissive wave of her hand. "Come on."

Sam followed her out into the parking garage. The rhythmic sound of rain against concrete accompanied them as they climbed into Michelle's car. The two talked easily during the drive, the conversation flowing as smoothly as the windshield wipers working overtime to clear the view ahead.

When Michelle finally pulled up to the curb outside Jess' apartment building, Sam thanked her and hopped out.

Water splashed up around her ankles, and she raised a hand to shield her face, squinting through the downpour to read the numbers on the doors. When she finally found the one Jess had sent her, she jogged toward it, stopping beneath the small overhang to shield herself.

She knocked once, pressing herself in close to the door.

Within a moment, the door swung open, and Jess' wide eyes and pale face stared back at her.

"Hey," Sam said slowly, her eyebrows pulling together. "What's wrong—"

Before she could get another word out, Jess surged forward. She threw her arms around her, pulling her into a crushing embrace.

Sam froze for a moment, confusion morphing into worry.

"What's—"

Jess suddenly pushed her back, still keeping a firm grasp on her forearms, holding her in place.

"Why would you do that?" Jess demanded, her voice trembling with equal parts panic and anger.

"What are you—"

"Why would you ride in the rain?" Jess cut her off, her voice rising.

Sam stared at her, blinking. She knew that panicked, detached look in her eyes. The pale sheen on her skin. She knew it all too well.

"I—"

"You didn't answer your phone," Jess snapped, her words spilling out too fast. Her hands shook where they gripped her arms. "I tried calling—you didn't— you didn't pick up and—"

The crack in her voice stopped Sam cold.

Jess stuttered, her breath catching as if she couldn't finish her thought. Sam could feel her trembling, could see the panic radiating off her in waves. That look in Jess' eyes, the raw edge to her voice—it wasn't anger. It was fear.

And then, finally, realization dawned on her.

"Hey," Sam said softly as she slowly slid her arms back, taking Jess' quivering hands in her own as she stepped past the threshold and into the apartment. "I didn't ride here. Someone drove me since it was raining."

Jess stared at her, eyes flicking over her face and body, as if they were still working to confirm once and for all that she really was there.

And that look alone was enough to cause a tidal wave of guilt to crash through every inch of her.

"You—" Jess shook her head slightly, blinking. "You said—" She shook her head again, the look of panic in her eyes finally waning. "And then you didn't pick up. I—"

Sam squeezed her hands gently. "My phone was in my backpack. I didn't know you called."

Jess looked down, her eyes seeming to focus on where Sam held her hands.

Sam waited a moment, watching her. Then finally, she looked up, scanning the cozy apartment to find the couch nearby.

"Come on," she said softly, leading her toward the couch and sitting them both down.

She took the helmet out from where it was still tucked beneath her arm and set it on the ground, shifting it out of sight behind the edge of the couch.

Then she released Jess' hands to shrug the backpack off.

She leaned forward, resting her elbows on her knees as she blew out a breath.

The silence stretched on for what felt like an eternity before Jess finally spoke.

"For months, after you left for MIT," she started, just barely above a whisper, "I had nightmares that I'd get a call saying you'd been in another accident."

A tight burn rose in Sam's throat, but she forced herself to swallow it away.

Jess hardly even moved as she continued, "I used to check the weather in the city you were living in." Her throat bobbed as she swallowed. "On rainy days—" she paused, blinking, as she released a breath. "I would check my phone constantly for texts from you." She swallowed again, the muscle in her jaw flickering as she whispered, "I could hardly focus on anything else."

The tight swell in Sam's throat grew into a throbbing ache in her chest. She'd always known the accident affected Jess more than she really ever shared or let on. But she'd never imagined how much.

"I'm sorry," Sam whispered, hating how inadequate the words felt.

Jess released a breath, leaning back into the couch as she ran a hand through her hair. She turned, her eyes drifting to the water-streaked window. She stared at it for a long moment.

"Even now," she continued, "all these years later, every time it rains, I still think of you."

Sam tightened her grip on the arm of the couch, resisting the urge to take her hand—to hug her—to hold her. To do anything that would take even a fraction of that pain and worry away.

Jess' eyes flicked back down to her lap, where her hands had begun to fidget. "I thought—" She paused, shaking her head slightly as she cleared her throat. "I thought it would get better after we stopped talking. Before—I mean." She shook her head again, this time seemingly more out of frustration. "And it did. Eventually." She released a deep sigh. "But it never went away."

Sam swallowed, watching the way her eyes glazed over with wetness. "Why didn't you tell me?"

Jess shook her head. "Why would I?" she breathed, wiping a hand across the edge of her face where the wetness had spilled down her cheek. "It wouldn't have changed anything."

Sam's jaw clenched as she looked away. "I could've helped. I could've—"

"You could've what?" Jess asked, her voice full of exasperation. "We both know you weren't gonna stop."

Was that true? Maybe. Or maybe not. She wasn't sure.

Riding had some hold on her. An ability to take her mind and free it from torment. No matter how hard things got, the second the whipping wind hit her face, it all fell away. She couldn't focus on anything but the ride—the road, the turns, the sounds, all of it.

The first time she'd ridden was unforgettable. The sudden sense of freedom—of control. It was something she'd never felt before. And something she never wanted to lose.

And that feeling never changed. It never went away.

Even after the accident.

Even when she wished it would.

"I knew how important it was to you," Jess whispered. "Even if I didn't understand it." She swallowed, turning to meet her gaze. "I wasn't going to guilt you into giving that up."

Sam loosed a breath, running a hand down her face. "I'm sorry. I—I don't know what else to say."

Jess nodded, a sad, defeated look filling her features. Then she stood from the couch.

"It's fine," she said, stepping around it toward the small kitchen area as she wiped another hand over her cheek. "Let's just forget it. We have stuff to go over."

Sam stood, following her to where she'd gone to her bag, where it sat on a circular white kitchen table.

"I can't—" she said quickly, stepping up beside her as she shuffled through her bag. "I can't just forget that and move on."

Jess sniffled, wiping a hand across her nose as she rifled through papers and folders in her bag.

"Jess," Sam said, reaching forward to stop her hand.

Jess paused, her eyes flicking down to where Sam's hand rested on hers.

"I'm sorry," Sam rushed, anxiety flitting through her bones. "I—I want to help. I want to fix this."

Jess turned toward her, releasing an exasperated huff. "I said it's fine—"

"It's *not* fine," Sam cut in, the anxiety spilling out from the cut Jess' frustrated tone left in her chest. She couldn't handle that. She couldn't handle Jess being upset with her. Not when she knew it was her fault.

Jess' phone buzzed where it sat on the table in front of them, but she didn't so much as glance in its direction.

"I don't know what you want. Just tell me what you want me to say." The words scrambled out of her in a frantic frenzy as her brain searched for a solution. Anything that would make Jess okay. Anything that would make things *between them* okay again. "Tell me what you want—"

"I want to stop worrying about you!" Jess snapped. She whipped her head up, eyes blazing as they locked onto Sam's. "I want to stop feeling crazy for still thinking about you every time I hear a motorcycle go by, or I watch a show with some software engineer in it. I want to stop wondering if it's you every time Scarlett laughs at a text on her phone." Exasperation filled every inch of her features. Like just saying the words out loud was a heartbreaking task. "Fuck, Sam, after all these years, I just want you to give me a reason to stop loving you!"

The swirling thoughts in her mind came to an abrupt halt.

Sam blinked, staring at the mix of intense frustration and despair in Jess' eyes.

The phone began buzzing again, and it was the only thing that pulled her from the circling thought. But again, Jess was either completely oblivious or choosing to ignore it.

Sam swallowed, the words turning over in her mind.

Jess glanced away, shaking her head slightly. "You broke my heart four years ago."

A tight twinge of pain crossed through Sam's chest.

"And I know nothing's changed," Jess scoffed. "I'm not stupid. You're the same person you were then. You want the same things. I know there's nothing that can work between us." She swallowed, shaking her head as she glanced down at their hands together. "But still, even knowing that—even with everything that's happened—all I can think about right now is how you're holding my hand." Jess squeezed her eyes shut, releasing a breath. "And how terrible it feels to not want you to let go."

Sam looked down at where their hands stayed intertwined.

She'd felt it too. The same want—the same *need*—
to be touching her. Like letting go would break
something inside her.

Something that could never be fixed.

"I don't want to let go," Sam whispered.

She looked back up at Jess, whose lips parted
slightly as her eyes widened with a mix of surprise
and—something else.

Jess shifted, their faces becoming dangerously close.
Closer than any friends would be.

Every muscle in Sam's body stilled as Jess raised a
slow, careful hand up to cup the side of her neck.

Then, ever so slowly, she ran her fingers a few
inches up into her hairline before dragging them back
down.

Sam's eyes fluttered closed as she leaned just a
fraction into the soothing touch.

And even though she knew she needed to pull
back—that the reasons they'd ended the last time
hadn't changed—it felt impossible in that moment.
Like Jess was the magnet that pulled her in, no matter
how far apart they were.

She released a tight breath, opening her eyes. And Jess was watching her, anguish etched throughout her soft features. But behind it was pure, unrelenting *want*.

Want that Sam had seen in her many times before. More than she could ever possibly count.

Although, she'd wondered if she'd ever be lucky enough to see it again in her lifetime.

"I know I shouldn't," Jess whispered, the words barely escaping her lips, "but if I don't kiss you right now—" Sam swallowed, her pulse instantly sprinting through her body. "I think I'll regret it for the rest of my life."

Sam released a shaky breath, waiting with more anticipation than she'd ever felt before.

Jess' eyes flicked over her face, as if searching for some answer to an unspoken question. But Sam couldn't take it anymore. She couldn't wait another second.

She tilted her head in, obliterating the short distance between them to kiss her.

Jess' hand cupped the side of her face, fingers trembling ever so slightly against her skin. There was hesitation, a softness that belied the hunger building between them, but it only made Sam want her more.

She deepened the kiss, pulling Jess closer, their bodies colliding like the answer to a question neither of them had dared ask.

It was heat. It was electricity. It was everything she didn't know she needed until that moment.

Sam's hands drifted to Jess' waist, gripping her like the kiss might be torn from them before it had truly begun. But Jess didn't pull away.

A soft sound escaped Jess. Something between a gasp and a sigh that went directly to her core. She pressed Jess back against the countertop, their lips never once breaking.

But something flickered in her chest, a warning that she couldn't ignore.

Sam pulled back, even though everything in her body screamed not to.

"Are—" she started breathlessly. "Are you sure this is a good idea? I mean—"

"Do you want this?" Jess asked, her face just an inch away.

Sam swallowed, taking in the dark, heated look in her eyes. "What about—"

"Right now," Jess whispered, leaning forward to rest her forehead against Sam's. "In this moment. Is this what you want?"

Sam's eyes slid closed, the feeling of Jess so close it bordered on intoxicating. If it were ever possible to be drunk off a person, Jess would be her drink of choice.

She nodded. And the second she did, Jess' lips surged against hers once again.

Jess slid a hand up around her shoulder and onto the back of her neck, holding her close. Then she slipped her tongue into her mouth as Sam turned her, pinning her body.

Jess' other hand dipped beneath the hem of her shirt, sliding up her bare back. And when it came back down, her nails dragged along her skin, leaving goosebumps in their wake.

When they reached her lower back, a surge of heat moved through her core, settling into a pulsing center below her waistband.

Her hips twitched forward automatically, moving entirely on their own as they reacted to her touch.

The corners of Jess' mouth moved upward against her lips in a smirk. She knew her body better than anyone. Like a programming language that only Jess had learned. She'd mastered every input to get the reactions she wanted.

And Sam knew how much she loved proving it.

Jess slowed the kiss slightly as she dipped the tips of her fingers below the back of her jeans, letting her nails trail downward ever so gently.

Sam barely stopped her hips from moving forward. But she couldn't stop the moan that whimpered past her lips.

Jess released a ragged breath, ripping Sam's hips toward her own with sudden urgency.

A loud knock suddenly pounded against the door, and Sam flinched as Jess froze, jumping back.

Sam looked at the door, then back at Jess. And before she could say anything, Jess pulled back entirely, her warm hands sliding away and leaving cold shadows in their place.

She crossed the short distance to the door, then leaned both hands against it, checking through the peephole.

Jess sighed, leaning back. "It's Scar," she muttered, running a hand through her slightly ruffled hair.

Sam stepped back, turning toward the door as she pulled the hem of her shirt back down and adjusted the top of her pants back into place.

Jess threw her one quick glance before pulling the door open.

Scarlett stood on the other side, not looking up as she typed something out on her phone.

"Hey," Jess muttered, before reaching a hand down to adjust her own shirt.

Scarlett finally glanced up from her phone, a smirk curling her lips as her eyes flicked between Jess and Sam. "Am I interrupting something?"

Jess forced a laugh, smoothing down her hair with one hand. "No, of course not," she said quickly, stepping aside to let Scarlett in.

Scarlett raised an eyebrow, clearly unconvinced, but she didn't push it. Instead, she made a beeline for the fridge, yanking it open like it was her own. "Right," she drawled. She grabbed a sparkling water, cracking it open and taking a long sip. "You weren't answering your phone. I had to come get my charger. I left it in your bag on the trip."

Jess frowned, shooting a quick glance at Sam. "Yeah, sorry, I meant to give it back to you yesterday," she muttered. "It's in my room. I'll go get it."

As Jess disappeared down the hallway, Scarlett leaned against the counter, taking another sip from the can as she studied Sam. "I'm glad you're here, actually," she said, releasing a deep sigh. "I need to vent about the wedding catering situation. It's a total nightmare."

Sam's pulse was still pounding in her ears, the remnants of the moment they'd just shared hanging heavy in the air. "What happened?"

Scarlett rolled her eyes. "The caterer decided to change the menu last minute," she said, letting out a huff of frustration. "Apparently, they can't source the seafood we picked. Now they want to substitute it with some fancy vegetarian option, but Terrence is freaking out because half his family is expecting crab cakes."

Sam forced a chuckle, stepping closer to the counter. "What are you gonna do?" she asked, hoping her voice didn't sound as shaky as it felt.

Scarlett sighed, taking another swig of the sparkling water. "No clue," she muttered. "I need to figure it out today, though. I'm this close to just saying fuck it and ordering pizza."

Sam cracked a grin at that, but her mind was only half on the conversation. She could still feel the ghost of Jess' touch, the heat of her body pressed against her own. And now, the sudden shift back to reality was like being doused with a cold bucket of water.

Jess reappeared, holding the charger in one hand. Her expression was carefully neutral, but Sam could see the tension in the tight set of her jaw.

"Here," Jess said, holding it out.

Scarlett took it, shoving it into her bag without another glance. "Thanks," she said. "Okay, I need you to help me handle this catering mess before Terrence has a meltdown."

Jess shot Sam a quick glance before looking away. And she couldn't tell if it was disappointment or relief in her eyes.

But either way, Sam knew the interruption was for the best. Even if everything in her body screamed the opposite, continuing what they'd started would've been a bad idea.

It was opening the door for a mess of unspoken feelings and who knows what else.

It wasn't something that could happen. And if it did, it definitely shouldn't just be on a whim of high emotion. They had too much history for that. Too many old feelings mixed in to make it casual.

"Okay," Jess said, moving to stand beside Scarlett. "Let's figure this out."

Sam nodded, stepping in closer as the three of them leaned over the counter. But even as they dove into a discussion about the wedding menu, she couldn't shake the feelings still coursing within her. And when she caught Jess's eye across the counter, she saw the same raw, unspoken tension reflected back.

Whatever happened wasn't over. Not by a long shot.

Chapter eighteen

Sam walked through the door into the busy bar and restaurant space.

Although it had been difficult to fit in Scarlett and Terrence's wedding events around her busy work schedule, this was a night she knew she couldn't miss.

They'd delayed their engagement party at the beginning, planning to hold it closer to the wedding when Terrence's friends could fly in. And Scarlett had double—and triple—checked that she'd be able to make it.

But now, walking in, she was filled with nerves.

She hadn't talked to Jess since their kiss earlier that week. She'd opened her phone half a dozen times, ready to text or call. But she couldn't do it. She didn't know what to say.

Or what *not* to say.

And as the days stretched on, and Jess didn't reach out to her either, the feeling worsened.

She wanted to talk to her. To talk about *it*. She had to. She couldn't just let it be what it was and never discuss it. With anyone else, she could've chalked it up to a onetime lapse in control. A moment of desire that got out of hand. But with Jess, it was different. It was more.

She scanned the area, searching for Scarlett in the crowd.

Within moments, she spotted the back of her dark wavy hair bobbing with her familiar infectious laughter.

She crossed the packed front bar to the back, where Scarlett stood at one of the many cocktail tables.

"Hey," she said, coming up beside her. "Sorry I'm late."

Scarlett turned to her with a beaming smile. "Don't worry, you're right on time. Everyone else just started getting here, too."

She waved a hand toward the back of the restaurant. "They're getting the tables ready for us in one of the back rooms. Should be a few more minutes."

Sam nodded, smiling as she greeted Terrence and introduced herself to the rest of the people standing with them.

"Hey."

Sam heard Jess' soft voice beside her, and she turned, her stomach instantly filling with nerves.

"Hey," she replied, a smile naturally tugging across her lips.

Jess gave her a tentative smile before sliding one arm around her waist and giving her a light squeeze of a hug.

Sam relaxed slightly. At least that felt normal.

She turned toward her, facing partially away from the rest of the group.

"How've you been?" Sam asked, hoping she didn't sound as timid as she felt.

"Good," Jess replied nonchalantly. "Busy week at work."

Sam nodded, contemplating whether or not that was the right time or place to bring up what had happened between them earlier that week.

She could wait, but who knew if they'd get another chance to talk without being at a dinner table surrounded by people?

She shifted a little closer to her, dipping her head slightly.

And Jess gave her a look that said she knew the exact words she was about to say.

"Do you want to talk," Sam started, her voice lowering, "about the other day?"

Jess' smile faltered, a flash of panic moving through her eyes before she smoothed it away.

"Not now," she replied, her voice barely audible above the clatter of glasses and the murmur of conversation around them. She pressed her lips into a thin line, a ghost of the easy grin she'd worn just seconds ago.

Then she smiled at a woman who waved at her from across the room.

Sam's chest tightened, the pit of her stomach twisting. "Okay," she managed, forcing a nod. It wasn't okay, but she wasn't going to push—not there, not with half of Terrence's friends within earshot.

Jess turned her head, looking back as a man greeted her. They hugged, immediately launching into conversation, and Sam took the opportunity to say hi to Jasmine, who stood by herself near the edge of one of the tables.

The room thrummed with energy, filled with the sound of clinking glasses, bursts of laughter, and the low murmur of overlapping conversations. A steady stream of people moved through the space, pausing to greet Scarlett and Terrence or mingle near the buffet table. The warm glow from the overhead string lights mixed with the camera flash as people took photos.

Sam leaned casually against the edge of a long table near the back of the room as she talked with a small group of guests she'd just met a few minutes before.

Jess approached from behind her, a drink in one hand, while the other trailed lightly across Sam's shoulder. "You disappeared on me."

Sam turned, surprised at both the gentle, almost intimate touch, and also the change in her tone from when they'd spoken before. Her expression seemed entirely different from when she'd first arrived. It was easy—casual. But it also held something else.

Jess' eyes lingered on her in a way that sent a ripple of warmth through her stomach.

A slow smile spread across Sam's face, the ease in Jess immediately seeping into her. "Figured you'd find me, eventually."

Jess smiled, stepping closer. And again, that smile stirred something. A deep anticipation. Her hand rested lightly on the back of Sam's chair, her presence warm and steady at her side.

"Having fun?" Jess asked, her voice low as she leaned a little closer.

Sam nodded toward the group she'd been talking to. "I think I've learned more about Terrence's college days in the last ten minutes than I ever needed to know."

Jess chuckled, her fingers brushing Sam's shoulder briefly as she shifted her weight. "He's probably left out all the best parts."

"Probably," Sam said, shooting her a wry smile.

One of the guests called Jess into the conversation, but she stayed where she was, her hand idly grazing Sam's arm as she leaned in, laughing along with the group. When Sam turned to her again, Jess' gaze hadn't moved.

"What?" Sam asked with a playful smile.

Jess shook her head, her hand falling briefly to Sam's arm as she leaned back. "Nothing," she said, her voice tinged with amusement.

Another wave of people passed by, one of them stopping to greet Jess with a quick hug and exchange of pleasantries. Jess answered them politely but briefly, her attention flicking back to Sam almost immediately once they moved on.

Jess' hand rested on the edge of the table, her fingers barely brushing Sam's as she adjusted her position.

The contact was fleeting, subtle enough that anyone else would've missed it.

"Not drinking?" Jess asked, nodding to her water glass.

Sam shrugged lightly. "Not tonight."

Jess gave her a knowing look as she nodded slowly. "Keeping your head clear, huh?"

Sam's smile softened. "Maybe."

Jess' lips twitched upward, and for a moment, neither of them spoke. The noise of the party seemed to fade as Jess' gaze settled on her.

"What?" Sam asked, the corner of her mouth quirking upward.

Jess stared at her for a long moment. "Just thinking about what would've happened if Scarlett hadn't shown up that day."

Sam stared back at her, the smirk on her lips dropping as nerves suddenly flooded her stomach. But it wasn't because of what she'd said. It was because of the look in her eyes. The hot, but carefully guarded longing in them.

She swallowed, unable to stop her eyes from flicking down to Jess' lips before yanking back up.

And this time, it was Jess who smirked. A smirk she instantly wanted to devour.

She reached a slow hand out, resting it against Sam's thigh beneath the table.

Sam tensed, her eyes flicking down as an anxious but pleasant feeling bloomed in her chest. But when Sam looked back up at her, she had a more serious but cautious look in her eyes.

And yet, she didn't pull her hand away.

Instead, she cocked her head slightly, eyes flicking down to her hand, then back up.

And even though Sam knew they shouldn't—that they should leave what happened the day before in the past—her body screamed for the opposite.

It begged to keep Jess' hand exactly where it was. It begged to feel her in any way it could—in *every* way it could.

And sitting there beside her, taking in the intensity in her eyes, it felt impossible to deny.

The corner of her mouth quirked upward, and instantly, the silent question in Jess' eyes turned into a heated gaze.

"Meet me in the bathroom," Jess murmured, her voice low and edged with urgency. Before Sam could respond, Jess pushed back her chair and slipped away, her movements deliberate but unhurried.

Sam's eyes followed her as she disappeared down a dimly lit hallway at the back of the restaurant.

Her heart thudded in her chest. She hesitated, taking a steadying sip of her water before setting the glass down and rising from her seat. She weaved through the crowd, her pulse quickening with every step toward the hallway Jess had vanished into.

At the bathroom door, Sam paused, her hand on the cool metal handle. She drew in a quiet breath, then turned it, stepping inside.

Jess was there, leaning against the porcelain sink, her fingers gripping the edge as if to steady herself. Her head lifted, and their eyes locked.

Jess didn't wait. She closed the space between them in an instant, her lips crashing into her with a heat and hunger that made Sam forget everything in the world but her.

Sam tangled her fingers up into her hair, deepening the kiss as Jess pressed against her.

She pulled her in, instantly forgetting her previous apprehension. It didn't matter. Even if they regretted it right after. This is what she needed—what they *both* needed.

Jess pulled back, gazing into her eyes with that same coy look she'd held all night. And she didn't break eye contact as she slowly slid her hands down and undid the button of her pants.

Sam tried to reach for the bottom of Jess' dress, but Jess grabbed her by the wrist, stopping her.

Sam looked at her again, brows furrowed. And Jess just gave her a teasing smile as she slid one hand down the front of her pants.

Sam inhaled sharply as her fingers slid over her. Her eyes fell shut, head bowing forward as Jess' fingers slid back and forth in lazy motions over her already wet center.

And she couldn't help the deep moan that escaped as Jess' fingers swiped her most sensitive area.

"Shh," Jess whispered. Then she snaked her free hand around Sam's neck, pulling her down against her shoulder. "Bite down if you need to."

Her hand worked back and forth over and over again as Sam felt herself drip into her fingers.

She turned her head into Jess' neck, hands seizing her hips. "Someones's gonna come in," she rasped, her breathing already ragged.

"Don't worry," Jess purred in her ear. "You're not gonna take long."

And maybe it was those exact words that made it happen, or maybe Jess just knew her body better than she did. Because the moment her voice drifted across her ear, a familiar tingling passed through her.

Sam tensed, both hands immediately sliding up the back of Jess' dress as her fingers dug into her bare skin. And this time, Jess didn't stop it. Instead, she pressed her body against her, letting out a soft whimper. Her hips twitched back, legs parting just enough to allow the tips of Sam's fingers to graze the center of her warm, wet thong.

But Jess didn't take it further. She didn't grind her hips farther back, like Sam had expected.

"I just want to feel you," Jess whispered. And this time, the words held no ounce of flirtation. They were vulnerable—yearning.

And they worked. *Fast.*

It reminded her of the first time they'd slept together. The shock she'd felt when her body raced towards its climax before she'd even realized it had begun.

Jess' hand slowed against her, and Sam almost groaned in protest.

But then Jess' other hand threaded through her hair, pulling her head back slightly. Sam looked at her, brows clenching with a pained strain as her body begged for more.

Jess gave her a tender, apologetic look. Then her hand began working again. It was expertly slow and careful. Everything she needed.

"Look at me," Jess whispered, her voice pleading like she was the one teetering on the edge.

And Sam saw it then. Whatever they'd both meant for it to be—a casual hookup, or something else—it would always be more.

She forced her eyes to stay open as each wave of feeling flooded her body.

"Fuck," she growled. But the word was swallowed away as Jess immediately surged forward, kissing her deeply through the orgasm.

Her entire body tensed, and she curled her hands deeper into Jess' body, letting her fingers flow farther over Jess' now soaking wet underwear.

Jess continued stroking, only slowing their pace once Sam's body finally settled against her.

They stayed like that for a moment, heavy breaths swirling between them.

Then she felt Jess' lips graze her ear. "Told you it wouldn't take long."

Chapter nineteen

Sam leaned back against her couch, legs stretched out on the coffee table as her eyes drifted over the darkened room. The laptop sat on her thighs, but she'd barely been able to focus enough to read even a single email. Her phone sat beside her, and the urge to pick it up and call Jess gnawed at her.

She rubbed a hand over her face, letting out a slow breath.

She'd already used work as a reason to call twice that week—once to ask a question she already knew the answer to, another time to double-check a detail for the PR campaign. And then there was the night before, when she'd called just to hear Jess' voice, and instead ended up stumbling through some half-baked excuse about a movie recommendation.

It was ridiculous. But she couldn't help herself. She wanted to hear her voice again—to feel that warm, easy connection between them.

She lifted the phone, her mind racing, searching for a reason, something believable that wouldn't seem too obvious.

Jess' words from before echoed in her mind.

We're friends. You don't need an excuse.

Sam swallowed, staring down at the phone. *Friends.* Although, after the last two times they'd seen each other, the word didn't seem as accurate as before.

She took a breath and pressed the call button.

It rang twice before Jess' voice answered. "Hey," Jess said, her voice low, with a slightly exhausted edge.

"Hey," Sam replied, the sound of Jess's voice immediately easing something tight in her chest. She rolled her shoulders back, drawing on her usual confidence. "Are you busy?"

"Not really," Jess replied. "I had a long day. Just got home from work. Why?"

Sam hesitated, clearing her throat as she glanced around the empty apartment. "Wanna come over?"

There was a beat of silence. "Yeah," Jess said, and she swore she could hear the hint of a smile in the word. "I'll be there in thirty."

Sam hung up, setting the phone down and running a hand through her hair. Nerves buzzed beneath her skin, but it wasn't the anxious kind. It was the thrill of anticipation, the kind she'd only just started letting herself feel again when Jess was around.

True to her word, Jess knocked on her door almost exactly thirty minutes later. Sam opened it, taking in the sight of Jess standing there in jeans and a faded T-shirt, her hair slightly mussed, like she'd run her hands through it on the way over. She looked tired, but there was an excitement in her eyes as she met Sam's gaze.

"Long day?" Jess asked, stepping inside.

"You could say that," Sam replied, shutting the door behind her. She felt the sudden urge to close the distance between them, to pull Jess in and kiss her, but she shoved her hands into her pockets instead. "You want a drink?"

"Water's good," Jess said, following her into the kitchen and leaning against the counter as Sam retrieved a water bottle from the fridge. "You okay?"

Sam handed her the glass, shrugging. "Yeah. Just—" she paused, forcing herself to be honest and not swallow away the words that wanted to come out. "Wanted to see you," she finished softly.

Jess' lips quirked up in a small smile that told her being honest was the right call. "So you finally got sick of trying to come up with excuses?"

Sam chuckled, looking down as she felt a slight heat rise in her cheeks. "Guess so."

They moved back into the living room, sinking onto the couch together. It was easy, familiar, the space between them closing naturally until their knees brushed.

"The wedding is coming up fast," Jess said, breaking the comfortable silence. "You ready for the trip back home?"

Sam snorted, running a hand through her messy hair. "Not even a little."

Jess chuckled, leaning back against the cushions. "Yeah," she drawled, looking away. "Me either."

Sam raised an eyebrow. "Why not?"

Jess hesitated, her fingers tapping lightly against the side of the water bottle. "My dad wants me to have dinner with him and his girlfriend."

"Oh," Sam said, nodding slowly. "How do you feel about it?"

"Yeah," Jess sighed, looking down at her hands. "It feels weird, I guess. I want him to be happy, but the idea of it, sitting there with them, it just.." she trailed off with a tight shrug. "I don't know."

Sam frowned, watching her. "It's okay to not be ready."

Jess' lips formed a tight line as she nodded slowly. "I feel stupid. It's been so long since my mom passed away. I should be ready for this. But—I'm not." She huffed a breath, shaking her head. "Especially not to sit there in our house and try to come up with things to say or ask."

Sam reached over without thinking, her hand resting on Jess's knee. "I can go with you, if you want."

Jess looked up, her face instantly brightening. "Really?"

"Of course," Sam said, squeezing her knee gently. "If that would help, I'll be there."

Jess' expression softened, a small, grateful smile tugging at her lips. Then her eyes flicked down, her expression changing.

Slowly, carefully, Jess leaned forward, trailing a hand up Sam's neck to turn her, instantly meeting her lips. And all at once, that deep need she'd felt since the last time finally felt some small relief.

Sam leaned into her, deepening the kiss like her very existence depended on it. Like she needed to taste every inch of her to satisfy the infinite craving. And for the first time, she wondered if maybe that's what it felt like to have an addiction. To want—*need*—something so deeply that nothing could satisfy the hunger.

Jess groaned softly as her hands tangled up in the hair at the back of her neck. She leaned in, swinging one leg over her lap and pressing the full front of her body against her.

Then she broke the kiss as she whispered, "Take me to your bed."

Sam smirked, instantly wrapping her arms around Jess' body and shooting up from the couch.

Jess giggled as she tucked her head into the crook of her neck, wrapping both arms securely around her shoulders. "Well, that was easy."

Sam grinned, easily trudging the distance down the hall with Jess' body tangled around her. "I haven't stopped thinking about—" her brain caught on the word *you*, and quickly substituted it. "*This*—since the engagement party. I'm not waiting another minute."

Sam stepped up to the edge of the bed, gently laying Jess down and settling in on top of her.

She kissed her again, even deeper than before. Maybe she should've been treating it more casual—the way she would any other hookup. But she couldn't.

She didn't want quick—she wanted *everything*. She wanted to taste and feel every detail.

Jess' body shifted, angling to the side as she felt her pushing upward. And Sam let her roll their bodies to the side until Jess was on top of her once more, legs hooked around her hips.

Sam sat up, reaching for her once again, unable to comprehend anything beyond the deep yearning for her lips. But Jess pulled back, the edge of her mouth turning up in a teasing smile before grabbing both of her wrists and pinning them down against the bed.

Jess watched her for a moment, as if daring her to try again.

But Sam couldn't do anything. She was in complete awe, staring into her beautiful gaze.

Jess slowly released her wrists, trailing her hands to the hem of her shirt instead. Sam instantly lifted her arms over her head as Jess slid her shirt up and off her body, leaving her completely bare.

Jess' eyes flicked down, taking in the sight for just a moment. But the teasing edge they'd held just seconds before had vanished, replaced with desire.

Jess' throat bobbed as she swallowed, finally tearing her eyes away as they zeroed in lower.

Her hand slid down her chest, nails grazing lightly down her bare skin, and Sam shuddered at the contact.

They stopped at the waistband of her gray sweatpants, then she hooked both hands inside, and Sam lifted her hips as she gently pulled them down, leaving her in just her black boxers.

Sam leaned forward, reaching for Jess once more, but she pulled back until she stood at the foot of the bed. Her eyes trailed down Sam's body, not looking away as she slowly unbuttoned her own jeans and tugged them down her legs.

Sam swallowed as her gaze flicked down to the thin red laced thong hugging her hips.

She looked back up to see Jess watching her intently, eyes burning into her own as she pulled her own shirt over her head, revealing a matching red bra.

Sam shifted to stand, but Jess paused, eyes narrowing in a mild warning.

Once she stilled, leaning back onto her elbows, Jess finally continued, hands hooking around her back to undo the bra and letting it fall to the floor.

Sam barely moved a muscle as Jess slowly stepped forward, kneeling onto the bed and climbing back on top of her. But before Sam could lift a hand, Jess grabbed her by the wrists again, pinning them down.

Sam stared down as she kissed her chest, lips brushing over the jagged, but smooth, scar tissue that cascaded down from her neck onto her chest.

Jess paused there, only for a moment, to leave one kiss before moving lower.

Her tongue glided down the exposed skin to the center of her abdomen, and she changed to an excruciatingly slow pace.

Sam shifted beneath her, hips jutting forward in a desperate attempt to get her tongue to a very different place.

But Jess pulled away just enough for Sam to make out the edge of a teasing smirk on her lips.

And then, ever so slowly, she pulled the boxers down, discarding them behind her.

She continued kissing down her body until she settled between her legs. She kissed her thigh, so softly she barely felt her lips against her skin. Then she moved closer, letting her lips just barely graze over her pulsing clit.

Sam squeezed her eyes shut, feeling a whisper of breath against her.

And this time, she didn't try to stop it when her hips automatically jerked forward, searching for the one mouth she wanted.

But Jess pulled back expertly, keeping her lips just close enough to skim against her without fully giving in.

Her hips fell back against the bed, and she could already feel the wetness trickling out.

Jess must've seen it too, because her eyes flicked up to her with a sudden hunger. As if whatever self control she'd maintained up to that point had begun to crack at the sight.

She dipped her head downward, and Sam instantly tensed, anticipation building as she waited to feel Jess' tongue finally hit her clit.

But it didn't.

Sam gasped, her mouth falling open as she felt Jess' tongue much lower, right where the wetness seeped from her slit.

Jess moaned, her tongue slowly twirling around her opening. It circled the edges before gliding slowly inside.

Sam gasped, her upper body springing forward. Her hand instinctively raised, stopping in midair behind

Jess' head. It paused there as she clenched it into a tight fist to stop from pushing her head down and grinding fully against her.

Sam bit down hard on her knuckle, squeezing her eyes shut as Jess's tongue slowed, running lazy circles around her opening.

Her chest heaved as she dipped her head back, blinking up at the ceiling as she felt herself tightening around Jess' tongue each time it entered her.

But even then, she entirely avoided any contact with her now aching clit.

"I—I—" She didn't even know what she was trying to say. She didn't know if she was about to plead or beg or command. It was too much. Too much want—too much *need*. Except, even *need* didn't feel like the right word. It wasn't just that she needed that contact there at that moment. She needed *Jess* there at that moment. Like nothing else—*no one else*—in the world would be able to satisfy that deep ache within her.

Then she felt Jess pull away.

She looked down, taking in the hungry look in her eyes.

Slick wetness glistened against her chin.

"Do you still have that strap?"

Sam's chest rose and fell rapidly as she stared down at her, barely comprehending anything, much less words, at that moment.

She blinked, her brain slowly working again. Then she nodded.

Jess gave her a satisfied smirk, leaning down to place a gentle kiss against her thigh.

"I want you to use it on me," she whispered into her skin.

Sam swallowed, watching every movement as if her life depended on it. And again, it took her brain a moment to process the meaning of what she'd said.

Jess looked up at her, keeping her mouth within an inch of her skin. "Where is it?"

Sam swallowed, her brain reeling. Then she nodded toward the drawer of her nightstand.

She turned toward it, but Jess reached out, placing a gentle hand on her arm to stop her.

Sam looked back at her, her brow furrowing in question. But Jess said nothing. Instead, she just moved up the bed, leaning over to open the drawer. She reached inside and, without a word, pulled the strap on out.

And again, when Sam tried to move, to stand, Jess placed a firm hand against her chest, pinning her down.

Sam watched as Jess moved back down the bed. Then she wordlessly placed the harness over each of her legs. Sam lifted her hips as Jess carefully moved it into place. Then she pulled on each strap until they tightened perfectly around her.

And this time, Sam didn't try to move. She waited as Jess moved up her body until she was straddling her, hovering just above it.

Jess trailed her hands up onto her neck, running her fingers into her hair.

She lowered herself slowly onto the strap, keeping her eyes locked with Sam's. The movement was painfully slow, as if Jess was working to savor every single moment. And as she continued, Sam could feel the base of the strap begin to press down against her throbbing clit.

Jess' eyes widened slightly, her lips parting as Sam felt her hips dropping closer.

And even though she knew Jess wanted to draw it out—to tease her as long as she possibly could—she couldn't handle it anymore. The look on Jess' face as her hips lowered the last inch against her was enough to send every coherent thought from her mind.

Her arm shot up, wrapping around Jess' hips.

And as if she instantly knew what she'd done—what dam she'd broken within her—Jess wrapped her arms around Sam's neck, leaning her body weight against her. Like she had lost every sense of the control she'd held onto up until that moment, and was now relinquishing it all.

Sam thrusted upward, pulling Jess' hips down against her.

The base of the strap ground against her clit, giving just a fraction of what it begged for.

And it wasn't enough.

Sam spun them in one fluid motion, pinning Jess against the bed as her hips thrusted violently, lacking any ounce of control.

"Fuck," Jess gasped, exhaling against her neck.

The sound of her completely unfiltered, raw want sent a new wave of need coursing within her. If she wasn't already so far gone, she would've slowed down. She would've forced herself to make it last as long as humanly possible so she could hear that sound forever.

But she was too far past that point. Her brain wasn't making any decisions. Her body had entirely taken over in a way it never had before. Not with anyone. Not even Jess.

Jess grabbed onto her back, clawing into her skin as her body writhed beneath her.

A string of profanities spit from her lips one after the next as her hips bucked upward, meeting each of Sam's thrusts. Then her whole body tightened against her, molding into her as if they were one, holding her so close she could barely pull her hips back even an inch.

And even though she knew Jess was close, she needed more.

Sam twisted her body, taking Jess with her as her legs dropped over the edge of the bed to the floor.

Jess clung to her as she stood, keeping one arm wrapped securely around Jess' waist, while the other hooked beneath one of her thighs.

She turned, immediately pinning Jess' back against the wall, holding the full weight of her body.

Then she drilled into her, losing awareness of anything else but the feel of Jess' body pressed against her own.

"Oh—my—god—" Jess panted.

Sam kept going, lifting her a few inches before yanking back down over and over again until a new intensity built in her core.

Then Jess released her arms from around her neck, pulling back to look at her instead. Her hands slid to Sam's cheeks, and Sam moved forward to meet her lips.

But Jess pulled back, just barely out of reach.

Jess looked at her then, with a yearning that almost broke her free from the carnal state she'd entered.

She softened each thrust just a fraction as Jess leaned her forehead against hers. Jess' brow furrowed slightly, lips parting as she watched her.

"Sam—I—"

Sam could see in her eyes what she was about to say—or maybe what she wanted to say.

Those three words.

The words that some deep buried part of her desperately wanted to hear. But there was another part that knew with certainty they couldn't be said. Because if they were spoken aloud, they would change things. They would turn it all into something else.

Something it couldn't be.

"I—" Jess paused, as if sharing those exact same thoughts, but deciding to say the words, anyway.

Sam tensed, her heart pounding with apprehension.

Then suddenly, Jess threw her head back, eyes squeezing shut.

"Fuck!"

Jess' legs trembled beneath her hands.

Sam continued stroking into her as she arched back, every muscle in her body tightening.

Then Jess slowly crumpled forward, arms draping over Sam's shoulders.

Sam slowed to a stop, adjusting her arms to wrap securely around her.

She stepped back from the wall, careful not to move too much while still inside her.

She moved back toward the bed, stopping when her knees hit the soft mattress.

Then she carefully leaned forward, laying her down against the bed.

Jess' legs remained wrapped securely around her waist, keeping her firmly in place. Sam pulled her head back, looking down at her as she pressed a gentle kiss on her now damp temple.

She reached one hand up, wiping a stray lock of hair back from where it stuck to her forehead.

Jess opened her eyes, blinking once, then twice, as awareness filtered back into her gaze.

Sam's heavy breathing finally began to slow, and she drooped her head forward, resting against Jess' neck.

She felt Jess' hands run across her shoulders, kneading against the now tight muscles.

Then they slid lower, running up and down the length of her back.

Sam lifted her head just enough to kiss the sensitive skin on the base of her neck, and Jess hummed, turning into the kiss.

She kissed her again, this time even slower, letting her lips drift over her skin.

Jess' hands eased down to the small of her back, and she just barely registered the movement before she felt her nails skim across the skin.

Sam whimpered, unable to stop her hips as they fluttered forward, sending the strap sliding back into Jess.

Sam pulled her head up fully then, concern instantly filling her as she checked to make sure Jess was okay with the movement.

Jess stared back with a look in her eyes that she'd never seen before. And she wondered then if Jess would finally speak the words she knew were about to come out a few moments before.

But even if she didn't, it wouldn't matter. The look in her eyes said more than any words ever could.

Before Sam could pull her hips away, Jess scratched her nails against her again.

Sam gasped, hips jutting forward again, this time faster—harder.

Jess' mouth fell open, a soft whimper escaping her lips.

She moved one hand up to the edge of Sam's jaw, running a thumb across her bottom lip, while the other scratched once again on her lower back.

Sam felt herself start to throb again—even more furiously than before.

She slid her hips back, ever so slowly, before pressing forward once more. The base pressed against her, right where she needed it most.

Her head drooped forward as she moved in and out of Jess at an excruciatingly slow pace.

And with every stroke, she felt the pressure in her core building.

Jess' soft lips brushed against her earlobe.

"Do anything you need, babe," she whispered. "It's okay, I can take it."

Something warm buzzed in her chest at the words, or—*word*—she'd chosen.

And that warmth spread down further, coming to a point between her thighs.

She pulled her hips back, then drove them forward, still slow, but this time much deeper.

Jess moaned in her ear. "Go as deep as you need."

The warm pulsing instantly morphed into a fierce, throbbing heat.

Sam's breathing went ragged as she pulled back once more before plunging back in. She pulled back, meeting Jess' focused gaze. And the way she was looking at her then was different. Her eyes dripped with desire. But that wasn't the only thing there. She looked at her like she was the only thing in the whole world.

"I—I think—" Jess rasped, her eyelids fluttering. "If you keep doing that—its gonna—its gonna happen again—"

Sam stroked in and out of her again, every nerve ending buzzing. And suddenly, she didn't care about getting what her body needed. She only cared about that look. About making Jess look at her that way every moment for as long as she lived.

But then Jess' eyes squeezed shut.

"S—Sam—im gonna—" Jess whimpered, biting down on her earlobe as she tightened her legs around her.

And that was it.

Sam groaned, body curling forward as her hips bucked wildly back and forth, a wave of pleasure crashing through her body.

She only managed to keep herself up for another second before collapsing forward.

She laid like that for a few moments as her breathing finally returned to a semi-normal pace. Then she slowly pulled herself out of Jess, rolling to the side and dropping onto her back on the bed.

Jess pushed up onto her elbow, leaning over her as she kissed her softly.

Sam kept her eyes closed, taking deep breaths as she waited for her heartbeat to return to normal.

Then she felt Jess moving down the bed.

She opened her eyes just as Jess began undoing the harness around her hips.

She watched her carefully loosen each side, then Sam lifted her hips slightly as Jess pulled it away, tossing it to the side.

Then she waited for Jess to crawl back up to her side.

But she didn't.

Instead, she settled back down between her legs.

Sam lifted her head, watching her curiously.

Jess' eyes flicked up to hers. Then, with their gazes still locked, Jess dipped her head.

Sam gasped, shooting upright as she felt Jess' tongue slide against her still throbbing clit.

Her hand instantly went to the back of Jess' head before she could stop it, and Jess moaned into her.

When Sam tried to pull her hand back, Jess placed her own over it, pushing it back down against her, cementing it in place.

And that alone was enough to take her right back to the edge.

She ground herself against the full length of Jess' tongue as her body released itself into her mouth.

When Jess' tongue swirled over her the next time, everything unraveled.

Chapter twenty

The neighborhood looked smaller than Sam remembered, its once familiar streets somehow shrunken by the passage of time.

As Scarlett's car rolled through the quiet, tree-lined neighborhood of Jess' childhood home, Sam felt a strange mix of nostalgia and unease settling in her chest.

Scarlett pulled up in front of Jess' dad's house, the high-pitched squeal of worn down break pads interrupting the silence.

Sam glanced up at Jess, who sat in the front passenger seat, and then back at the house, its front porch light glowing softly in the gray evening air.

Sam opened the car door, sliding out into the street before grabbing their bags from the trunk.

"I'll text you about the timing for the rehearsal dinner tomorrow," Scarlett called out to Jess as she slowly rounded to the back of the car to where Sam stood waiting.

"Kay," Jess mumbled, her face a mask of tension as she glanced up at the house.

She followed as Jess trudged up the driveway, her suitcase rolling behind her. Then she waited a few steps behind as Jess knocked before her father opened the door.

"Hi," he said, his deep voice commanding attention even in its low volume.

"Hey dad," Jess said, stepping forward and wrapping her arms around his thick torso in a tight hug.

Fine lines now marked his face, and deeper shadows etched permanently between his brows gave him a more weathered appearance. The light brown hair that once carried only a hint of gray had faded almost entirely to silver.

He let go after a moment, straightening up as he stepped aside to let her past the threshold into the house. Then he looked at Sam with a tight smile that was laced with more awkward discomfort than it was unfriendly.

"Sam," he said, nodding once.

"Hey Mr. Miller," she said with a warm smile, easily navigating the awkward tension she'd grown accustomed to over the years. "It's good to see you again."

She held out a hand, and he took it, his palm calloused and grip firm as he gave her one solid shake.

"Yeah," he said, clearing his throat. "You too."

She stepped past him over the threshold, following Jess inside, her duffel bag and backpack weighing against her shoulders. The house smelled faintly of cedar and something savory from the kitchen.

A black-haired, middle-aged woman stood in the kitchen, grinning up at them from where she was drying her hands near the sink. Her tan skin carried a healthy glow, though the faint lines around her mouth and eyes hinted at her age. Her black bob cut framed her face neatly, the ends just brushing her shoulders in an effortlessly tidy way that seemed to suit her perfectly.

"You must be Jess," she said, dropping the towel on the countertop and making a beeline toward them.

She paused a few steps away from her, and Sam could read the apprehension clear across her face. Like she was deciding whether or not to go for the hug or the handshake.

"Yeah," Jess said, her own voice sounding more nervous than Sam had heard it in a long time.

"I'm Suki," the woman said, her smile softening into something more understated.

Jess reached out, shaking her hand. "It's nice to meet you."

Suki nodded, her expression steady but kind, as if she understood how difficult this moment was for her. She turned to Sam then, her warm smile still firmly in place, though there was a hint of curiosity in her gaze as she looked her over.

"I'm Sam," she said quickly, grinning at the woman as she reached a hand out.

Suki nodded, smiling as she took it. "It's wonderful to meet you, Sam." Then her eyes flicked back to Jess, who seemed to be almost frozen in what she guessed were awkward nerves.

And Sam couldn't blame her. She couldn't imagine how it would feel to meet the first woman her father had dated since her mother passed. Especially in her childhood home.

Sam cleared her throat, looking back at Suki. "Thanks for letting me crash your dinner," she said with a light laugh. "I hear you're an amazing cook."

Suki chuckled softly. "You're very welcome," she replied, her voice smooth and low, with just a touch of amusement. "I wouldn't call myself amazing, but I do enjoy it." Her dark eyes flicked back to Jess. "And it's nice to finally meet you both."

"I'll take your guys' bags up to your room," Mike's gravelly voice cut through as he stepped up behind them.

"Oh—" Sam muttered, pausing when he held a hand out for her duffel bag. "That's okay. I'm actually staying at a hotel nearby."

He nodded, unfazed, turning to grab Jess' suitcase instead.

"Thanks dad."

"I'm just so grateful you guys were able to come," Suki said as Mike dragged the suitcase up the stairs and out of view. "I'm sure your schedule is packed with all the wedding festivities."

Jess gave her a small smile that seemed just slightly less tense than before. "Yeah. Lots to do."

Suki watched her, an expectant smile on her lips as if waiting for more.

And when a couple of seconds ticked by in silence, Sam broke it for her once again.

"Is there anything I can help with?" she asked. "I'm not great in the kitchen, but I can definitely follow instructions."

Suki laughed, waving her to come forward as she turned back toward the kitchen. "I would love some help."

Sam dropped her bags by the bottom of the stairs, then walked back toward the kitchen, running a gentle hand across Jess' lower back as she passed.

Jess gave her a grateful smile, releasing a breath as her shoulders dropped slightly into their normal relaxed state.

Suki began directing her on what to do, and they quickly fell into an easy rhythm, talking as they worked.

"So you're a software engineer, is that right?" Suki asked as she poured breading into a large bowl.

Sam glanced up at her in surprise. Then her eyes flicked to where Mike and Jess sat in the living room talking. Maybe Mike had paid more attention than he'd really let on those handful of times they'd spoken. But even if he had, she was even more surprised that he would've brought it up to Suki before they'd arrived.

"Yes," she said, looking back down as she continued chopping the cabbage. "I work on software for financial analytics right now."

Suki hummed, placing raw chicken breasts on a plate beside the bowl of breading. "My oldest son is a software engineer, too. He's always enjoyed it. Although, I'll be honest, I have a hard time following most of what he tries to explain about his work."

"I understand," Jess' voice floated to them as she entered the kitchen. "I feel like she's speaking another language when she talks about it," she said, nodding toward Sam in a way that was far more composed than when they'd first arrived.

Suki chuckled, looking up at her with an excited grin, as if she'd also picked up on her change in demeanor. "Exactly."

Mike followed behind Jess, grabbing a beer from the fridge.

"Want me to take over?" Jess asked, nodding down at the cabbage she was chopping. "So you can give your hand a break."

"Yeah," Sam replied with a smile, knowing that meant Jess was finally ready to have some time to get to know Suki.

"Beer?" Mike's gruff voice asked from the other side of the island, holding one out toward her.

"Sure," she said, moving around the kitchen to take it from him. "Thanks."

She followed as he made his way back to his recliner in the living room. And the corners of her lips quirked up in a smile, hearing Jess and Suki talking and laughing behind them.

She sat down on the couch opposite of Mike, taking a sip of the ice cold beer. The low murmur of announcers floated out from the TV, where a hockey game was playing on the screen.

"You follow hockey?" Mike asked, keeping his eyes off the screen as he took a big gulp of his beer.

"Not really," Sam answered. "But I like watching most sports. I can get behind anything competitive."

Mike huffed, throwing a nod over her shoulder while still keeping his eyes glued to the screen. "Just like that one."

Sam smirked, nodding to herself. "Yeah, she might be the only person I've ever met that's more competitive than me."

Mike hummed, taking another swig of his beer.

Calm silence fell between them as Sam leaned back into the couch, trying to savor the rare downtime where she didn't have to think about work.

After a while, she caught Mike glancing at her out of the corner of her eye. Then he shifted in his recliner, clearing his throat.

She looked up at him, curious, as he threw a glance back to where Jess and Suki were still talking in the kitchen.

"So," he started, his voice slightly lower and somehow more timid than she was used to. Almost—nervous—in a way? If that was even possible for him.

"You guys are uh—" He looked at her with a question in his eyes, then nodded once over his shoulder. "Again?"

Sam's heart rate ticked up a notch, the question catching her entirely off guard. If there was anything she expected him to ask that night, that definitely wasn't it.

"Uh—we're" she stammered, scratching the back of her neck. "We're friends. Just—friends."

He watched her for a moment, and she was suddenly transported back to years before when she'd first met him and he'd questioned her about the incident at the clinic. Like he was searching for what she might have been concealing in the words.

But it was true. They were friends. And she sure as hell wasn't about to give him the full explanation of what they'd been doing that might have blurred those lines.

He hummed, nodding once. Then he looked at Jess once more.

"She doesn't—" he paused, looking down at the beer bottle in his hand, as if carefully measuring his words. "Tell me much about who she's dating these days."

Sam wanted to ask if she'd *ever* told him much about that. But it didn't seem like the right response. Not with that being the most serious thing he'd ever really said to her in all the times they'd interacted.

"I wouldn't take it personally," Sam said with an easy chuckle. "Pretty sure Scarlett is the only one that gets all the details."

Mike nodded, giving her what was probably the closest thing to a smile she'd ever seen on him.

"Dinners ready!" Suki called out from the kitchen.

***

Sam rested her shoulder against the weathered wooden railing of the back porch steps, her eyes fixed on the streaks of pink and orange spreading across the horizon where the sun had just dipped out of sight.

Dinner had gone better than expected. Once Jess had worked through her initial nerves, the night had flowed with easy laughter and conversation, each story and shared moment bridging the gaps between them.

Mike had left to drive Suki home after they'd all finished dinner and tidied up, leaving her and Jess with some time to themselves.

"So, what did you think?" Sam asked, turning to look at Jess, who sat beside her on the top step.

She nodded slowly, a small smile forming on her lips. "I like her. She's sweet."

"Yeah, she is."

Jess glanced down at the cup between her hands. "It's weird, though. I've never seen him like that with someone." Her throat bobbed as she swallowed, brow furrowing slightly. "He seemed—*happy*."

"Yeah," Sam muttered, the conversation between them resurfacing in her mind. "He was definitely—*different*."

Jess looked at her, cocking her head to the side in question.

Sam opened her mouth to explain, but paused as a laugh worked its way out instead. "He um—he asked me about us."

Jess' brow furrowed. "Asked *what* about us?"

"He asked if we were like—together."

Jess' head whipped to the side, eyes widening. "Are you serious?"

Sam laughed, shaking her head in shared disbelief. "Yep."

"What did he say exactly?" Jess asked, turning her whole body toward her.

"He just asked if we were a thing—I guess. Or I mean, I think that's what he was trying to get at."

Jess blinked, staring at her as if waiting for more. "What else did he say?"

Sam shrugged lightly. "Nothing, really. You know him. Pretty sure he's never said more than like one sentence to me at a time."

Jess nodded slowly. A beat of silence passed, then she asked, her voice low and careful, "what did you tell him?"

Sam swallowed, looking away. "I said we were just friends."

Jess was quiet for a moment, and Sam glanced back at her, studying the reaction. But her face betrayed no emotion.

"Is that—I mean, was that okay?" Sam asked slowly. "I didn't really know what to—"

"No—yeah," Jess replied, shaking her head. "Yeah. That's fine."

Sam nodded, looking out into the backyard as she took a sip of her water.

"I'm just surprised," Jess muttered. "He's never asked me about any of that stuff before."

"Did you tell him about Liz?"

Jess shrugged. "I told him at the beginning, when we first started seeing each other. But we never talked about it after that. He never asked."

Sam nodded, letting comfortable silence fall between them.

After a minute, Jess exhaled, leaning into her slightly as she shivered in the dusky cold air. "How do you feel now that you're back?"

Sam thought about it for a moment—how it felt seeing the familiar road as they drove up to the house.

The memories of every time she'd picked her up and dropped her off there when they'd first met.

It felt like an eternity had passed, but each memory was crisp enough in her mind that it could've been hardly any time at all.

"It's weird," Sam said quietly as her gaze drifted across the darkened sky above the wooden fence.

"What're you going to do after you sell the company?"

Sam tilted her head back, releasing a sigh. "I haven't really figured that out yet. I've just been so focused on what comes before that I haven't really been able to see past it."

Jess threw her a teasing smirk. "Retire on a beach somewhere?"

Sam snorted a laugh. "Pretty sure I wouldn't be able to make it more than ten minutes without getting bored."

Jess smiled knowingly at her.

"I don't know," Sam continued. "I guess maybe start another software company? Probably with Caleb again. And then just see what happens."

Jess arched one brow at her. "So, exactly what you're doing right now?"

"Well, not—" Sam paused, her mouth remaining open for a moment. Then she closed it, cocking her head to the side. She'd never really thought about it before. But—yeah. That's what she wanted her days to look like. Exactly what she was already doing. Minus the constant travel and stress of hyper-growth.

She let out an amused chuff. "Okay, yeah. I guess so."

Jess laughed, shaking her head as she sipped her drink. "Are you gonna stay in Seattle?"

Sam glanced at her, wondering if there was a specific reason she'd chosen to ask.

"I don't know," she answered quietly. "I never thought I'd end up back here. Or at least, end up this close to where I grew up." She ran a hand across the back of her neck. "I never really planned on coming back once I left."

Jess gave a slight nod.

"But it's also been—nice," Sam continued. "Better than I expected. Being around friends and everything."

She sighed, resting her elbows against her knees.

"Did you miss it?" Jess asked quietly. "I mean, did you miss Scarlett and—" she trailed off, but Sam knew what she was really asking.

"Yeah," she whispered. "I missed—everyone—a lot." She swallowed, tapping a finger against the edge of her glass. "But I think I've always just had this tunnel vision. Ever since I graduated. I knew what I wanted and—it's like I could only ever think about getting it. I never let myself think about any of the other stuff. Any of the stuff I—" she swallowed, realizing for the first time how true it was. "Gave up."

Chapter twenty-one

Sam walked through the familiar hallway toward the desk she'd spent so many days and nights at in the past.

The second Scarlett had told her the wedding would be held back in their hometown, she knew she had to stop by the clinic to see Laura. Really, it was the only thing she actually looked forward to about being back.

Laura was one of the few constants of the town that only brought along pleasant memories.

She made her way to the end of the hall where a young woman stood at the side, looking down at her phone.

Sam cleared her throat as she approached.

The woman looked up at her, then smiled softly. "Hi," she said, nodding toward the open meeting door behind her. "The next meeting doesn't start for another thirty minutes or so, but feel free to wait inside."

"Oh," Sam muttered, "uh—actually, I was looking for someone. She works here. Laura. She runs the program."

The young woman cocked her head slightly, thinking for a moment. "Oh! Yeah. Laura. I remember her." Then her smile dropped, replaced with an apologetic frown. "Sorry. She hasn't worked here for a while. She moved away last year."

"Oh," Sam muttered, a pang of disappointment running through her chest.

"The program is still running, though," the woman said. "If you want to come to the next meeting, we'd be happy to have you."

Sam forced a polite smile. "That's okay. Thanks, though."

She turned, trudging back down the hallway and out the double doors.

Her eyes floated over the mostly empty parking lot. And even that looked entirely different than she remembered. The asphalt had worn down even further, creating jagged cracks and potholes. And the paint had faded to the point of barely being able to tell where one spot ended and the next began.

Her drifting gaze landed on the old building of the diner. The windows were boarded-up and the lettering of the logo had been half-removed. There was a sign stuck up near the edge, labelled with some construction company. And she knew by the look of it that probably meant the building would be demolished at some point. It might even be the last time she saw it standing.

One of the places that housed the few truly happy memories of her childhood, ready to be torn down. Ripped away, like it had never existed at all.

She stared at it for a long moment.

Then she pulled out her phone, mapping to the one place she never expected to go back to.

***

Sam sat on the grass, staring at the headstone in front of her.

Richard Garcia. Loving husband and father.

Her eyes traced each letter of the words.

The first time she'd seen it at his funeral, she'd barely been able to read them without feeling an overwhelming sense of anger. And she realized then how long that anger had lasted. It didn't truly dissipate until years later, when she'd seen it for the second time. And instead of anger, she felt a deep sadness.

Not for herself—but for his daughter.

For what she must have gone through.

And now, as she sat there, reading over the words once again, she felt an even deeper sadness for what she must be going through now as she grew older. As she grew to an age where she would finally begin to understand what really happened.

A faint vibration jolted her from her thoughts, and she instinctively reached for her pocket.

Her phone buzzed again as she pulled it out, the glow of the screen illuminating Jess' name. She watched it for just a second, before swiping the screen and raising the phone to her ear.

"Hey," she said, her voice coming out much more strained than she'd expected.

"Hey," Jess answered, "My dad said I could use his truck today to drive to Scarlett's for the rehearsal dinner. Do you want me to come by the hotel early? Then we could go to Scarlett's together."

Sam cleared her throat, trying to regain her normal tone. "Yeah, sure. Sounds good."

"Great," Jess said as the phone crackled with her movement. "I can pick you up in like ten minutes."

"Oh," Sam muttered, clearing her throat again. "I'm—not there right now. But I could order an Uber and probably be back in like an hour or so."

"Where are you?" Jess asked, the phone crackling again. "I can pick you up wherever."

Sam swallowed, glancing back up at the headstone, her eyes tracing over the words once more. Each jagged letter stared back like they held a permanent imprint of her previous anger.

"Sam?" Jess asked, her voice now more focused as the sounds in the background diminished.

"Yeah," she mumbled, running a rough hand down her face. "Sorry. I'm uh—I'm at the Crest View Cemetery."

A beat of silence passed, and Sam tensed, waiting for her reaction.

It wasn't that she didn't want to tell her. It was just that she didn't want it to have to *mean* something.

She wasn't even really sure why she'd chosen to go in the first place. Stopping there wasn't part of the plan. But then, when she'd seen the diner closed down, she just needed—something.

The world had entirely moved on—erased every trace of her only good memories in the town. And at one point, when she was younger, she wanted nothing more than to have it all wiped away. To start fresh without any reminders of the past. Because maybe then, she could finally feel settled.

But now that it'd happened, it just left her feeling— empty.

"Do you want to be there for a while longer?" Jess' gentle voice asked. "I could pick you up whenever you're ready. It doesn't have to be now."

Sam frowned, shaking her head. Although Jess' caring voice soothed that deep empty feeling that had built, something in her didn't want to hear it.

"No," she said, her voice finally returning to its normal state of strength. "It's okay. I'm ready now."

Jess was quiet for a moment before she replied, "Okay. I'll come get you."

***

Soft footsteps crunched behind her.

Sam glanced over her shoulder with a frown. "You didn't have to come all the way in. I could've met you out front."

She was about to stand, but Jess placed a soft hand on her shoulder, stopping her as she sat down beside her in the grass.

"That's okay," Jess said with a soft smile before turning toward the headstone. "Is that.."

Sam nodded, eyes trailing over the letters of his name. "Yeah."

Jess stared silently. "I'm sorry. I should've known you might want to visit him while you were here. I would've offered to drive you."

"It's okay," Sam replied, clearing her throat. "I didn't really think of it until earlier when I was leaving the clinic."

Jess turned to her, her brow wrinkling. "You went to the clinic?"

Sam nodded slowly. "I went to see Laura." She shifted, pulling her knees up to her chest and resting her elbows against them. "She wasn't there, though. I guess she moved, or something."

"Oh," Jess said quietly, frowning. "So you left and came here instead?"

"Yeah," Sam muttered, biting the inside of her cheek. She didn't know how to explain why she'd ended up there. Even though she knew Jess would be the only person to understand.

Jess studied her for a long moment. "Did you visit him the last time you came home?"

Sam stiffened slightly, caught off guard by the question. She'd forgotten about their conversation at the hotel.

She glanced over to the far side of the grounds, to the memorial wall. Although she'd been there that last time, visiting his grave that day wasn't the reason.

"Yeah," she whispered.

She could've left it at that. She didn't have to tell Jess the whole story—the reason why she'd come home in the first place. And Jess would never know the difference.

Or maybe she would. She'd always had a way of reading through the things she left unsaid—of knowing her, even when she didn't really know herself.

And maybe that's why she felt the need to tell her, then.

"I—" she started, her voice coming out soft and weak in a way she hated. She cleared her throat. "When I came back that last time, it was for my mom."

Although she kept her eyes on Ricky's grave, she could feel Jess' silent gaze burning into her.

She shifted beneath the weight of it.

"I bought a memorial space," she continued, casting a pointed glance at the wall she now couldn't stand to go to. "And I came back after they installed the plaque."

Jess stayed quiet, her gaze expectant, like she was waiting for Sam to fill the silence. When the words didn't come, Jess tilted her head slightly, her voice soft as she finally asked, "She didn't have one before?"

Sam shook her head. "She didn't leave behind any money." She paused, shifting in the grass as she loosed a deep breath. "And we didn't have any family to cover the costs. Chris was deployed, and even if he was here, I don't think he would've paid for it, anyway."

A chilled wind blew past, sending crisp russet leaves tumbling across the grass.

Sam pulled the sleeves of her hoodie down to cover her bare forearms as she continued. "When she died, the city cremated her. They sent the ashes overseas to Chris." She tilted her head back slightly to feel the brisk air against her cheeks. "I think he just spread them wherever he was at the time."

Jess placed a tender hand on her thigh. Sam looked down, watching it for a moment before taking her hand and lacing their fingers together.

"Did it bother you?" Jess asked, peering up at her. "I mean—not having somewhere to visit when you wanted to feel close to her again."

Sam thought for a moment before turning to look at her. "Honestly? No. I didn't understand that she wasn't getting something that most other people did. I just thought it was normal."

Jess nodded slowly, her eyes deeply focused on Sam's, as if searching to see if there were any words she was leaving unsaid.

And she must have found whatever she was searching for, because her eyes changed with that knowing look she always got whenever she saw something within her that she couldn't see herself.

"Did you visit the memorial today?"

Sam's eyes flicked past Jess to the wall in the distance behind her. "No."

Jess watched, her expression unchanged. And Sam knew then that she'd already known the answer.

"I thought," Sam started, "that it would make me feel different somehow. Like closure or something." She shook her head, brows tightening in frustration. "But— it didn't."

Jess nodded, her eyes flicking down to where their fingers intertwined. "I don't know if anything ever really brings that closure," she said softly.

Sam watched her, taking in every tiny detail in the way her eyes and brow tightened just the slightest bit. It reminded her of the first night they'd ever spoken about it. The first night Jess had really felt like more than just some girl she volunteered with.

"Did you visit your mom's grave a lot when you were younger?"

Jess nodded slowly, her eyes still entirely focused on their hands. "I made my dad take me constantly, for a while." She released a deep sigh. "But I could always tell something about it made him uncomfortable. Like he had to force himself to go every time I asked."

She bit the edge of her lip, her eyes taking on that distant look Sam had seen many times before when they'd first met.

"Eventually," Jess continued, "he started just waiting in the car while I would go in and visit. Back then, I thought he just didn't care. I remember feeling so angry with him for it. But now—" She paused, an almost guilty look flashing over her face. "Now I know it wasn't because he *didn't* care. It was because he cared too much."

Sam watched the flash of pain move through her features. Like she single-handedly blamed herself for causing him that pain.

She squeezed her hand gently, and Jess looked up at her, a pained smile barely gracing her lips.

"You never really told me about what happened back then," Jess said quietly, her expression both careful and comforting all at once.

Sam swallowed, looking away toward the far off tree line surrounding the gates of the cemetery. "I don't really think about it much."

It wasn't a lie. She barely left time in her day to think about anything more than the very necessities of work. And after she'd moved away, it made it even easier. There was rarely a reminder of those days.

Jess nodded slowly. "I can't imagine how hard that would've been. To watch your parent do that—" She paused, as if catching herself. "Or—go through that."

Sam shrugged, her mouth pressing into a tight line. "Every time she would relapse, it was almost better. I was less anxious then."

Sam shifted, releasing a breath as certain memories floated through her vision, blocking everything else out.

"When she was sober," she continued slowly, "the first couple days would always be good. It was like the way you feel before the weekend—the excitement on a Friday afternoon."

Her eyes swam through the thick fog of memories, flickering to the memorial wall.

"But then," she went on, "when you wake up Sunday morning, it feels different. Like you can't even enjoy the last day of the weekend because you're stuck thinking about Monday morning."

Jess rubbed a light thumb across the back of her hand. "You knew what was coming."

Sam pursed her lips, nodding once. "The longer it lasted—the longer she'd stay sober—the worse it was."

Her head dropped slightly as a twinge of familiar guilt worked its way through her chest. "I think sometimes I almost wanted it to happen," she whispered. "Just so I could stop obsessing over *when* it would happen."

Jess turned to fully face her, placing her other hand on her thigh.

"And the longer it went on," Sam continued, releasing a frustrated breath, "God, it felt like *I* was the one relapsing. I was so on edge all the time, and after a while it would just turn into this crazy rage."

She closed her eyes as she exhaled, trying not to get lost in the guilt of those memories.

"Then she'd relapse and everything would go back to normal. Or at least, *our* version of normal. And I could finally stop worrying about when or how it would happen. I could focus on other things again."

Sam took a deep breath, focusing in on Jess' hand in her lap, like a tether that kept her from being consumed by the past.

"You weren't wrong for feeling angry," Jess whispered.

"I know," she breathed.

And that was the truth. She did know. But knowing didn't change anything.

"She'd always be such a mess on those first few days. She'd cry and apologize and say how horrible of a mom she was." Sam sighed. "And I just had to pretend—to tell her it was okay. Because if I didn't, if I got upset or angry, it would just make things worse."

The last memories of her mother forced their way into her mind.

She swallowed, using all the strength she had to keep the sickening guilt at bay.

"I picked a fight with her," Sam whispered, her throat suddenly feeling tight and raw.

She swallowed, keeping her eyes glued to Jess' hand in her lap.

"That day—the morning before I went to school. She'd been sober for almost a month. The longest she'd lasted in a while. She wanted to walk me to school."

The back of her eyes began to burn in a way she hadn't felt in years. Or maybe even longer.

"I could tell she was trying to be a good mom. Trying to pretend like walking me to school was normal."

She closed her eyes, seeing it play out in her mind. Seeing her mother's face, and the healthier glow it'd finally begun to regain.

"And I just—broke," she whispered. "I was *so* angry with her. It all felt like a lie. Like I was some toy she wanted to take out and play with whenever she felt like it."

Sam shook her head. No matter how many times she thought about it—turned every thought and reason over in her head—it didn't matter. Because no matter what the reasons were, it all still ended the same.

Good reasons didn't change a bad outcome.

Sam hesitated, her eyes scanning Jess' face, searching for any sign of judgment. Then she pressed on, the words crawling out like they were being dragged against their will.

"Everything I'd held in came out. I said—*horrible* things to her."

Sam's jaw tightened, the next words getting caught somewhere between her throat and her stomach.

Her hands fidgeted at her sides, brushing against the fabric of her jeans like she could scrub the memory away. "I thought she'd yell, or scream, or even cry. But she didn't." Her voice broke, the images flashing behind her eyes with cruel clarity. "She just looked—defeated."

Jess squeezed her hand gently.

Sam's chest rose and fell in a shallow breath, and she cast a reluctant look toward the far side of the grounds.

"When I got home from school that day, she wasn't there." Her voice softened, becoming almost detached as she forced the last words out. "The cops showed up later that night."

She took a deep breath, waiting for the crushing guilt to rush through her like it always did.

"Look at me," Jess said, raising her hand and placing it on Sam's cheek.

Sam looked up and saw a glassy sheen covering Jess' eyes.

"You didn't make that choice for her."

Something in her eyes kept her grounded there. Not in the way it did when she forced herself to focus on something and drown out the thoughts she wanted to avoid.

But something else.

Something in Jess' eyes—in her *everything*—kept her there. Kept her from being overtaken by the memories.

She'd never told anyone about that morning with her mom. Or at least, not the details. Not the parts that threatened to devour her if she let them linger for too long.

Even when she'd talked to Jess about it before, she'd kept those parts to herself. The worst parts.

And now, seeing that look in her eyes, she realized maybe that had been a mistake. Because if there was anyone she should've trusted with those parts of herself—it was the girl she'd loved more than anything.

Sam slowly leaned forward, closing the small gap between them.

She pressed her lips against hers. Not even wanting to kiss her, but instead just to feel her. To know that she was right there with her. That she wasn't walking away.

She pulled her lips away, leaving her head resting against Jess' forehead as she let her eyes close.

Jess' hand ran up the back of her neck, nails scratching lightly against the skin in the way that never failed to soothe her.

Her other hand ran up the side of her jaw, past her temple, her fingers tangling in her hair as she stroked it back.

Sam released a breath, her shoulders relaxing for what felt like the first time since they'd arrived the day before. "I love it when you do that," she whispered, leaning into the touch.

"I know," Jess whispered, tilting her head to the side as she brushed her lips against her temple. "Stay with me tonight."

She kissed her temple, then her cheek, before pulling her head back.

Sam raised her head slowly, blinking away the exhaustion that had begun to build in her eyes.

"My dad won't be there," Jess continued softly. "He's going with Suki to some event for her work. He said they'll be gone late."

"Okay," Sam answered, not even bothering to consider the alternative. It wouldn't be any use, anyway. Even if she knew it might not be a good idea—that they shouldn't be spending so many nights together when they still hadn't talked about what any of it meant—or how it would end, she knew she wouldn't be able to say no.

She wouldn't be able to stay away from her.

Chapter twenty-two

Sam carefully tied the last knot in the ribbon around the vase, tugging on the ends until they were even.

"Perfect," Jess said, placing another picture of Scarlett as a child into the vase.

She glanced around the backyard of Scarlett's parent's house, where different friends and family members gathered around white folding tables, laughing and talking as they each worked on different decorations.

Scarlett had insisted that they have the rehearsal dinner there and they build the centerpieces for the wedding tables themselves. She'd explained when they'd first arrived that night, after leaving the cemetery, that she'd always imagined the night before her wedding. She wanted that one night where their family and friends could get together and build something that would be there for their big day.

"Well," Scarlett said from where she and Terrence sat across from them at the table, "It'll definitely work. But I wouldn't say either of you should leave your jobs to become decorators anytime soon."

Sam snorted a laugh, peering across the table at the nearly perfect vase Scarlett and Terrence had assembled. "Well, maybe if you'd given us some more direction, it would've come out better."

Scarlett grinned, adjusting the already perfectly tied bow they'd put on theirs. "That would defeat the whole purpose. I want it to be whatever you guys want to make. That's what makes it special."

Jess hummed, her brows furrowing as she tried and failed to cut an even edge around the next picture she'd chosen. "Well then, you can't blame us for our decorating skills," she murmured. "Or—*lack* of skills."

"She just picked something she knew she'd be better than us at," Sam said, throwing a challenging smirk across the table. "She's trying to make up for all those nights she lost to us at beer pong in this house."

Jess laughed, leaning her head over to rest on Sam's shoulder for a moment as Scarlett glared across the table at them.

"Whatever," Scarlet muttered. "You guys are both just like—freakishly good at sports."

Jess chuckled, placing the photo carefully inside the vase with the others. "Sam's freakishly good at a lot of things."

The corner of Scarlett's lips quirked upward, her head cocking to the side. "Oh, yeah?"

Jess must've caught the tone in her voice, because her hands froze where they were on the vase. "I mean—with—" she stuttered. Then she stopped, shaking her head as she rolled her eyes. "You know what I mean."

Sam chuckled as she picked up her soda can and tilted it back, finishing the last few drops. "I'm gonna get another drink," she said, pushing her chair back in the grass. "You guys want anything?"

"I'm good," Jess answered. "Thanks, though."

Terrence shook his head, smiling up at her. "Nothing for me."

"I'm ready for another," Scarlett said, standing from her chair.

"I can grab you one—" Sam started, but Scarlett instantly waved her off.

"I'll go with you," she said, walking around the table. "I don't know what I want."

Sam nodded, turning to follow her into the back of the house. They went through the sliding glass door, crossing the living room where a few people sat, talking on the couch.

Sam approached the island, looking over the different beers that had been laid out.

"Wanna do a shot like old times?" Scarlett asked with a mischievous smirk.

Sam laughed, instantly remembering the first time she'd been in that kitchen. "I think I'll save that for the wedding tomorrow."

Scarlett hummed, grabbing two beers instead. "You sound like Terrence."

She held one beer out to her, but when Sam reached for it, she pulled it back slightly out of reach.

Sam arched a brow, taking in the still mischievous look in her eyes. "What?" she asked slowly.

"You know what," Scarlett answered with a small smirk.

Sam cocked her head, waiting for an explanation.

"You and Jess," she said, her voice dropping slightly.

Sam looked away, a soft laugh bubbling out. "She told you?"

"She didn't have to," Scarlett replied, handing her the beer. "I know her—and I know *you*."

Sam hummed, cracking the cap off against the edge of the countertop.

"When?"

Sam took a sip of the beer. "When what?"

Scarlett rolled her eyes. "You're so hard to get information out of. When did you guys—you know?"

Sam looked away, thinking back to the day it had happened. "A few days after the bachelorette weekend."

Scarlett hummed, nodding slowly as she took another drink. "Took longer than I thought it would."

Sam squinted at her. "You expected it to happen?"

"Obviously," Scarlett muttered with an incredulous look. "You know, you guys are both the smartest people I know. And somehow you're also stupid as shit when it comes to each other."

Sam snorted a laugh, taking another sip of her drink. "Thanks."

"Seriously," Scarlett continued, leaning back against the countertop. "I don't know how you guys thought it would go any other way. You're like magnets. If you're near each other, you're definitely not gonna stay apart for long."

Sam bit the inside of her cheek, looking down at the beer as she swirled the bottle. "So how'd you know something happened?"

"You guys look happy," Scarlett said with a shrug. "Don't get me wrong, I've seen her happy without you, too. But—" she paused, pursing her lips. "It's different when it's with you. Makes all the other times seem like nothing."

That feeling wasn't exclusive to Jess. Sam had felt it within herself, too. Ever since she'd been back—since she'd seen Jess again—she'd felt an inner happiness that paled in comparison to anything else.

"Yeah," she breathed. "I know the feeling."

Scarlett tipped her drink back, taking a long swig. "So what happens next?"

Sam shrugged, leaning forward to rest her elbows on the countertop. "I don't know. We haven't talked about it."

"Well, it's perfect timing, right?"

"What do you mean?"

"You're about to sell the company," Scarlett answered, as if it was obvious. "Won't you finally be able to stop moving constantly? You can finally settle down and stay for a while."

Sam glanced down, turning the thought over in her mind. "Yeah. I guess."

Scarlett squinted slightly, giving her a pointed look. "Then what's the problem?"

Sam scratched the back of her neck. "I don't know," she said with a sigh. "What if the timing still isn't right?"

She expected an instant rebuttal from Scarlett about how she was being ridiculous, or why she was overthinking things. But instead, she just watched her intently.

"I mean," Sam continued, straightening back up, "I still don't feel like I'm where I want to be yet in life. I still have so much I need to figure out, and what if that messes something up?" She sighed, shaking her head. "What if I do something wrong and she changes her mind or—"

"So what?" Scarlett cut in. "You'd rather keep doing this thing you guys have been doing for the last eight years? You'd rather never give it a real shot?"

Sam closed her eyes, letting out a breath. "That's better than doing it too soon and messing it all up for good."

"But what does that matter if you never actually end up going for it?"

Sam picked at the edge of the label on the bottle. She knew what Scarlett was thinking. That she was being stupid. And really, she could understand why. But it wasn't that simple. The reasons why they hadn't worked out in the past weren't simple.

"Having the possibility of something working in the future is better than trying and failing and knowing for certain it didn't work out."

Scarlett's eyes softened a touch as she looked at her. "But," she continued, her voice more gentle than before, "what if it *did* work out?"

Sam stared down at the bottle in her hands, letting the question hang silently around them. She thought back to that first night they'd spent together in Scarlett's house.

"For some reason, it felt easier at the very beginning," she whispered. "When she didn't really want me."

Scarlett frowned, a dark look flashing through her eyes. "She always wanted you. She just didn't know how to handle it."

"I know, I know," Sam sighed. "But honestly, back then, I don't think I ever really believed that she would choose me at the end of it all." She paused, thinking back to those days that now felt like another lifetime. "Or at least, I never let myself believe that she would."

Scarlett frowned, stepping forward and squeezing her shoulder gently.

"Even the accident makes me feel guilty," Sam whispered, staring down at her hands. "Like something I did to her." Her jaw tightened involuntarily. "I caused her so much pain, without meaning to. I wouldn't have blamed her for walking away."

She felt Scarlett's eyes on her, her expression looking slightly torn for a moment. Then she sighed. "She would kill me if she knew I was telling you this." Sam watched her intently. "But even if she doesn't know it, she was waiting for you. All that time, all those years, I think she was waiting for you to come back."

A pleasant burn sizzled in her chest at the words, but an equally strong feeling of guilt surrounded it.

"But you know," Scarlett continued, her voice low and careful, "she won't wait forever. Even if she wants to." Scarlett let out a sigh, leaning away. "Eventually, one of you will have to choose. *Really* choose. Because just doing this," she motioned between Sam and the backyard, "it can't last forever."

***

The front door of Mike's house creaked open, and Sam followed Jess inside.

She flicked on the light, and Sam's gaze drifted across the familiar row of framed pictures that lined the walls, landing on one she'd look at every time she'd been in the house. It was Jess as a kid on Mike's shoulders, holding a trophy, her blonde waves pulled back in a messy ponytail.

Jess tossed her keys onto a table by the door, and Sam looked up at her as she gave her a soft smile and nodded toward the staircase.

Sam followed, her boots echoing softly against the wooden steps. The air felt heavier upstairs, the kind of weight that came with memories embedded in the walls. Memories she was a part of.

Jess reached the second floor, then went down the hall, pausing in front of the open bathroom door. "I'm gonna take a quick shower."

Sam leaned against the doorway, arms crossing as she watched Jess disappear into the bathroom. The sound of the faucet twisting on filled the silence, followed by the rush of water. Sam shifted her weight, unsure if she should wait in her bedroom or wander back downstairs.

Jess poked her head out, a small, knowing smile tugging at her lips. She moved closer, her bare feet silent against the hardwood.

"Just gonna stand there?" Jess asked, with a teasing lilt in her voice.

Sam smirked, watching her. "Maybe."

Jess' smile softened. Then she reached one hand out, her fingertips brushing Sam's wrist before trailing up to her shoulder. Sam held her breath, soaking in the touch.

Jess leaned in, her lips finding Sam's.

The kiss wasn't heated or rushed. It was careful—deliberate. Like she had all the time in the world as her hand slid to the back of Sam's neck and pulled her closer.

Then Jess pulled back just enough to whisper, her voice a low murmur that sent chills down her back. "Shower with me?"

Sam swallowed, her gaze meeting Jess' as she nodded.

Jess smiled up at her softly as she tugged at the hem of Sam's shirt, lifting it gently over her head. Sam raised her arms, the fabric sliding away before dropping onto the floor. Her hands skimmed Sam's waist, undoing the button of her jeans with an ease that reminded her how many times she'd done it before.

Jess knelt slightly, guiding the fabric down Sam's legs before standing again.

Sam watched through the clouded steam as Jess quickly discarded her own clothing before stepping into the shower.

When they moved beneath the spray of hot water, Jess turned to face Sam, her hands instantly finding her waist. She drifted closer, letting her fingers slide up Sam's back, pressing their bodies together as the water ran over them.

Sam closed her eyes as Jess threaded her fingers through her wet hair, massaging her scalp in a slow, careful motion. Sam exhaled, curling her head down into her neck. And with every stroke of Jess' hands, long held stress and tension rinsed away.

Jess leaned forward, lips brushing against Sam's jaw and lingering there before moving to the hollow beneath her ear.

Neither of them spoke at first. There was no need to.

But eventually, Jess broke the silence.

"Have you thought about it?" she asked softly, her hands resting lightly on Sam's back.

Sam opened her eyes, meeting Jess' gaze. "About what?"

Jess hesitated, her thumb brushing against Sam's collarbone. "What we're doing. What it means."

Sam swallowed, looking away. At the beginning, that was all she could think about. The fear that they were making an irreparable mistake. That they were ruining the one shot they had to finally be back in each other's lives. Even if it was just as friends.

But now, talking about it was the last thing she wanted. There were too many things between them left unsaid. She didn't even know where to begin.

But more than that, she didn't know how it would end.

"I thought you didn't want to talk about it," Sam said softly.

Jess looked down, leaning her head into Sam's bare chest. "I didn't," she whispered. "But maybe we should now."

Sam ran a hand up her back, resting it on the base of her neck as she tried to hold on to the calm she'd felt just moments before. "Why now?"

Jess shifted slightly, her arms tightening around Sam's waist. "Because I don't want to hold back anymore," she admitted. "I don't want to stop myself from kissing you or touching your hand just because there are other people around. I don't want to hide this just because I'm trying to make it not mean anything."

A sharp ache flickered through Sam's chest, her emotions twisting and coiling in ways she couldn't untangle.

"I'm not saying I want to talk about the future or something," Jess continued, her voice steady. "I just want to feel this—feel us—without worrying about if I'm doing too much. Or if it's going too far."

Sam nodded, understanding the feeling all too well. It was exactly how she'd felt when they'd first met. Every action or reaction had to be carefully measured. And it almost tore her apart.

"Yeah," Sam whispered. "I get it."

"I want to enjoy this time together," Jess said, pulling her head back to look up at her. "The wedding tomorrow, our friends, and everything that comes with it. I don't want to spend the whole time overthinking it anymore."

Sam searched her face, finding nothing but sincerity in Jess' eyes. She reached up, her fingers brushing Jess' cheek. "Okay," she whispered.

Because even if that made everything harder—if it crossed a line they couldn't return from—if that's what Jess needed, she'd do it without question.

Chapter twenty-three

Sam stared down at her cell phone where it sat on the small wooden table of the hotel room, adjusting beneath the smooth material of the button down and blazer she'd chosen to wear to the wedding that evening.

The screen ticked off the seconds of the conference call.

"I'm sorry," she murmured, clearing her throat as she glanced back at her notepad. "Can you repeat that last number?"

Howard recited each crucial detail of the formal offer he'd just given.

Sam blinked, staring down at the paper before adding one more zero at the end of the buyout price he'd just officially given them for the company.

"Thank you," she muttered, working to maintain her professional composure.

"Now," Howard said, his voice booming through the small phone speaker, "there is one other matter we need to discuss."

Sam glanced back at the phone screen, forcing herself to focus on anything other than the number she'd just written.

"During the due diligence process, when we were looking into the employee structure of your company, we noticed a recent trend in the employment."

Sam swallowed, a twinge of uneasiness bubbling in her stomach.

"You seem to have an uptick in employee turnover as of late."

She loosed a breath as he paused. "Yes," she said, working to keep her voice even. "There's been some—discontent—around the prospect of the company being acquired."

"Right," Howard said nonchalantly. "That's the way it usually goes with these things."

Sam nodded slowly, eyes glued to the phone.

"But of course," he continued, "that poses some additional risk for us, as I'm sure you understand. Our main priority is to have a smooth transition. And if some key members of your team decide to leave after the buyout goes through, then that could put us in a tough situation."

Sam nodded again. "Right. Well, we—"

"So to mitigate that risk," Howard cut in, "we'd want you and Caleb both to come to London. And to be here at the headquarters to work with us throughout the transition period."

Sam stared down at the phone. She opened her mouth to speak, but the words failed as her brain struggled to understand.

"The—transition period," she repeated slowly. "How long is that, typically?"

"I'd expect a year at least," he answered. "Perhaps two."

Something deep in her chest constricted at the words.

"Of course," he continued, "we'll include a salary that I think you'll both find more than fair."

No matter how hard she tried, she couldn't find the words to respond.

Any other time, she wouldn't have even thought twice about it. The 'yes' would've sprung from her in an instant. But for some reason, this time, it refused to come out.

Howard cleared his throat, for the first time sounding as if he detected a problem in the conversation. "That is a non-negotiable part of the deal," he added.

Sam stared at the phone, her brain firing off a thousand different thoughts at once. But none of them gave her a clear answer.

"Of course," Caleb cut in abruptly. She'd almost entirely forgotten that he was also on the call. "That won't be a problem at all, right Sam?" He let out a chuckle that sounded all too forced. "The travel is nothing new to us."

She swallowed against her suddenly dry throat.

"Great," Howard answered, although she could detect a certain hesitance in his voice. "Well, we're eager to get things in motion, as I'm sure you are. Everything has already been cleared on our end, so I can have one of our lawyers in Seattle meet with you. I'll speak with them and see when they can make it there."

"That's perfect," Caleb replied, his words tumbling out in clear elation. "Just let us know when. We'll be here and have everything ready to go."

Sam cleared her throat, finally regaining enough sense to speak. "Yes, that sounds good."

"Wonderful," Howard said with a tone of finality. "I'll send you the scheduling details, and then we'll connect again after everything has been signed."

"Great," Caleb said quickly. "Thank you. We look forward to hearing from you."

Howard said something in response before the line went out, but Sam couldn't comprehend it. Her brain was still stuck on what he'd said—the final term of the deal she'd worked toward relentlessly for the last year.

A few beats of silence passed, and she glanced down, seeing Caleb still on the call.

"Sam?" he asked. "You there?"

"Yeah," she muttered.

He burst into an explosion of ecstatic laughter. "Oh my god, I can't believe it!" He yelled something on the other end that came through as a muffled crackle of noise. "We did it!"

A timid smile ghosted across her lips. "Yeah. We did."

He continued hollering and laughing on the other end for a few moments before dying down. "Holy shit," he muttered with a deep breath. "It's finally done."

"Yeah," she whispered.

It was done.

A door in her life finally coming to a close, once and for all.

***

Sam undid her seatbelt as the car rolled to a stop at the curb of the wedding venue, her chest tightening with a mix of nerves and anticipation.

The building loomed ahead, a rustic yet elegant estate wrapped in climbing ivy, with tall arched windows that glowed in the dim evening light.

She stepped out of the car, the cool evening air brushing against her face as she adjusted her blazer.

The path leading up to the entrance was lined with delicate flower arrangements in glass vases perched atop wrought iron stands. Twinkling string lights arched above, casting soft, golden hues on the cobblestones below. She slowed her pace, trying to take it all in, even as her mind tugged at her—pulling her back to what she knew she needed to do.

Jess had been there since the early morning, tucked away with Scarlett in the bridal suite, doing all the traditional pre-wedding things Sam couldn't even begin to imagine.

And now, she was glad for it.

She needed to tell Jess. She needed to tell her about the offer—and the one specific detail that came with it.

But it wasn't the right time. It needed to wait until after the wedding.

And selfishly, maybe she wanted to wait as long as possible. Because the second she told her, everything would change. They'd no longer be able to avoid the hard conversations. It would all come to a head.

It would all come to—an end.

She reached the large wooden doors, surrounded by huge windows on all sides, looking into the main waiting area and dining hall.

The door opened with a creak, and the faint scent of roses and eucalyptus flowed out, mingling with the distant hum of music.

A server passed by, balancing a tray of champagne flutes, the delicate clinking of glass barely audible over the soft buzz of voices. Sam followed the sound of laughter and conversation, crossing through an archway into a wide cocktail room.

Small, round tables draped in white linen filled the space, while clusters of people leaned against the bar or gathered near the sprawling windows that overlooked the estate's gardens.

She scanned the room, instantly finding a few familiar faces.

The hum of conversation swirled around her, an indistinct buzz of laughter and clinking glasses that only amplified the restlessness in her chest. Her eyes skimmed over clusters of people, scanning each face with a rising urgency. She didn't even realize her fingers had started fidgeting with the edge of her blazer until she forced them still.

And then she saw her.

Jess stepped out from the far side of the room, moving toward one of the cocktail tables to set down an empty glass.

For a moment, all the surrounding noise seemed to fall away.

The soft glow of the chandelier lights caught the subtle shimmer of her dress as she tucked a strand of blonde hair behind her ear. She paused, straightening, and glanced across the room.

Then their eyes met.

The grin that broke across Jess' face was nothing short of magnetic, and Sam felt her feet move without thought.

Whatever tension had been simmering beneath her skin since she'd arrived immediately melted away.

"Hey," Jess said with a warm smile as she approached, her lightly curled blonde hair flowing down the front of her tight, dark blue dress.

"Hey," Sam replied as Jess slipped her arms around her waist.

"Sorry," Jess said softly, pulling back but keeping her hands resting on her hips. "I would've found you sooner, but it took longer than I thought it would to get ready."

"All good," Sam said, smiling back at her as her eyes instinctively trailed down, admiring the beautiful woman before her. She caught herself a split second later, pulling her eyes back up as she cleared her throat.

And she knew by the amused look in Jess' eyes, she'd been caught.

Jess leaned in closer as she whispered, "Dress looks better than you remembered?"

Sam released a soft laugh, bowing her head slightly as a twinge of heat spread into her cheeks. "Sorry."

Jess' smirk instantly grew into a wider grin. "Don't be," she said in a low, coy whisper. "That's the reaction I was hoping for."

Sam smiled back at her as a pleasant warmth bloomed in her chest.

Then, one thought blew past it, obliterating it entirely.

London.

The smile on her lips fell, even as she tried to force it to stay.

Guilt replaced every other feeling, sinking into her gut.

She had to tell her. And it had to be as soon as possible. Because no matter how badly she wanted to savor one last night together, she couldn't do it with Jess not knowing the truth.

She cleared her throat, frowning slightly as she lifted a hand to scratch the back of her neck.

Jess' head tilted to the side as she watched her, and Sam knew right then that she could see something was wrong.

"Okay everyone," an older woman called from the end of the room as soft music began to play. "Its time to move into the ceremony hall."

Jess turned back to her, the previous look entirely gone and replaced with that easy smile once again. "I'll come find you after," she said, squeezing her hip lightly.

Sam nodded, forcing a smile. "Give Scar a hug for me."

Jess leaned forward, pressing one soft kiss to her cheek before retreating toward the opposite side of the room.

Sam watched her walk away, savoring every bit of that interaction as if it was the last they'd ever have. Because maybe it would be. Or at least, maybe it would be the last time Jess looked at her that way.

***

Sam took a sip of her drink as she set her fork down beside the untouched plate of food in front of her.

She leaned her elbows against the table, half-listening to the conversations taking place at their circular table.

Then the music slowly faded out, replaced with the high squeal of a microphone.

"While you all finish eating, we're going to start the speeches," the DJ announced from a small table behind the dance floor. "First up," he continued, making his way to one of the small tables near Scarlett and Terrence, "we'll hear from the Maid of Honor."

Sam instantly straightened in her seat, craning her neck to see where Jess stood from the table, thanking him as she took the microphone from his hand.

"Hi everyone," Jess said softly, lifting the microphone to her lips. "For those of you that I haven't gotten to meet yet, I'm Jess."

Murmurs of 'hi Jess' floated through the crowd.

She smiled, looking down at the paper in her free hand.

Then she cleared her throat, her voice steady as she began. "Scarlett and I have known each other for as long as I can remember. It feels like every major moment in my life has had her in it." She glanced down, a fond smile tugging at her lips. "We've played on the same team, won championships together—while Scarlett probably earned the record for most yellow cards in a single season." The crowd chuckled, and Scarlett nodded with a wide, proud grin from her seat beside Terrence, one hand wrapped tightly around his.

The corner of Sam's lip quirked up as she recalled the endless days she sat in those bleachers watching the games of their last season.

"We've fought together, celebrated together. We've seen each other at our best—and our worst. And somehow, even at my worst, Scarlett was always there, reminding me of who I was." Jess' voice wavered for just a second, and Sam felt the room grow quieter, more focused.

Scarlett smiled up at Jess, her eyes glassy with tears. Sam watched the way Jess' expression softened as their eyes met, a silent conversation passing between them that no one else would ever understand.

Jess cleared her throat again. "What I admire most about Scarlett—and I've always admired this—is her ability to love fearlessly. She never holds back. When she chooses someone, she chooses them with her whole heart. She dives in, no matter how uncertain the waters might be." Jess smiled, her eyes flickering toward Terrence, whose grin widened as he looked at his wife.

"Terrence," Jess continued, turning to him with a smile. "You're one of the lucky ones. You've earned her love, her trust, her devotion—and I know you'll never take that for granted." Her voice faltered, just barely.

"There's a kind of love," Jess said softly, her voice lowering, "that endures everything. Distance, time, doubt. It just *stays* through it all."

Jess' gaze drifted over the crowd, and for a brief second, their eyes met. Sam's heart lurched, and in that instant, it felt like Jess was speaking directly to her.

"That's the love Scarlett and Terrence have. They're proof that when two people are meant to be together, nothing can come between them."

A dull ache entered Sam's chest. She was talking about Scarlett. But there was something else in her tone. She spoke about the one thing neither of them had ever seemed to be willing to do at the same time. When one of them was ready, the other wasn't.

Every word Jess spoke felt like a reminder—of what they'd never had the courage to say, of the moments they'd both let slip away.

"There's a statistic that says the one person you choose to spend your life with will determine up to eighty percent of the happiness you feel in your lifetime." She tilted her head, smiling back at Scarlett and Terrence. "And if that's true, then I think you both are about to live extraordinarily happy lives." She reached down, taking the champagne glass from the table and holding it in the air. "Here's to you. May we all be lucky enough to hold on to our one person in this life."

***

The reception was winding down, and with it, the dance floor had thinned, leaving only a few couples swaying to the soft, lilting melody that poured from the speakers.

Sam stood at the edge of the floor, watching Jess laugh at something an older relative had said. Then she excused herself, making her way across the room toward her.

Sam watched every movement. She watched Jess carry the same effortless grace she always did, but this time, it seemed amplified.

Like the world was giving her one final look at what she was about to lose.

Jess' gaze met hers, and she gave her a warm smile as she held one hand out toward her. Sam hesitated for only a second before taking it.

She led her onto the dance floor, slipping her arms up around Sam's neck as the music shifted to a slower song. Sam's hands found Jess's waist, settling lightly as they began to sway.

For a while, they didn't speak. But Sam could feel it building inside her, that gnawing truth she'd been carrying all day. Like the moment she let her guard down, it would come spilling out, changing everything. And yet, she couldn't bring herself to say it aloud, not yet. Not with Jess looking at her like that, with warmth and tenderness so palpable it felt like a physical weight pressing against her.

"You know," Jess said softly, "I don't know if I've ever felt this lucky. Being here, seeing Scarlett so happy, and—" Her fingers grazed lightly along the back of Sam's neck. "Having you here with me."

Sam's throat tightened. She managed a faint smile, but it felt fragile, like it might shatter under the weight of Jess' words. Her grip on Jess's waist faltered slightly, and she forced herself to steady it.

Jess leaned closer, her forehead brushing lightly against Sam's. "Everything feels better when I know you're there."

Sam's chest felt like it was caving in. The lump in her throat grew unbearable, and she fought to keep her expression neutral. It was both everything she wanted to hear, and everything she didn't.

The music faded into a quiet instrumental bridge, and Sam swallowed hard. "I need to talk to you about something."

Jess' brow furrowed slightly, but her smile didn't fade. "Yeah?"

Before Sam could say another word, a vibration buzzed against her hip.

Then another. And another.

She hesitated, releasing one hand to glance at her phone. Caleb's name flashed on the screen, followed by a string of frantic texts.

Her heart sank as she glanced back at Jess, whose expression had shifted to one of concern. "I'm sorry," Sam said, stepping back reluctantly. "I just—I need one minute to handle this. Then I'll be right back. I promise."

Jess gave her a smile that was so understanding it almost pained her to see. "It's okay. I want to check on Scarlett, anyway. Make sure she doesn't need anything."

Sam nodded, guilt clawing at her chest as she slipped away toward the quiet edge of the room. Jess gave her one last glance over her shoulder before making her way through the crowd of people.

Sam took one deep breath, then forced herself to turn away and walk back out to the entry area.

A few people lingered, laughing as they said their goodbyes and flowed out through the front doors into the darkened night.

Sam pulled her phone out, scrolling through the string of texts from Caleb. She began typing out a quick message when the main door creaked open once again.

She glanced up, expecting to see more wedding guests filtering in and out.

But instead, a much more familiar face looked back.

Liz stood there in an outfit similar to her own, except the blazer she wore was a creamy white.

"Oh," Liz said, surprise adorning her features.

Sam blinked, staring at her as her mind went completely blank.

A beat of uneasy silence passed between them as Liz stepped fully through the doorway, looking just as uncomfortable as Sam felt.

"Uh—what.." Sam trailed off, not entirely sure that she should be the one questioning why she was there.

Liz smiled in a painfully awkward way that told her that question would've been expected. "Um," she started, glancing cautiously around the empty area. "Is Jess here?"

Sam stared at her, dumbfounded. "Yeah," she said slowly, drawing the word out into a question.

Liz nodded as she glanced down at the ground, her throat bobbing as she swallowed.

"She's with Scarlett," Sam continued, not caring to dull the edge in her words.

Liz nodded, sucking in a deep breath. "Right. Yeah, of course."

Sam watched her closely, examining the way she uncharacteristically fiddled with her hands.

"Did she ask you to come, or.." Sam left the rest of the question hanging in the air, already halfway knowing the answer. Because she knew that if she did, Jess would've told her.

Liz frowned, her eyes lingering on the floor for an extra second before looking back up at her. "No," she said quietly.

Sam cocked her head, waiting for an explanation.

Liz released a deep breath. "She—she hasn't called me back. And I—I just—I need to talk to her. So we can figure things out. We need to—"

"And you thought this was the best time to do that?" Sam cut in, her jaw clenching involuntarily.

Liz's eyes tightened a fraction, as if ready to shoot back with some biting words of her own.

But then she looked away. And that challenging look in her eyes morphed into one that resembled embarrassment—or maybe even shame.

A look she'd never seen on her before.

And selfishly, that gave her a small hint of satisfaction.

"I know," Liz whispered, squeezing her eyes shut for a moment. "I know it's stupid. I just—" she paused, mouth open as she shook her head, then tilted it back as if trying to keep tears from falling. "I messed up."

When she lowered her head again, the tears Sam had suspected were clear in her eyes.

"I didn't think—" she stopped, shaking her head again as she blew out a frustrated breath. "We've been off and on again so many times before, I just assumed this time wouldn't be any different. I thought we'd just, I don't know, take time apart for a few weeks and then get back together, just like before."

"So you thought it would be a better idea to show up unannounced at her best friend's wedding?" Sam asked, utterly failing to keep the cutting tone out of her words.

Liz shot her a dangerous glare. "You wouldn't get it," she huffed. "You're—*you*."

The corners of Sam's eyes tightened, her head tilting slightly. "What does that mean?"

Liz let barked out a laugh that seemed to hold more irritation than humor. "You're *Sam Hayes*," she said, waving a hand in the air as she looked her up and down. "Everyone's favorite. The one who never screws up." She shook her head, letting out a disgusted puff of air.

Sam pulled her head back a fraction.

"My friends always loved you. My parents loved you. And now even my damn girlfriend—" she paused, shaking her head as she scoffed, rolling her eyes. "You get everything handed to you. While I work my ass off, and still I have to show up here just to get—" she stopped again, clamping her mouth shut as her jaw flickered—anger rolling off of her in waves.

There were so many things she could've said. So many things she *wanted* to say. So many pent up words of anger.

But they didn't matter. They could've seen and experienced the exact same things, and still, they would've looked at it differently.

Like two people staring at a freshly painted wall, one seeing red, and the other seeing blue.

Sam let her eyes fall to the ground as she let out a deep breath. One that felt like it'd been held in since the first moment they'd seen each other again.

"I guess we both wanted things the other one had," she said quietly.

Liz's gaze softened slightly, as if she'd been expecting a different response. She looked away, clenching her jaw. "Yeah," she said, the word clipped. "I guess so."

Then Liz stopped, her eyes suddenly widening as they flicked past Sam to somewhere behind her.

Sam turned, following her gaze to where Jess stood in the doorway.

Chapter twenty-four

Jess stood there, frozen, her face a mix of surprise and confusion. "Liz," she said slowly. "What are you.."

Liz took one tentative step toward her. "We need to talk," she said in a shaky, pleading voice. "Please."

Sam watched Jess' expression carefully as the confusion grew. But she just stared silently back at her.

Liz threw a nervous glance at Sam, as if silently begging for her to leave them to talk in private.

Sam was about to look at Jess, to see what she wanted, if she wanted her to leave them, but before she could, her phone began buzzing in her pocket.

She looked down with a frown, seeing Caleb's name on the screen.

"I have to take this," she said, casting a quick glance at Jess, who looked back at her with a blank, still confused stare. "I'll be right back."

She strode to the front doors, pushing them open and stepping out into the chilly evening air.

Then she swiped the phone open, holding it to her ear. "Now's not a good time—"

"Did you see Howard's email?" he cut in immediately.

She stopped mid-step. "No. I'm not exactly trying to work during the wedding," she growled, unable to contain the annoyance. She turned, glancing back through the window into the entry area where Jess and Liz still stood, now closer together. "Why?"

"He sent the details on when their lawyer will be here with the paperwork," he said quickly. "It's tomorrow morning."

"What?" Sam asked, releasing a frustrated breath. "I can't—"

"I know, I know," he interjected. "But is there any way you can come back late tonight to be here in the morning?"

She shook her head in frustration.

This was the outcome she'd been catapulting toward for what seemed like ages. And now that it was finally happening, it suddenly felt like it was all moving too fast. Like she barely had time to think through one step before the next had already come and gone.

"No."

Caleb was quiet for a moment, probably too stunned by the answer she'd never really given him before.

"No?" he asked, confusion thick in his voice. "But, what about—"

"Caleb," she gritted through clenched teeth. "I don't care what you have to tell him. But I'm not leaving my friend's wedding early just because he wants it to happen tomorrow."

He fell quiet again, but she didn't care. She didn't care what he was thinking. This was one time she wouldn't give in to the urgent demands and needs of anyone else.

Finally, he cleared his throat on the other end. "Okay," he murmured, his voice losing its urgency. "I'll—tell him we need to reschedule for later this week or something."

"Kay," Sam mumbled, only half paying attention as she turned back, peering through the window once more. She scanned the room until she found Jess and Liz again, now in the far corner, slightly more hidden.

"Sorry," Caleb murmured. "I just thought you'd want it to happen as quick as possible."

She squinted, eyes dropping to where Liz's hand now held Jess' in her own.

"Its fine," she said into the phone. And now, seeing how close Jess and Liz stood, their hands locked together, she was glad she'd had an excuse to walk away.

"I'll text you after I know the new day and time."

Sam listened as he mumbled something else, perhaps some form of a goodbye, but she was too distracted to listen.

She stood there with the phone still pressed tightly to her ear for a few moments before she realized the call had already ended.

And even then, she left it there, still watching Jess and Liz through the window.

Then Liz began to lean forward.

Sam's heart lurched into her chest as she watched Liz slowly bend forward, placing a kiss on Jess' cheek. A kiss she didn't pull away from.

And that was it. She couldn't watch anymore.

She turned, blinking the image out of her mind as she made her way to a small wooden bench a few yards from the entrance.

She tucked the phone into her pocket as she sat down, her mind reeling one moment, then going utterly blank the next.

She should've been thinking about the meeting she'd just turned down. Or the agreement they'd sent that she still needed to look over.

But all she could think of in that moment was what might have been happening inside.

And then another thought entered her mind.

London.

She had no right to be angry. She had no right to have any opinion on what Jess did—or what she chose.

She was going to leave. Again.

Maybe it would be better this way. Because Jess deserved better. She deserved someone who would stay.

And maybe—eventually—Liz would be that person. No matter how much Sam hated that thought, if that's what was best for Jess, she would choose it in a heartbeat.

The door of the entrance pulled open.

Sam's head whipped to the side, seeing Liz step out and trudge down the short path to the parking lot without so much as casting one glance in her direction.

She watched her the entire way until she was out of view.

Then the door opened again. And this time, it was Jess who walked out.

Sam watched as she looked around outside, then stopped once her eyes fell on the bench where Sam still sat.

She frowned, but looked relieved as she walked toward her before wordlessly dropping onto the bench. She stared out blankly into the parking lot, looking more worn and exhausted than she'd seen her in weeks.

Sam watched her intently, waiting. But as the seconds ticked on, she realized she wasn't going to get the explanation she was looking for.

"So," Sam said quietly, "you guys.." She trailed off, leaving the question hanging in the air.

Jess released a deep breath. "She wants to work things out—get back together." Her eyes flicked down to her lap as she bit her lip. "She said things would be different now. That she'd be working less and would have more time to focus on our relationship."

Sam's jaw tightened as the image of Liz kissing her cheek flashed through her mind.

"You deserve that," Sam said quietly, hating each word as it came out. "You deserve someone who will give you that. And I—" she looked away, swallowing down the reluctance in her throat. "I understand."

Jess turned to her then, her eyes tightening a fraction. "What do you mean?"

Sam loosed a breath, running a hand over the back of her neck. "I mean—you don't have to justify it to me. If that's—if that's what you're going to do."

In an instant, the confused look in Jess' eyes turned to something resembling anger. "Is that really what you would say if I ended up with someone else?"

Sam watched her carefully, her mind searching for where she'd apparently gone wrong in her previous words. "What do you want me to say?"

Jess scoffed, shaking her head as the anger built within her eyes. "I guess that's my answer."

She stood suddenly, as if about to walk away. Then she stopped, whirling back around.

"And I guess that's the difference between us, Sam," she said, spitting each word out. "Because I'll tell you right now, if I saw you with someone else today, I sure as hell wouldn't just let you go." The muscle in her jaw twitched, her eyes flaring with anger. "I would fight for you with everything I have."

Sam shook her head slightly, confusion swirling in her mind. "You want me to tell you what to do?" she asked, standing as she lifted a palm in the air. "You want me to tell you not to get back together with her?"

"I want you to stop pretending like it doesn't matter to you!" Jess shot back.

Sam stared at her, her mind twisting with every word she wanted to say. With everything she felt. But one thought overtook them all.

She was leaving. Again.

So none of that mattered. *Again.*

She swallowed the words down, looking away as the guilt crept back into her chest.

They stood there for a moment in silence before Jess finally shook her head. "In high school," she said quietly, her voice frail as if she was holding back tears, "you needed time. I could see it in you that you weren't ready. And I thought it was because of me." Her voice cracked as a tear fell down her face that she quickly wiped away. "I thought it was because of what I'd done, and how long it'd taken me to come to terms with who I really was. What I wanted." She paused, shaking her head. "But now I know it wasn't that. It wasn't my fault. You would've left regardless of what I did. Because that's what you do."

Sam's head yanked back, her eyes narrowing. Something in the words broke a piece within her. Something that felt like it'd been built up for an eternity.

And instantly, that guilt she'd felt before was entirely replaced with a burning rage.

"You think what happened between us in high school was my fault?" she asked, her voice falling to a deathly quiet.

Jess' eyes flicked to hers, a new cautious intensity within them.

"You have no idea how that felt," Sam seethed as every long buried wound resurfaced. "You have no idea how it felt to fall so helplessly in love with you. All while you changed your mind every single day about wanting me back."

A pained look flashed across Jess' face.

But Sam couldn't stop. Everything she'd forced away years before came flooding to the surface.

"You have no fucking idea how much it hurt to have the girl you loved more than anything treat you like the love of her life one day, and absolutely nothing the next."

Jess' lips parted as her eyes filled with tears. "You know that's not how it was," she whispered, her lip trembling. "You know I never meant to make you feel like that."

"I don't care if that's how you *meant* for it to feel," Sam spat, ignoring the urge to hold back the words. Ignoring everything in her that screamed to stop. That screamed to do whatever it took—say whatever needed to be said—just to make Jess stop hurting.

"That's how it was, Jess!" she continued, pain rushing through her bones. Pain that had been long suppressed, but never once forgotten.

"No matter how much I understand it. No matter how much I understand how hard it was for you." She shook her head. "It doesn't change how hard it was for me, too. It doesn't take away the pain of having my heart ripped back and forth for months while you figured it out."

Jess looked at her with more defeat in her eyes than she'd ever seen before. Guilt seeped through them.

"You have no idea how it feels to not be wanted by the one person you want more than anything."

A tear rolled down Jess' cheek, but this time, she didn't bother wiping it away. "I want every part of you," she said as she stepped forward. "I did then, and I do now!" Jess shook her head, her eyes filled with an almost desperate looking frustration. "God, I want you to give me your last fucking name, Sam!"

Sam's body froze, and with it, so did the anger that coursed through her.

She stared at Jess, who seemed to be just as shocked by the words as she was.

Jess blinked, her throat bobbing as she swallowed and glanced down at the ground between them. She shook her head slightly, her voice lowering. "That's how much I want you," she whispered, shutting her eyes as she released a sharp breath. "I don't just want you when we're in the same city. I want you every month. Every week."

She shook her head, as if every word she'd spoken had drained the remaining fight within her.

"Every day," she whispered.

Sam couldn't think. She couldn't move. It was as if she'd been split in half. And part of her was begging to stay—to take Jess in her arms and never, ever let go.

But the other half screamed against it. Screamed like it never had before.

Jess' eyes finally found hers once again. A blue eyed warning sign. "And I've forced myself to swallow all of that down for the last four years."

There were so many words she could have said. So many things she wanted to say. But none of them would take away what had already been set in motion.

"It doesn't matter anymore," Sam whispered, the words scraping out of her throat.

Jess' eyes tightened slightly, caution flickering through her features.

"We got the official offer today," Sam said, her voice so weak she wondered if the words had even made it past her lips. "I'm moving to London."

Jess stared back, her face evening out into a blank, confused look. And with every second that passed, Sam could see her slowly begin to understand.

The rest of the tears that had built in Jess' eyes spilled over, leaving sparkling streaks down her face.

Then she tipped her head back slightly, letting out an almost pained scoff. "Of course you are."

Sam took a step toward her, although she didn't know why. She didn't know what to do—what to say. There wasn't anything else.

It was utterly and entirely empty. *She* was empty.

And it was only then that she truly realized how much of their past she'd been holding onto.

How much hurt and anger had lingered for so long, exiled to the deepest parts of her.

"Then I guess it also doesn't matter that I would've never said yes to getting back together with Liz," Jess whispered, her eyes a broken mixture of anger and despair.

If she'd heard those words a few minutes before, she might've felt relief. But now, she only felt a deep swelling guilt.

She looked away, an unfamiliar feeling burning in the back of her eyes.

Jess turned, taking a step back before stopping. She opened her mouth, then paused, as if fighting with herself.

"We both know that for all those years, I would've done anything to be together," she said with a calm that reminded Sam of the ocean after a bad storm had finally passed. "Ten miles, or ten thousand miles, I would've been yours." Jess swallowed, wiping the tears from her cheeks. "It was you who walked away. It was you every single time." Her jaw flickered in the dim light as she released a breath. "You always made sure you stayed just out of reach."

Jess looked at her then, her eyes already distant and guarded behind the impenetrable wall that had risen between them. "I don't know why I thought that would ever change."

Then she turned, walking away.

Sam watched every step, not daring to follow.

Because there was nothing else left.

Everything had finally been laid out for both of them to see. Feelings she didn't even know still existed within her.

And now, there was just—nothing.

She stumbled back a step, dropping onto the bench.

She waited for the thoughts to come racing through—to drown her beneath the waves of guilt from being the cause of Jess' pain.

But—they didn't.

Nothing came.

And maybe that's what she had really needed. Because even if those words hurt to say, it was the

433

truth. No matter how much it hurt both of them, maybe all that time, they'd been waiting to come out.

She wasn't sure how long she sat there, mind blank, as she stared out into the parking lot.

But eventually, the door opened again.

She looked up and saw Scarlett peering back.

Sam blinked, instantly forcing a painful smile on her lips. "Hey," she said, clearing her throat as she tried to hide the anguish in her voice. Because no matter what, she couldn't let any of what happened take away from Scarlett's happiness. "What're you doing out here?"

Scarlett gave her a grim look as she walked toward her. She sat down beside her on the bench, and Sam knew then that she'd failed.

"So," she said in a low, calm voice, "London?"

Sam sighed, leaning forward to rest her elbows against her thighs. She ran both hands over her face, pressing her palms into her tired eyes.

"Yeah," she breathed. And she didn't know why, but she needed Scarlett to understand. "I didn't know," she whispered, her voice shaking slightly. "I just found out this morning."

"If I—" Sam continued, her voice cracking. "If I had known, I never would've—"

And that's when she broke.

Everything she'd held back, everything she'd held together as she'd spoken with Jess, came rushing to the surface.

The burning in her eyes became unbearable, and she blinked away the foggy wetness that came with it.

She sucked in a sharp breath, her chest trembling as the pain radiated within her. "I'm so sorry," she whispered. "I didn't mean for any of this to happen tonight."

"I know," Scarlett sighed, her voice tender and soothing. "I know. It's okay."

Scarlett's hand ran up and down her back in a soothing motion as Sam failed to keep the tears from falling.

She took a shaky breath, wiping a palm against her cheeks.

"Do you want to go?" Scarlett asked quietly.

"It's part of the deal," Sam rasped, straightening up as she leaned back.

"Yeah. But do you *want* to go?"

Sam shook her head in frustration. "It doesn't matter what I want. That's how it has to go. I can't give this up. This is what I've been working for—this is what I've given *everything* for."

Scarlett took a slow breath, her eyes heavy with understanding. "You gave everything to build something incredible. But that doesn't mean you have to lose yourself in the process."

Sam clenched her jaw, irritation swirling in her gut. She wasn't in the mood for platitudes, not now. Not after everything with Jess, not with the weight of London hanging over her like a storm she couldn't outrun.

Scarlett's hand remained on her shoulder. "You keep talking like this is all there is," she said softly. "Like this deal, this move—it's the only thing that matters. But I know you, Sam. You're more than this company."

Sam stared ahead, her chest tightening. It all felt like a lie—like everything she'd been working for, everything she'd sacrificed, had led her to this moment where suddenly nothing fit anymore.

"I've already made my decision," Sam muttered, her voice flat.

Scarlett sighed beside her, but didn't pull away. "I get it. But are you doing it because you *want* to? Or because you're scared of—"

"I'm not scared," she snapped, her voice sharp.

But even as the words left her mouth, something bitter settled in her throat. She didn't want to hear it. Didn't want anyone picking apart her choices, especially when it suddenly felt like she barely understood them herself.

London was clean. It was clear-cut. It had no strings attached, no history, no—anything.

Scarlett watched her for a long moment, the silence almost unbearable. "You're really going to walk away from this again?"

Sam's heart clenched, the image of Jess standing there, tears in her eyes, flashing through her mind. She'd been ready to say something—*anything*—to stop her from walking away. But then what? They'd been there before. They'd stood at the edge of the same cliff, and every time, it ended the same way.

One of them always jumped. And the other always stayed.

Maybe it was because of Jess. Or maybe it was because of her.

Maybe Jess had walked away from her so many times when they'd first met that she couldn't even tell whose fault it was anymore.

"It's better this way," Sam whispered, barely able to say the words aloud.

Scarlett shook her head slowly, disappointment etched into her features. "You really believe that?"

Sam didn't answer. She couldn't.

The truth was, nothing about it felt right.

The gap between them had grown too wide, and this deal was the only thing she could control.

Scarlett let out a long, slow breath. "You earned this. You deserve everything you've accomplished," she said, her voice calm but firm. "But don't convince yourself into thinking you *need* this. It won't change anything."

Sam bit the inside of her cheek, trying to keep her emotions from rising again. "It's not about changing anything," she said, her voice cold. "It's about moving forward."

Scarlett's eyes darkened with something Sam didn't want to face—pity, maybe. Or sadness. "If that's what you think you need," she said quietly.

Scarlett's hand slipped away from her shoulder, the weight of her absence settling in as she made her way back into the wedding venue.

And as she sat there, the cold night air biting into her cheeks, she felt it sink deeper—that familiar isolation.

The only constant she had left.

Chapter twenty-five

The streets outside the coffee shop bustled with late-morning energy, a mix of business professionals and students weaving their way through the sidewalks.

Two painstaking weeks had crawled by since the wedding, each day stretching endlessly.

Luckily, work had been her saving grace—a relentless, all-consuming distraction she clung to like a lifeline.

After Caleb had cancelled the meeting, Howard had rescheduled for a couple weeks later. And they'd spent every waking moment of that time poring over details. But finally, that morning, she couldn't take it anymore. She needed a break. Just a few minutes to clear her head before diving right back in.

Sam tucked her hands into the pockets of her hoodie, the crisp air nipping at her face as she turned the last corner to the nearby coffee shop.

And right when she did, she froze, her lips parting in surprise.

Jess was walking toward her from the opposite way, about to open the door.

Jess' eyes flicked to Sam, then darted away just as quickly. Her body tensed, and for a moment, it looked like she might turn around and flee the opposite direction.

"Hi," Sam said before Jess could escape, her voice coming out more rushed than she intended.

Jess hesitated, her lips pressing into a tight line before she nodded slightly. "Hi."

Sam stepped forward, opening the door and holding it for her. Jess hesitated again, then slipped inside with a quiet, "Thanks."

The line was uncharacteristically short for what she expected at that time in the morning, with just two people ahead of them.

Jess stood in front of Sam, her shoulders stiff and her gaze fixed firmly on the menu board above the counter. Sam studied her for a moment, the uneasy silence stretching between them.

They didn't need to talk. Sam could've waited there in silence, gotten her coffee, and left. She could've written it off as just one more bullet on the long list of poorly timed surprises.

Really, it would've been for the best. There was nothing else to say between them, anyway.

But still, standing there behind her, catching the faint scent of her familiar perfume, she couldn't help herself. Even if it was just a few words, she wanted to hear her voice.

"How've you been?" Sam asked finally.

"Fine," Jess replied, the word clipped as she remained with her back to her.

Sam swallowed, trying to keep the conversation going despite the brick wall of tension between them. "How's work been?"

"It's fine," Jess said again, her tone no warmer than before.

Sam bit back a sigh. She didn't know what she'd expected—that two weeks of silence would be wiped away with a few polite questions?

When they reached the front of the line, Jess stepped forward and placed her order—a black coffee, nothing else. As the barista started ringing her up, Sam stepped beside her, pulling out her wallet.

"I got it," she said quickly, adding her and Caleb's coffee orders to the order.

Jess glanced at her, but said nothing as she stepped aside to let Sam finish paying.

The barista handed back Sam's card with a look that felt more than friendly. "Here you go. I'll remember your order for next time so you can skip the line."

Sam forced a polite smile, mumbling, "Thanks," as she grabbed the receipt and moved to the pickup counter beside Jess.

"How's it been with the wedding planning being over?" Sam asked quietly, not sure if she could handle another clipped response but feeling the need to try.

"Less busy," Jess muttered.

Sam opened her mouth to say something else, but the barista called out their orders before she could. She reached for the cups, grabbing two at random as Jess picked up the third.

Jess turned the cup in her hands, eyes narrowing as she spotted something written on the side.

Her lips pressed into a tight line, and she rolled her eyes, holding the cup out toward Sam. "This is yours."

Sam's brows knitted in confusion as she took it from her. Then she saw the phone number scrawled in black ink on the side.

Jess pushed the cup into her hands before taking a stiff step back.

"Jess—" Sam started, but Jess had already turned, making a quick exit for the door.

Sam rushed to follow, her heart already thudding in her chest. She quickened her pace, catching up to Jess just as she strode down the sidewalk. "Jess, wait."

Jess slowed to a stop but didn't look at her, her eyes fixed on the street ahead.

"I'm sorry," Sam said, the words tumbling out. She hesitated, her breath unsteady as she scrambled for the right way to say how she felt.

Jess stiffened, her head tilting ever so slightly in acknowledgment, but she didn't turn around.

"I'm sorry for what I said the other day," Sam continued, her pulse racing. "About how things were when we first met."

Jess turned to look at her then, her brow furrowing in confusion as if that specific apology was the last thing she'd expected. "What?"

Sam swallowed hard, wondering where she'd gone wrong. "I didn't mean to—" she stammered, her voice catching as Jess stared up at her, eyes narrowed in a deep, questioning gaze.

She wasn't entirely sure what she wanted to say. But she needed to say something. She couldn't leave their last conversation untouched. Not when those words had so clearly hurt Jess.

"Sam," Jess said, her tone soft but firm. She stepped closer, her eyes searching Sam's face. "Did you mean what you said?"

Sam stiffened, the question twisting into her gut. She thought back to the argument, to every word she'd spoken. She had meant it—all of it. But she hadn't meant to upset her, to bring up old wounds in a way that felt so raw.

"Yeah," Sam admitted, her voice barely above a whisper. She dropped her gaze to the sidewalk, unable to meet Jess' eyes. "But I'm sorry for how I said it. I didn't mean to hurt you."

Jess sighed, her expression softening. "Of course it hurt." She looked down at the ground between them, staring for a long moment. "I didn't realize how much I'd hurt you back then. And I hated knowing I'd done that. But—" She stepped closer, her voice lowering. "You don't need to apologize for telling me the truth."

Sam blinked, her throat tightening as the words washed over her.

"Listen to me," Jess said firmly, enunciating every word.

She stared deeply into her eyes, like she was trying to force her to understand something even deeper than what was between them. Like all she needed in the world at that moment was for her to listen. To really hear what she was about to say.

"Sam, it wasn't your fault."

The intensity in her voice settled deep in Sam's chest, a balm to the rawness she hadn't realized was still there. And by the way she said it, the deep look in her eyes, she wondered if she was still talking about them. Or if she was talking about something else entirely.

She nodded slowly, her lips parting to say something, but before she could, Jess' gaze shifted, her guarded walls sliding back into place.

"I have to go," Jess said, stepping back. Her voice was steady, but the way she avoided her eyes was enough to let her know how forced that was.

Jess swallowed, her jaw flickering. "Good luck with everything."

Then she turned and walked away, her figure disappearing into the crowd.

***

446

The coffee was lukewarm, barely touched as it sat between her and Caleb on the conference room table. The papers spread out before them blurred together in her mind—legal jargon and dotted lines that felt more like shackles than opportunities.

"Okay," Caleb said, staring down at the organized chaos, "so remember, we need to ask about the details on page three." He flipped through the copy of the agreement he'd printed and scribbled notes all over. "And we probably need to clarify this section on page twelve, also."

Sam sipped the stale coffee, barely processing what he'd said as her mind replayed the run in with Jess that morning.

She looked up, blinking, when she realized he'd gone quiet.

He stared at her, as if waiting for an answer to a question she'd missed.

"Sorry," she muttered, straightening up in the chair. "What?"

He let out a deep sigh, dropping his pen on the table as he leaned back. "Okay, what's going on?"

"Nothing," she said, shaking her head. "Keep going. I'm listening."

He frowned. "You haven't listened to a single thing I've said since you got back."

She sighed, grinding a palm into her tired eyes. "I'm sorry. I just—I feel like I can't think straight right now."

He watched her for a moment, then flipped the stapled contract closed. "Wanna take a break and go over some of the other work stuff we need to talk about instead?"

She nodded, finally feeling some small ounce of relief. Talking about the software always made her feel better. Something about focusing on the fine details and inner workings of the code calmed her. It all made perfect sense, even when the other things in her life didn't.

"Okay," he said, letting out a breath. "Starting with the bad news."

She glanced up at him, the ease she'd felt just a moment before instantly evaporating.

"Han quit."

"What?" Sam hissed.

Han was by far her favorite developer on their team. He was one of the people she loved working with. It was people like him who made all the work they collaborated on so enjoyable.

And that was one of the reasons why she loved doing what she did—collaborating with exceptional minds who pushed her to think in entirely new ways about what she was trying to build.

"Yeah," Caleb muttered with a tight frown. "Sorry."

He continued onto the next string of things they had to catch up on. But Sam couldn't grasp any of it.

All she could think about was what the next two years of their lives would look like.

Relentless work with none of the people they enjoyed. Working for a huge corporation where they were just one of thousands of tiny pieces on the board. In another new place. A place where they wouldn't have anyone they knew.

No one they cared about.

Caleb leaned back in his chair, arms crossed, watching her carefully. "What're you thinking?"

Sam rubbed her temples, staring down at the contract but not really seeing it. "I'm just trying to think it through," she muttered.

"Are you?" Caleb asked, his tone curious rather than accusatory.

Sam looked up, meeting his gaze. There was no judgment in his expression, only concern. She hesitated, then leaned back in her chair with a long sigh. "I miss how it was at the beginning."

He watched her for a moment, then sighed. "I miss it too. Sometimes."

She looked up at him, surprised. "You do?"

He loosed a breath, frowning. "Sometimes I wonder if we made the right call." He gave her an apologetic look, and for the first time, she could see an edge of remorse in his eyes. "I know I pushed it on you. When we first started getting clients. All the moving and—"

He stopped, shaking his head. "Those first few months after we left New York," he continued, his voice soft and careful in a way she rarely heard. "You seemed so—*miserable*." He shook his head, staring down at the table between them. "I thought maybe it was because you'd left Jess."

Her body constricted instinctively at the sound of her name.

"But then," he continued, "after we hired Han and some of the others, you seemed—better. I thought maybe you just needed more help. And if we kept getting new clients and hiring, then you'd go back to your old happy self." He looked up at her. "And you did. Or—well, you mostly did."

She swallowed, thinking back to that first year after New York. He was right. She had been miserable. She'd thrown herself so deeply into the work that she couldn't see anything else—couldn't think about anything else. And she was happy—or at least, content. In her own way.

Caleb stared at her, his lips pursing. "Do you remember what I told you when we first quit and started this company?"

Sam let out a dry laugh. "That we were broke and needed money?"

Caleb chuckled. "Okay, yeah, I probably said that too," he admitted. "But no. I'm talking about when you asked me what my vision for all of this was. What I wanted out of it."

Sam's brow furrowed as she thought back. She could still picture the dingy apartment they'd rented, the smell of takeout that had fueled those late nights. But slowly, the memory came into focus.

"That all you wanted was to work with the most brilliant people in the industry," she said, her voice soft with the recollection. "To see how they thought, and felt, and operated. What drove them to be who they were."

Caleb nodded, his eyes taking on a fond look she'd never seen in him before. "Do you know who I was talking about?"

Sam blinked, caught off guard. "Uh—I don't know. The clients?"

Caleb smiled softly. "I was talking about you."

She stared at him, her brow crinkling as she absorbed the words. "Me?"

Caleb nodded, his smile softening into something more earnest. "I knew it the day I met you. That first time we talked—you just—had it. The way you think, the way you solve problems, the way you care about the work and the people doing it. That's almost impossible to find in a person."

Sam looked away, her throat tightening.

Caleb was quiet for a moment before releasing a deep sigh as he leaned back in his chair. "I didn't care if we eventually sold, or if we just coasted along, or even if we went bankrupt. Because every day, I got to do what I always wanted from the start."

Sam swallowed hard, the weight of his words pressing against the emptiness in her chest.

"Maybe you need something more than that," Caleb continued, his tone gentle. "But I can't imagine anything greater than what we've already built. Not because of the company, but because of the people in it. And because of you."

She stared down at the table, the words turning over in her mind.

She thought about everything she'd been chasing—the deals, the contracts, the validation that came with success. But sitting there, with Caleb's unwavering belief laid bare, she felt something crack open inside her.

"What if it's not enough?" she asked quietly.

Caleb's expression softened, but kept its serious edge. "What if it is?"

The words hung in the air, sinking deep into her chest. She thought about the long hours, the sleepless nights, the sacrifices she'd made to get there. And then she thought about the team they'd built, the people who had come and gone. The ones who stayed.

"It's a lot to handle," she admitted, her voice barely audible. "I used to love it. Building something bigger than myself. Now it just feels—I don't know. Different."

Caleb smiled, quiet and understanding. "Then let's change that. You don't have to do it all alone. You never had to."

The warmth of his words easing the icy knot in her chest. "Thank you," she said, swallowing. "Not just for this. But—for everything."

"Anytime," he replied easily, leaning back in his chair with a satisfied grin.

She glanced down at the papers on the table once more, her eyes flitting across them. "I think I need to clear my head," she said quietly. "Go for a ride and think about things."

He smiled knowingly, as if he'd expected that from the start. "Do whatever you need."

***

The city skyscrapers blurred past as she wove through the streets, the rare warm air of the day drifting over her bare arms. The rides were a reset button. A way of finding clarity when everything felt like too much.

But this time, it wasn't working.

She pushed harder, twisting the throttle and feeling the surge of power beneath her. The engine's roar drowned out the noise in her head, but it didn't quiet it.

Her thoughts chased each other in endless circles: the deal, Caleb's words, Jess, the wedding, the fight. It all spun together in a chaotic storm she couldn't outrun.

She turned down a familiar street, one that usually soothed her with its winding arcs. But even the rhythm of the ride—leaning into the curves, shifting gears, letting the machine and the road work in harmony— didn't bring the relief it usually did.

Frustration bubbled under her skin like a restless itch. She gritted her teeth, hands tightening on the handlebars as she accelerated onto an open stretch of road. The wind tore past, sharp and burning, but it did nothing to cut through the raw cold in her chest.

The traffic light ahead turned red, and she slowed, her breaths coming shallow and uneven as she looked down at the glowing controls of the bike.

Then one unexpected thought made its way into her head, swirling with the others. And even when she tried to shut it out, it persisted. Something she didn't want to do—but for some reason, felt the overwhelming *need* to do.

She released a frustrated breath, shaking her head as the light turned green. Then she twisted the throttle again, the engine snarling in protest as the bike shot forward.

Finally, with a sharp exhale, she made a U-turn, heading to the last place she would've expected to want to go.

Chapter twenty-six

The office was quiet when Sam arrived, the hum of fluorescent lights and the faint tap of keyboards the only sounds in the otherwise still space.

She stood outside Liz's door, debating whether to knock or turn around and walk away.

The impulse to go there had been sudden, overwhelming, and completely without reason.

But she was there now. And turning back no longer felt like an option.

Sam knocked lightly, pushing the door open without waiting for a response. Liz looked up from her desk, her expression tightening when their eyes met.

"Sam," Liz said, her tone neutral but clipped. "What are you doing here?"

Sam stepped inside, awkwardly shoving her hands into her jean pockets. "I was in the area," she said quickly, her voice too forced. "Thought I'd stop by. See how the software's working out."

Liz blinked at her, the silence stretching just long enough to feel uncomfortable. "It's fine," she said finally, setting a pen down and leaning back in her chair. "No issues."

"Good," Sam replied, nodding. She shifted her weight, her gaze flicking around the large office. "That's good."

Liz cocked her head, her sharp gaze cutting through the awkward air. "That's it? You came all the way here just to ask that?"

Sam hesitated, her mouth opening and closing before she shrugged. "Just wanted to check in."

Liz rolled her eyes, pressing her lips into a thin line. "Right."

The tension in the room was suffocating, and Sam felt the sudden urge to leave. She turned toward the door. "Anyway, I'll let you get back to—"

"You know," Liz interrupted, her voice sharp and tight, "you might not believe me, but I really did want to try being friends again when you first showed up here."

And there it was. The tone she'd had at the wedding. The undercurrent of whatever tension that seemed to simmer between them since that first moment she'd seen her again.

She could've left it at that. Gave some noncommittal reply, and left.

But she couldn't. Maybe it was some need to argue against what Liz had said at the wedding. The words she'd kept to herself, still begging to be released.

Sam paused, half turned away. Then she said carefully, "Did you mean what you said at the wedding?"

Liz eyed her, the edges of her mouth twitching. "Is that really so hard for you to believe?"

A flare of frustration ignited in Sam's chest, heating her tone. "I never did anything to you," she said through gritted teeth, her jaw flexing as the words came out. "How can you hate me for—"

"I never said I hated you," Liz said sharply, her brows wrinkling in a look of distaste. As if she wanted to make sure Sam knew she didn't care enough for hatred.

The dismissive edge in her voice was like a slap, wiping away the last of Sam's patience. She shook her head, glaring off to the side as if looking anywhere but at Liz might stop her from saying something she'd regret. But it didn't.

"You and your parents both act like nothing happened back then," she said, her voice low and biting. "And that's fine. Pretend it never happened. But you can't have it both ways. You can't act like I stole your life somehow and also act like me leaving didn't mean anything to you."

The words hung heavy in the air, and Sam braced herself for a retort, something to cut just as deep. But Liz didn't say anything. She stayed seated, anger rolling off her in silent waves, her jaw clenched so tightly it looked carved from stone.

The silence stretched on until Sam realized Liz wasn't going to say anything at all. And maybe that was for the best.

With a short breath, she turned toward the door, grabbing the handle.

"Wait."

Sam froze, her grip tightening on the doorknob. Slowly, she glanced back over her shoulder. Liz was standing now, arms crossed defensively over her chest, her gaze locked somewhere on the floor.

Sam hesitated a moment before letting go of the door, her hand falling to her side.

The room fell into a strained quiet again. Liz's gaze drifted somewhere far away, her expression clouded and unreadable. For a moment, Sam thought that might be the end of it. That Liz had nothing else to say.

But then Liz let out a slow, shaky breath, her arms uncrossing and falling to her sides. She looked down at her hands for a long moment, as if needing to ground herself.

"I know you asked them to stay," she said softly, her voice quieter now, though still tight with resentment. Her eyes darted to the side, refusing to meet Sam's. "And I know they said no."

Sam looked away. Maybe it was out of surprise. Or shame. But either way, she had no words.

And maybe that's what Liz wanted. To take one last strike at her before they were out of each other's lives for good.

Liz's sharp gaze lingered on Sam for a moment longer, the anger in her eyes softening into something quieter, harder to place. Finally, she let out a deep sigh, her focus dropping to her desk. "After you left—when child services came to take you—I was upset. Obviously." Her voice carried a flatness, like the memory was something she had rehearsed into numbness.

She tilted her head back, shaking it with a hint of exasperation, as though the emotion itself was an inconvenience. "My dad took me out that night. Bought me new cleats to cheer me up."

Liz inhaled sharply, shutting her eyes for just a millisecond before looking at her again. "When we got home, I went looking for my mom to show her the cleats." She swallowed, her voice now threaded with something closer to vulnerability. "I found her in the bathroom, crying."

Sam stilled, her mind coming to a halt.

Liz released another deep breath, and some of that cutting anger seemed to flow away with it. "I think she thought she did a good job hiding it. She never talked about it, at least not to me." She paused, eyes flicking away once more as she crossed her arms back over her chest. "But sometimes," she continued, her voice dropping, "I'd see her in her room, looking at a picture of us. The one from our last game together."

Sam's chest tightened, the weight of Liz's words settling heavily in the air between them. She didn't know what to say, so she didn't say anything.

Liz finally glanced back up at her, and for the first time, her expression wasn't sharp or dismissive. It was unreadable, layered with emotions that Sam didn't recognize. And for the first time, she didn't remind her of the girl she'd known as a child. She looked different. Like the years that passed since their childhood had added new layers to her features.

"I just—" Liz started, her words catching like she wasn't sure if she wanted to continue. She exhaled hard through her nose. "It wasn't nothing. At least, not to her."

Sam swallowed, her throat too tight to speak.

Liz held her gaze for a moment longer, then her expression softened. It wasn't a smile, but maybe it was the closest alternative she could muster. And in that look were words that didn't need to be said. A forgiveness that neither of them was willing to voice aloud.

"Anyway," Liz said, shaking her head as she regained her regular nonchalant attitude. "I have to finish this so I can make it to pilates on time."

Sam nodded slowly. She turned, stepping back to the door before pausing. She threw a glance over her shoulder, casting one last look at her old childhood friend. "Bye Liz."

***

Sleep didn't come that night.

She'd laid out on the couch, staring at the ceiling for hours.

But by the time the sun had finally begun to rise, her thoughts had finally settled, crystallizing into something clear.

The faint sound of movement in the kitchen pulled her from her thoughts. Tiana's groggy voice broke the stillness. "God, you wake up way too early."

Like Sam had expected from the start, Tiana was leaving once again. After the short few months in Seattle, she'd decided to try out Miami instead. And although Tiana said it'd be a short trip, that she'd come back eventually, Sam didn't entirely believe it. But she didn't blame her, either. She'd once felt that same urge to leave, too—the want to bounce around, never staying in one place too long.

The friend Tiana had been crashing with since arriving in Seattle had moved into a smaller studio apartment, and when Tiana had asked to stay with her

464

in the short time before she left for Miami, the answer was an easy yes.

She didn't mind Tiana crashing at her place. In fact, she liked it. The loud company, the effortless banter—it made the apartment feel less empty. And with everything going on, that was something she needed.

Sam sat up, the corners of her lips twitching into a small smile. "Couldn't sleep."

Tiana shuffled into the living room, a blanket draped over her shoulders like a cape. "Well, whatever new crisis you're having, don't involve me 'til at least ten AM," she mumbled, flopping onto the armchair across from her.

Sam chuckled softly.

Her phone buzzed on the coffee table, the screen lighting up with a message.

Caleb: Let me know what you decide.

Sam stared at the message for a long moment, her thumb hovering over the keyboard. But this time, she didn't overthink it. She'd already thought through everything all night long.

She typed out a response, hit send, and set the phone down.

Chapter twenty-seven

Sam sipped the steaming cup of coffee before setting it down on the small table in her living room.

"So," Tiana started, tossing the last of her clothes messily into her black duffel bag, "you gonna miss me?"

Sam smirked, quirking an eyebrow at her. "Yeah, but it'll be nice having my couch back."

It'd been one week since she officially turned down the offer.

And although she'd expected a new onslaught of worries and stress to hit, it hadn't.

Actually, for the first time in as long as she could remember, things felt—calm.

Sure, it brought up an endless string of new questions and problems they needed to solve. But it wasn't the same as before. For the first time, it felt like she actually knew what she really, truly wanted. And with that clarity came a new vision for how she wanted to run the company. A vision for how they should move forward.

Tiana hummed, pulling the zipper across the top of the bag. "So you can finally stop having an excuse to not ask Jess to come over?"

Sam frowned down at the cup on the table. They hadn't spoken since the run in at the coffee shop a week before. And every time she'd thought about texting or calling, she came up with some excuse as to why it was a bad idea.

But she'd be lying if she said it wasn't absolutely killing her every day that passed by.

"She wouldn't want me to ask her to come over," Sam muttered.

"Well, maybe that would change if you told her you weren't leaving anymore."

Sam let out a deep sigh, rolling her head back to lean against the couch cushion. "You didn't see how she was last week. I think it'll take a long time before she's ready to talk to me again."

Tiana rolled her eyes, shooting her an irritated look. "That woman is hopelessly in love with you. She doesn't want time. She wants *you*."

Sam swallowed, feeling just slightly better at hearing those words. "Even if that were true, it's not the right time to talk about it. Things need to settle more."

Tiana groaned exaggeratedly, standing from where she'd been crouched beside the bag on the ground.

She crossed the living room in two easy strides, then dropped onto the couch beside her.

Tiana grabbed the coffee cup Sam had been sipping on, taking a large gulp. Then she set it back down before turning to Sam with an intense gaze.

"What?" Sam asked with a sigh.

Tiana opened her mouth to speak, then paused, closing it again as if rethinking the words. "Every time Jess changed her mind when you first met and walked away from what you guys had, did you want to have to keep chasing after her?"

Sam's brows pulled together. "Of course not."

"And even after things were good between you guys, did you just instantly trust that they'd stay that way?"

Sam pursed her lips, glancing away.

"No, you didn't," Tiana continued. "You needed her to prove it. You needed her to show up and prove to you that it would work. That she *wanted* it to work."

Sam loosed a breath, about to argue, but Tiana continued.

"So why the hell are you still sitting here?"

Sam's eyes flicked up to her. "Fine. I'll call her tomorrow."

Tiana let out a disgusted scoff. "Please, Sam. You're so much better than that. Go see her. Now."

"I have to give you a ride, remember?"

"Right," Tiana muttered, standing to grab the last of her things from the kitchen. "Because there's no other way in the world for me to get to the airport."

Sam frowned, hands fidgeting in her lap. Maybe Tiana was right, and Jess really would want to see her.

Or maybe seeing her was the absolute last thing she would want. In which case, showing up would only make things worse.

"I don't know," she mumbled.

Tiana rolled her eyes, shaking her head before trudging back to where Sam waited on the couch.

"I'm ordering an Uber," Tiana said, tapping something on her phone.

Sam opened her mouth to argue, but Tiana's firm look cut her off.

"Sam," she said in a low, serious voice. "I'm only going to say this one more time. Do not fuck this up again. Go get your girl."

***

Sam barely noticed the street as she walked, her feet moving almost on their own, her mind racing through everything she wanted to say to Jess. When she finally reached the familiar apartment building, her nerves prickled to life.

She probably should've called or texted first to actually make sure she was there. But she'd been more concerned with what she was going to say once she got there.

Then an old memory sprang into her mind.

The corners of her mouth turned up in a smirk as she pulled her phone out of her pocket and easily found Jess' contact.

She clicked the call button and pressed it to her ear, listening as it rang.

And not even halfway through the second ring, it stopped.

"Hi," Jess answered, her voice lacking all of its usual warmth.

"Hey," Sam breathed, scratching a hand over the back of her neck.

Jess was quiet for a moment before she asked, "Everything okay?"

Sam smiled to herself as that long ago memory played in her mind. "Yeah." She paused, clearing her throat as she peered back up at the building. "Are you home?"

"Yeah," Jess drawled, curiosity clear in her voice. She didn't sound happy to hear from her, but she also didn't sound as clipped as she had the week before. So at least that was a win.

"Why?" Jess asked.

The corner of Sam's mouth twitched upward as she answered, "I'm outside." Seconds of silence ticked by, and Sam had to fight to keep from holding her breath. Then finally, when it seemed like Jess might not respond at all, she added, "Can we talk?"

A soft exhale came through the phone. "I don't think that's a good idea," Jess muttered.

Her stomach suddenly felt heavy at the sound of resignation in her voice. She knew it. Showing up was a terrible plan.

But even as she realized that, even as her brain told her to turn around and walk away, she couldn't. She had to at least know that she really tried.

"I understand," Sam said quietly. "And if you want me to leave, I will." She paused, taking a deep breath to calm her nerves. "But please, just give me one minute."

The phone felt quiet once more, and Sam waited, her heart pounding in her chest with every second.

Then suddenly, the phone beeped as the call ended. Sam pulled it away from her ear, glancing down at the black screen as every last bit of hope she'd held onto dried up.

She released a breath, shutting her eyes, letting that rejection seep into her bones instead of immediately pushing it away. She had to. No matter how painful it was, she couldn't run from it.

She opened her eyes again, giving herself a few more seconds to recover. Then, right as she began to turn away, the door to Jess' apartment opened.

Her head snapped up, lips parting in surprise as she watched Jess step outside, glancing around.

Then Jess paused as her gaze fell to her.

She looked down at her for a moment, and even from that distance, Sam could clearly see the way she seemed to steel herself before walking down the short flight of stairs.

Sam's legs began moving on their own before she registered it, bringing her to the bottom of the stairway as Jess descended the last few steps.

Jess watched her with a timid look, crossing her arms over her chest as if holding herself together. "How does it feel being on the other end of that call this time?"

Sam released a tight breath, smiling slightly as she shook her head. "Terrifying," she said with a laugh.

Jess hummed, her face still a hard mask. "You have it easy. You don't have to worry about knocking on the door and having Chris open it."

Sam laughed again. "Yeah, I definitely didn't give you enough credit for that."

A tiny flicker of amusement crossed Jess' face before it immediately evened back out to its emotionless state.

Sam cleared her throat, glancing away as she worked to summon some tiny ounce of the confidence that usually came so easily to her. "Sorry," she mumbled. "If you were busy or—"

"Sam," Jess cut her off with a pointed look. "What do you want to talk about?"

Sam let out a deep breath, running a hand over the back of her neck. "I um—"

Her mind was reeling, searching for the best way to ease into it. The best way to explain how things had changed.

"I'm not going to London," she blurted suddenly, as if the words refused to be held in even a second longer.

Jess blinked, staring at her. Then she blinked again, her brows furrowing as if it had taken a second to understand. "What?"

Sam swallowed, watching her. "Yeah."

Then a mixture of something resembling guilt and panic flashed through Jess' eyes.

"Not because of you," Sam added immediately. "Or—I mean—" She shook her head. "There were a lot of reasons. It wasn't the right choice to make."

Maybe they'd have more time at some point, and she could tell her the details. But now wasn't that time. The details didn't matter. All that mattered was that Jess knew.

Jess looked down, nodding, her brow still slightly furrowed. "So you're staying?" she asked slowly.

Sam nodded once. "Yeah. At least, for now. Caleb and I still need to talk through the details and really figure out what it means and how we're gonna move forward," she rambled, the words tumbling out of her mouth. "But—" She swallowed as their eyes locked together again. "Yeah. I'm staying."

She wasn't sure what she'd expected Jess to say or do after she told her. But the still guarded, careful look in her eyes was a surprise.

"And what does that mean, exactly?" Jess asked.

Yeah, she definitely should've thought the whole thing through more before just showing up.

"I—don't know," Sam muttered, every last bit of her confidence draining out with the inadequate words.

Jess' lips pursed together as she let out a small breath, her shoulders dropping. "Okay."

Sam swallowed against a sudden dryness in her throat. "I just—I wanted to tell you."

Jess nodded slowly, her eyes flicking away. "Well, I'm happy for you. If that's what you ended up wanting."

Sam pursed her lips, looking down at the ground. "Thanks."

The word felt hollow. Everything about what she'd said felt hollow—meaningless. And she hated herself for thinking it would've felt different—been different.

Of course it didn't change things. She'd already broken what they had. It was ridiculous to think she could fix that.

When she looked up again, Jess was watching her with guarded eyes. But behind that, she could see the hurt. And even though she felt that same deep sorrow, just looking at her made it better. Like being near her was enough to ease the pain.

"I'm sorry," she said, watching the way Jess' blonde hair fell perfectly out of her messy bun and around her face. "I know you didn't want to talk."

Jess stayed quiet, watching her with a deep intensity.

Sam swallowed, releasing a long exhale. "I just—I miss you."

The carefully guarded mask of Jess' features slipped slightly. Like those three words had tugged it from its place.

Jess stared for a long moment, studying her in the way she always did. Then she swallowed, looking away. "I don't know where you wanted to go from here. But I don't think this changes things."

Sam felt her chest sink.

"It's not that I don't want it to," Jess added, closing her eyes as she inhaled. And Sam could see the split emotions on her then. The carefully caged want. "But we've been here so many times before, Sam."

Her voice cracked on her name, and it took every ounce of will she had to keep from reaching for her.

Jess took a deep, steadying breath. "How am I supposed to trust that you're really in it this time?" She paused, shaking her head in frustration. "That something else won't come up and I'll wake up one day to you leaving again."

Sam looked away to the darkened skyline. She couldn't blame her. If anything, she understood completely. Even more than she realized. It was a feeling she knew all too well.

"I need time," Jess whispered.

"Yeah." Sam swallowed down the tight burn in her throat. "I understand."

Jess stood there for a moment, her eyes on the ground. Then she took a step back, and that one single step felt like a thousand miles.

Sam watched her, wondering if that was how Jess felt each time she'd left. Each time she'd shoved her feelings down and walked away. And if it was, then she couldn't blame her.

But they'd had time.

Too much time.

Excruciating years of it.

And she wasn't about to let her slip away. Not again.

"I've loved you every minute for the last eight years."

Jess' gaze shot back up to her, lips parting as if that was the last thing she expected to hear.

The same clarity she'd had over the last week came flowing back to her. It wasn't complicated. Not anymore. Jess was her person. And no matter what happened—no matter what they were—she needed her to at least know that.

"You're it," she continued. "You always have been. No matter how hard I've tried to move on, it's always been you."

Jess watched her, the guarded look now completely gone and replaced by pure shock. But Sam continued, feeling more confident than she had in weeks.

"If you need time, that's fine. Take all the time you need. But I don't. I know exactly what I want." The corner of her mouth quirked up in a soft smirk. "I've known since the first time you kissed me." She shook her head, releasing a deep breath. "Time won't change that. It never has. At least—not for me."

Jess looked at her, her gaze softening as something deeper flickered in her eyes. She took a slow, steady breath and stepped closer, close enough that Sam could feel the warmth radiating between them.

"You're really not leaving?" Jess murmured, her voice just above a whisper, as if saying it any louder would break the moment. Her fingers brushed against Sam's, tentative, then bolder as she took her hand.

Sam's pulse kicked up as she tried to hold her ground, feeling the intensity in Jess' touch, in the way she looked at her.

"I'm not leaving," Sam whispered, trying to keep her voice steady.

Jess let out a slow exhale, her thumb tracing a soft circle over Sam's knuckles.

Sam swallowed, the soothing touch spurring her on. "I want this. Us."

Jess lifted her other hand, brushing a loose strand of hair back from Sam's face, her touch lingering. The silence between them grew charged, each second stretching.

Then slowly, softly, Jess leaned in.

Sam stilled as Jess' warm lips met hers. It wasn't hesitant or uncertain—it was purposeful, as if Jess were pouring years of unspoken feelings into that single, aching moment.

Then slowly, Jess pulled back, breaking the kiss.

Sam's heart pounded as she opened her eyes, watching Jess release a slow breath.

"I missed you too," she whispered, her hand sliding to rest against Sam's cheek. Her thumb traced along her cheekbone as she held her gaze.

The corners of Sam's lips turned up in a smile as the last of the overwhelming nerves in her stomach finally dissipated.

Jess leaned forward, sliding her arms around Sam's waist and leaning her head against her shoulder.

Sam wrapped her arms around her in a tight embrace, savoring the feeling she'd missed for weeks.

"You know," Sam said, unable to hold back the grin that tried to break across her lips, "Jess Hayes does sound pretty good."

Jess groaned into her shoulder, then chuckled, pulling her head back to look up at her. "You just couldn't wait to bring that up, could you?"

Sam grinned back at her. "No, I couldn't."

Jess shook her head as she laughed. Then she stopped, looking up at her with some mix of adoration and amazement.

"What?" Sam asked, cocking her head to the side as she chuckled.

Jess bit the edge of her lip, still staring at her. As if she was looking for the very first time.

"Hearing you say it," she whispered. "I don't think I realized how good it would sound coming from you."

Chapter twenty-eight

*T*_{*wo Years Later*}

Sam adjusted the collar of her shirt for what felt like the hundredth time, staring at her reflection in the small mirror perched on the table. The suit she'd chosen was a deep charcoal, crisp and perfectly tailored, though she kept fiddling with it as if the right fold or tug would settle her nerves.

Tiana and Caleb bickered in the background, their voices filling the small room with an easy, playful energy.

"I'm just saying," Caleb protested. "I'm the best man. I should get to stand next to her at the altar. Besides, you got to throw the bachelorette party, so I should get this."

"Of course I got to throw the party," Tiana shot back, glaring as she adjusted a stray petal of the flower pinned to Sam's suit pocket. "You wouldn't know the first thing about having a good time."

Caleb rolled his eyes, adjusting the sleeve of his shirt. "The point is, *I* should be beside her," he said, crossing his arms. "You got the party. I get the prime position. It's fair."

Sam chuckled, turning around to watch them, feeling the warmth that only people who knew her inside and out could bring.

The door creaked open, and Chris stepped in, his military dress uniform pressed and immaculate as always. He gave her a once-over, his expression as unreadable as ever. Then he strode over, tilting his head as he reached out to straighten her tie.

"How're you feeling?" he asked.

Sam managed a weak smile. "Nervous."

Chris nodded. "From what I've heard, that's normal." His eyes softened just a fraction as he gave her tie one last tug. "You look good."

She nodded, swallowing back a sudden lump in her throat. He offered a brief, approving smile, patting her shoulder before stepping back.

"You ready?" he asked, squaring his shoulders.

Sam stepped out into the hallway, Caleb, Tiana, and Chris trailing behind her. As they closed the door, Sam caught sight of Mike waiting at the end of the hall. He stood there, shoulders tight, with his hands tucked into the pockets of his suit pants. His expression was solemn, yet softened by a certain depth in his eyes as he looked at her.

Caleb and Tiana exchanged a quick glance, then took a step back, allowing him the space to approach. Chris remained close, arms crossed as he watched intently.

Mike walked up, stopping just in front of her. He glanced down for a brief moment, as if gathering his words.

"Big day," he began, his voice low and gruff.

"Yeah," Sam said with a small smile, tucking her hands in her pockets. After years of dating his daughter, she'd grown used to his awkward tendencies. It almost felt comforting now, in its own way.

He cleared his throat, nodding as he looked around the room. "Jess is—" he paused, his gaze shifting, as if the sentiment was larger than the words he could find for it. "Lucky," he said finally. "But I am, too." His hand came up, giving her shoulder a firm, brief squeeze. "Glad it's you."

Sam felt her chest tighten, a mixture of gratitude and relief warming her as she nodded. "Thank you, Mike," she murmured, meeting his gaze with sincerity. The words might not have seemed like much to anyone else. But she knew him. Even better than she ever would've thought possible. And those words carried the weight of all the years they'd known each other, of everything she and Jess had fought through to get to that day.

Mike gave her a final nod before stepping back, his hands finding their way into his pockets once again.

The wedding coordinator approached them, clipboard in hand. "Alright," she said, glancing from Sam to Chris and then to Jess' father. "Let's get you all in place."

They followed her instructions, and as they moved toward the garden, Sam felt a renewed calm settle over her, each step bringing her closer to the moment she'd been waiting for.

Sam and Chris stopped where they'd been instructed, then Caleb and Tiana took their places in front of them before the two wide wooden doors.

Her heart raced as the first note of the song they'd chosen began to hum from the other side of the doors.

Chris nudged her elbow, giving her a single nod as the doors opened, and Caleb and Tiana immediately began their slow ascent up the aisle.

Once they reached the altar, the coordinator gave them the signal to begin.

The venue was open air, a garden surrounded by tall, whispering trees and filled with rows of guests seated on wooden chairs decorated with wildflowers. The late afternoon sun cast a soft, golden glow over everything, filtering through the leaves.

As she walked, her eyes scanned the crowd, catching familiar faces. She spotted Laura in the fourth row, her eyes already misty as she watched.

At the front of the aisle, two empty chairs adorned with delicate arrangements of white lilies and baby's breath sat side by side. On one chair sat a beautifully framed picture of Jess' mother.

And on the other, was the one good picture she had of her own mother. It was carefully taped to the center, and from that distance she could make out the small details of her genuine smile.

Having the memorial made after all those years had never really felt real. It hadn't felt like anything, really. But seeing that empty chair in the front row, with her mother's picture—that felt real.

When they reached the end of the aisle, Chris gave her an approving nod before stepping back. She took her place at the altar, heart racing as she turned to face the crowd. And then the music shifted, softening.

And when she looked up at the end of the aisle, her breath caught in her throat.

Jess had one hand resting lightly on her father's arm, her white dress flowing around her in soft, unbroken lines. She looked radiant, her face illuminated by a mixture of nervous excitement and overwhelming happiness that Sam felt deep in her chest.

Their eyes met, and the world around them faded, leaving only the soft glow of the evening. Mike walked Jess slowly down the aisle, each step measured.

When they reached her, she extended a hand to him.

Mike glanced down at it for a moment, the corner of his lip turning upward. Then he stepped forward, wrapping his arms around her with a tenderness that caught her off guard.

She hugged him back, catching Jess' equally surprised, but wide, grin over her shoulder.

Mike released her, stepping back as he gave one last look at Jess, reaching out to squeeze her arm.

Then, as he strode away, Jess turned to face her, both hands extended. Sam took them, warmth filling her chest as their fingers intertwined.

Chapter twenty-nine

J ess leaned against the terrace railing, gazing out at the softly lit garden below. The hum of laughter and conversation drifted through the air as the last few guests began to say their goodbyes, waving and hugging each other in the warm glow of the evening. The night was winding down, but Jess felt more awake than she ever had.

She spotted Sam standing near the bar, one hand resting on her hip as she laughed at something Scarlett was saying. Tiana leaned in, adding to the story, her hands animated as she gestured wildly, and Sam's head tipped back in laughter. That unrestrained, genuine sound Jess loved so much.

She couldn't help but smile.

Her thoughts drifted back to the first time she'd seen it—the first time she'd really seen *her*. The real her. The quiet confidence. The way she'd listened more than she spoke, and yet somehow, always managed to make Jess feel like she was the only person in the world worth listening to.

It had taken years to get to this day. And they'd both earned every second.

She glanced over to where her father was sitting, arm resting on the back of his chair as he spoke with Suki.

He'd seemed different that night. His usual stoic presence softened with something lighter. He'd even laughed during the speeches, eyes crinkling at the corners in a way Jess hadn't seen since before her mom had passed. And maybe some part of him was finally truly healing. Just like it had for her years before.

"Having your own party out here?" Sam's voice cut softly through the quiet, and Jess looked up to find her standing there, that familiar half-smile on her lips.

Jess smiled, reaching out to take Sam's hand as she joined her on the terrace. "Just thinking," she murmured, glancing down as she laced her fingers with Sam's. "About how we got here."

Sam leaned her shoulder against Jess', following her gaze out to the garden.

Jess turned to look at her, taking in the soft glow in her eyes. "Remember when we first met?"

Sam chuckled, squeezing her hand. "When you yelled at me in the parking lot?"

Jess snorted a laugh, rolling her eyes. "After that."

Sam shot her a teasing look, cocking one eyebrow. "When I got punched in the face and then your dad showed up and interrogated me?"

Jess burst into a full deep laughter then, shaking her head. "Oh my god," she said, pulling one hand away to push Sam's chest lightly. "Fine. Not at the very beginning, then."

Sam looked at her with a dazzling smile, leaning in as she waited.

"After the football game at the clinic," Jess continued, keeping one hand resting against Sam's chest. "When we were at Scarlett's party. Remember when we talked on the bench outside?"

Sam nodded, her grin falling into a more serious, but loving, gaze.

Jess peered up at her, taking in every tiny detail of the clear and overwhelming love in her eyes.

"I think, even then, I loved you," she whispered.

The air filled with quiet memories, the long journey they'd taken to get to that exact moment. Jess could feel it in the space between them—the weight of every choice, every time they'd found each other, over and over again.

Sam lifted their joined hands, pressing a light kiss to Jess' fingers. "I think I did, too."

if I could tell you then
what we know
when mom finally sinks
six feet below
leaving you
a victim
of her vices
when safety
sounds like love
and liquor
tastes like laughter
sometimes it takes years
for seasons to change
and when they do
I'd tell you
not to shake
when she thinks you're a sin
I swear
it's not your fault
she'll be too scared
to let you in
but when you
fly too far
and don't land right

take too long

and put up a fight

I promise you

it'll be okay

because one day

when we hear her velvet voice

in the sea

of scorching smiles

we'll finally know

how it feels

to come home

Printed in Great Britain
by Amazon

57226580R00280